# ABANDONED SHORES

## A TALIONIS SERIES COMPANION NOVEL

CJ MILACCI

JOURNEY PERSPECTIVE PUBLISHING

Published by Journey Perspective Publishing

Philadelphia, PA, USA



ISBN: 978-1-958230-08-4 (printed softcover)

ISBN: 978-1-958230-10-7 (printed hardback)

ISBN: 978-1-958230-09-1 (ebook)

Cover design by GetCovers

Editing by Becca Weirwille

Typesetting by C.J. Milacci

Find out more at www.cjmilacci.com

*To all the little ones who call me "Aunt Carli"*

*Although you may not be old enough yet to read my stories, one day I hope they take you on grand adventures and inspire you to be men and women who do justice, love mercy, and walk humbly with your God. Your names are scattered throughout my books on purpose, and I love each of you so much!*

The weight of the golden gown pulls at me as I enter the heart of the Upper District. It's probably the thousands of minuscule lights the Inventors wove into the material to make me shimmer with a soft glow. The color offsets my olive skin, and my hair is twisted into an elaborate updo with so many diamond-studded pins I'm not sure how I'll ever get them all out. I frown, wishing I could be anywhere else right now.

But Grandfather would tear into me if he even suspected my wish. I shudder at the thought and step further into the Welcoming Party. He's probably waiting for me on the platform at the center of the party. But I'm not ready to join him.

Yet.

I'll go over soon.

For now, I take in the party's opulence. Hundreds, if not thousands, of candles flicker in the darkness, along with chandeliers strung over the open square, lights dimmed low to add to the atmosphere. Every light, both those powered by electricity and fire, is placed and set strategically so that the Upper

District shines like a glimmering jewel. Especially compared to the rest of the compound.

The buildings stand tall, lavishly decorated. Wealth oozes from the pores of the streets—golden lamp-stands, bejeweled signs on shops, rich garments for sale for occasions such as this. Although no garment can ever compare to what I wear. A different gown for every Welcoming Party or elaborate occasion.

Such a waste, when those in the Lower District are practically starving.

But the Princess of the Raiders must stand out. My nose wrinkles at the thought, and I slink into the shadows between two shops.

The party is in full swing as everyone in the compound awaits the Raiders returning from their missions, bringing the loot, supplies, and riches Grandfather tasked them to retrieve. If only that was all they brought back.

The scent of roasting meat, garlic, and freshly baked bread wafts through the air, and wine is already freely flowing among those present. More men and women arrive with each passing moment, their clothing chosen to shout their wealth and power on nights like this.

I'd give anything for the black leathers I usually wear. The leathers *everyone* usually wears.

"Well, don't you look fancy, Princess Catori." My best friend Gabby sidles up next to me and loops her arm through mine.

Some of my tension eases, and I grin at her. "You found me."

I squash my jealousy at her attire.

Gabby is still in Raider leathers. Her older sister, J, runs one of the most elite crews in our compound—in *all* the compounds. And they're always dressed in leathers, ready to go out on a mission at a moment's notice.

Even during a Welcoming Party.

Gabby rolls her eyes. "Please. You're literally *glowing*. Everyone can see you standing over here."

I stick my tongue out at her, even as my stomach knots. She's right. And I'd better enter into the festivities before Grandfather notices my sulking in the shadows.

I let Gabby lead me out of my hiding place and deeper into the swirling dresses and tailored suits of the guests. Some I pass can barely contain their disdain, others give me wide and sweeping bows, but all let me through.

Gabby guides us to a table overflowing with freshly baked bread. She picks up a roll and smiles at me. "Still warm." She hands me one, then gets another for herself.

I break off a piece but don't eat it.

"Look," Gabby says, elbowing me lightly. She nods to our left. "Ms. P. seems to be having a good time."

I snort a laugh as I glimpse our teacher dancing. Her bright blue dress, festooned with feathers and glittering gems, makes her look like an oversized bird. And the woman has no rhythm. Her movements are awkward and completely out of step with the band playing off to the side.

"Class, this is how you dance," Gabby says in the high-pitched voice she uses to mimic Ms. P. She breaks out into a disjointed dance, her limbs flailing.

The sight is so preposterous, a snort of laughter bursts from me. "Stop. Someone will see!"

Gabby flips her hair back over her shoulder. "I'm okay looking ridiculous if it means giving you a chance to loosen up."

I roll my eyes. "Yeah, because all I ever wanted was my best friend to make a complete buffoon of herself in front of everyone in the compound."

Gabby sticks out her tongue. "You're always so miserable at these parties. You just gotta embrace the fun."

She focuses on Ms. P. again, and I do too. Anything to keep from explaining to my friend—again—why I don't like Welcoming Parties.

"I'm glad I only have two weeks of classes left with her," Gabby says. "I'm sick of sitting around when there's more important work to do."

I swallow the emotions her comment rouses. Gabby is training more and more with her sister now that we're almost nineteen. Which means our lives are taking different directions.

After all, as Grandfather regularly reminds me, the princess does not go on missions. Not that I'd want to, anyway. The very idea makes me sick.

I give my head a small shake. I can't let myself go there. Not tonight. I have to put on a good face. Miriam's words from earlier today filter into my mind, but I shove them aside. I love my sweet, old mentor, but she doesn't understand how things work here. Not fully.

Gabby and I move through the party, giggling as we spot various men and women making fools of themselves. The tension of the evening ebbs as I walk arm and arm through the crowd with my friend.

"Miss." A Roamer—Parreu, according to the nameplate on his suit—clicks his heels a step in front of us, forcing Gabby and me to a stop.

I know why he's here before he says his next words and stiffen my spine to prepare for what's coming next.

"Your grandfather is looking for you." His words are tense

and laced with an edge. Disdain for the fact that I'm not where I should be, maybe?

I incline my head. "Very well."

Gabby releases my arm and drops into some ludicrous curtsey. "We shall reconvene later, my princess." She winks.

I smirk, but it dies. Staying with Gabby this long was a mistake, but after the day I had, I needed some fun.

Hopefully, I won't pay too dearly for it.

I trail behind the Roamer as he cuts a path through the crowd and directly to the platform where Grandfather waits with his top advisors and the few he's chosen to bestow his favor upon tonight. I clamp my hands together to keep them from shaking. According to Grandfather, my place is among them— the elite of the elite. But every day I spend with Miriam and those in the Lower District makes me believe that less and less.

I climb the stairs to the platform, lifting my flowing gown so I don't trip on it. The stiff fabric scrapes against my skin, and again I wish for Gabby's leathers. The dress is less cumbersome than one would expect with the thousands of minuscule lights woven into the fabric. A testament to the Inventors' skill. But that doesn't mean it's comfortable.

I pause at the top of the steps and straighten my shoulders. Grandfather is several feet away in conversation with Briggs, my uncle and his chief advisor. I take a few tentative steps toward them, then stop and wait.

A servant from the Lower District carries a tray overladen with a selection of foods up onto the platform. She keeps her head bowed low, but I instantly recognize her. Marsha. I want to approach her and say hi, but refrain.

It wouldn't do her or myself any good if I showed any display of kindness and care towards her tonight. She makes her way to each of those on the platform, offering food. Every person acts as though she's nothing more than a machine or piece of moving furniture. No one looks her in the eye or offers a thank you. I clench my hands into fists.

How can *people* be beneath other people? They can't.

Yet, that's exactly how the Raiders, Roamers, Inventors—everyone in the Upper District—treats those of the Lower District. Like slaves.

Marsha makes her way over, and I glimpse the shimmering black and blue of a new bruise on her left cheek.

Thick swarms of emotions chase their way through me. I want to ask her what happened, demand someone be held accountable for their cruelty. But I would be laughed off this platform at best. And even worse would befall this woman who I consider my friend.

She stops in front of me, and I hardly notice the array of foods on the tray.

"Hi, Marsha." I keep my voice at a whisper.

She gives me a hesitant smile and lifts the tray higher. "We made your favorites."

I finally focus on the tray. She's right. They *did* make my favorites. Honey glazed chicken. Spinach turnovers. Roasted potatoes. I take one of each, even though my appetite is nowhere to be found.

"Set some aside for me in the kitchen," I say, glancing around to make sure no one is close enough to hear. "I'll bring them to your family tomorrow."

She gives a brief nod, before moving onto a nearby group. I want to talk with her more, make sure she's okay, but I can't. Not here. Not tonight.

"There you are, my dear," Grandfather says from just behind me.

I swirl around, pasting a smile on my face and praying it hides the guilt creeping its way up my spine.

"Grandfather." I dip into a low curtsey, fiddling with my dress. Worry over Marsha fades as I wait for Grandfather to approve of my attire.

"You look lovely." His voice is almost soft. Well, as soft as it ever is for him.

He's pleased.

I stand back to my full height, releasing a full breath.

He snaps his fingers, and one of his personal servants materializes at his side with a box in hand. Grandfather takes the box, opens it, and withdraws a diamond studded necklace.

A group nearby stops their conversation to stare as Grandfather leans forward and puts the necklace on me. The weight is instantly suffocating, and the gems cling to my skin like leeches, but I can feel the barely contained jealousy of the surrounding women. Grandfather always presents me with an elaborate gift at these functions. Proof that I'm one of the wealthiest in the compound. I want to yank it off and cast it in the trash. This one item would be enough to feed most of the Lower District for a month.

Instead, I swallow and force a smile that I pray looks sincere. "Thank you, Grandfather. It's stunning."

He tilts his head. "As are you, Catori."

Marsha approaches with the tray of food, freshly refilled. She keeps her head low.

Grandfather swats at the air, and Marsha flinches. "Light more candles up here!" He bellows. "The mosquitos are everywhere."

He snatches a skewer of meat from Marsha's tray, and dismisses her with a wave of his hand.

Her shoulders visibly lower as she heads off the platform.

I watch her walk away. When I'm able to leave without making a scene, I'll go to the kitchens and retrieve the leftovers from the party to bring to the Lower District tomorrow. And I'll bring salve for Marsha's bruise.

The men and women of the Lower District starve as we live off their labor. And the wealth stolen from any town or village the Raiding parties enter.

The rich scent of the pig roasting in a pit in the center of the square turns my stomach, and the raucous shouts of the party ring in my ears.

"Are you ill, Granddaughter?" Grandfather's rough whisper at my elbow jolts my attention to him.

"No, of course not." Being ill is unacceptable. Even if I *was* sick, Grandfather wouldn't let me take my leave for the evening.

He grips my arm, his clasp almost painful. "Then smile, Catori. You look miserable, and this is a celebration." His weathered face creases into a smile, but his eyes remain hard.

"Yes, Grandfather." I smile at him, hoping I look as pleased as he wants me to. The last thing I need tonight is to upset him.

"Good." His grip loosens, and he pulls me into a hug. "Now go, enjoy the party. And keep your eyes out for any suitable matches, hum? You're nearly nineteen. Time for you to marry so you and your husband can help me rule this place."

My smile falters, so I duck my head into a nod.

Marriage to one of the men in this compound is the last thing I could ever want.

Despite their utter lack of morals in every other area of life, all Raiders take marriage seriously. Once you marry, they believe you are bound to that person for all eternity. All you possess becomes your spouses, and once a bond is made, it isn't severed. Even if the husband or wife dies, the remaining mate never marries again.

Grandfather enacted the law after my grandmother died years ago. According to all accounts, he loved her fiercely, and her death nearly killed him. He swore he'd never marry again and declared that no Raider could marry a second time.

Many hate the law, but all obey it. They obey every command from Chief Jehoram, whether or not they like it. Although despite the apparent eternal bond, faithfulness to one's spouse is…less common.

How can I ever pledge my life to a man Grandfather deems worthy? It would go against everything I've come to believe. Maybe Miriam can give me some insight.

A servant approaches Grandfather. "The Raider parties have entered the far west gate."

Grandfather pulls the white-pearl-handled pistol from the leather holster at his waist and shoots it three times into the air.

Most people would flinch at the deafening blast of the gun shooting mere feet away from me. But I don't. Because it's normal.

A raucous cheer explodes from the crowd.

Why is this my life?

Servants from the Lower District weave through the swarms of people, serving appetizers and refilling wine goblets. They're shoved, spit on, and screamed at. A woman nearby backhands a servant I know—Sienna—all because the woman didn't like the appetizer she chose for herself. I step toward them.

I should do something, stand up for Sienna. She's a *person*. And no person should be treated with such disdain. I glance toward my grandfather, his deep scowl emphasizing the thick lines on his face as he peers in the direction the Raiders will enter from. There's a gleam in his eyes as he watches, waiting to see the loot his men and women have for him.

No. I can't stand up for Sienna. It's too risky. Grandfather will feel shamed. And it will be worse for both me and her.

I turn my back to the woman who is now cursing out Sienna and swallow bile. Later. I'll find a way to help her later.

My earlier conversation with Miriam floods my thoughts, unbidden.

*"Remember, child. Every command we follow reveals the one we serve."*

*"Sometimes we don't have a choice," I said, desperation lacing my words.*

*She caressed my cheek with her thumb, then dropped her hand. I immediately missed the warmth and comfort of her touch. "There is always a choice, dear girl. Both our actions and our lack of action determine the course of our lives."*

*Her words held the same pressure as they always do. A weight of truth and a call to press deeper into what I know is right. Which is why I get lessons from her...right?*

*But, as much as I love Miriam, she can't understand that some things must be done to protect not only myself but her.*

A slow clapping begins, breaking me from my reverie.

The first Raider has been sighted.

The ground rumbles as the thunder and high-pitched whir of dozens of mechanical horses nears.

Carver, the Raider at the head of the company, enters the square. He's one of the cruelest men in Grandfather's compound...and the one everyone says I should marry.

A chill whispers through me, despite the relative warmth of the evening. Both from Miriam's words *and* the sight of Carver.

I can't act. Not now. Not here. Right?

*God, what am I supposed to do?* The prayer rushes through my mind, but a part of me is terrified of what His answer might be.

The rest of the Raiders enter the square, followed by a dozen or so more captives.

My heart clenches.

Amid the captives is a little girl, and she's crying.

I freeze, unsure of what to do. My chest burns, and my shoulders tighten. They took a *child*. Why would they take a child?

"The child is going to be as worthless as that old woman," Grandfather scoffs to Briggs.

I tense, knowing he's referring to Miriam. But maybe he'll listen to me about the little girl like he has about Miriam. If I'm careful not to upset him too much.

The crowd shifts, and the girl disappears from my view, but not from my mind.

Grandfather stands and spreads his arms. Silence steals over the crowd instantly. I force my attention to him, working to keep my face the placid expression of a doting grand-daughter even as fury burns in me.

"Welcome home, my warriors!" Grandfather's voice reverberates in the silence, and he pumps his fist into the air.

The crowd cheers, and falls quiet again a moment later.

"Tonight, we celebrate. But first, we remember." He pauses, his gaze sweeping the crowd. "We are who we are because we evolved into the people we needed to be in order to survive. When North America was destroyed in the Demise, when all we knew was snatched from us, when our own neighbors stole what was never rightfully theirs," he speaks the words through clenched teeth, "we learned a powerful truth. And it is the one we *live by!*" He shouts the last words, and there's another roar from the crowd that burns with anger.

I press my lips together. All my life I cheered with them, but not anymore. I've heard Grandfather's speech countless times, but my time with Miriam, what I've learned of the God she serves, the God she's taught me to trust—I know Grandfather's ways aren't right. I ease toward the edge of the platform, slipping behind some of Grandfather's advisors.

Grandfather grips the rail at the front of his platform and leans forward, eyes narrowed. "All of us have lost someone or something, and it has taught us this valuable lesson: take before someone takes from you. Steal what you need and what you want. Rule by fear. And understand that power is the richest commodity there is!" His words increase in volume and intensity until he's practically screaming.

The crowd erupts in cheers and shouts, creating a cacophony that threatens to shatter my eardrums. I stare at the group of captives huddled together, shaking. Many crying.

The little girl—she can't be more than six or seven—is sobbing. They've never brought back a captive younger than fourteen. Every captive must work. So why would they take a little girl?

I clench my hands into fists, as Grandfather once again quiets the crowd.

This isn't okay.

None of this is okay.

But I don't know what to do.

Grandfather paces to the left of his platform, making eye contact with the men and women in the crowd. "I was among the generation that lost everything in the Demise of America. Family. Friends. Every possession. I found other survivors in the North after the attacks, and we banded together, desperate to just live another day."

He tells the same story at every Welcoming Party, but no one quiets him. It would be the last thing they ever did.

Yet, at the moment, I *wish* someone would dare to stop him. I shift back slightly, deeper into the crowd.

"We found a life, but one day that changed. Jonas Reptation," he spits the name like it's a curse, "wanted to return to the life of luxury he'd lost more than he cared about helping others survive." Grandfather's face is carved into lines of hatred. "One day when I was out, he murdered a dozen people in our group, stole everything he could and left to find the life he'd lost. He—"

The little girl lets out a sob that cracks through the air.

Grandfather's face twists. "Shut the brat up!"

Sienna rushes to the little girl, picks her up, and takes her out of the square before any of the Raiders can respond.

I release a sigh, thankful she reached the little girl first. Because I shudder to imagine what might happen to the child if someone like Carver tried to stop her crying.

Before Grandfather can continue with his speech, I ease down the steps and deeper into the crowd. With cautious movements, I slip out of the square.

I can't listen to more of the speech about Grandfather's loss and how he's used it to fuel his rage and create the Raiders. How our compound was the first—and remains the fiercest and most advanced—of the dozens of compounds that now litter the ruins of North America, bringing every village of survivors they find into captivity.

Don't want to listen to the chants and excitement of the crowd as they revel in their own bitterness and greed. Can't bear another lecture on the evils of Eryndale and the scouts who attempt to stand against the Raiders. How they have, so far, kept them from spreading their rule further to the east. And I refuse to witness the parading of the captives as they're stripped of all their possessions, their lives, and forced into slavery.

This compound is now their life, where they will live and die. And I don't want to witness the defeat I'll see echoed in their eyes, just like every other group of captives I've watched brought in.

I reach into the skirts of my gown, find the battery unit, and yank out the cords. My dress goes dark, and I breathe a relieved sigh. The Inventors won't be happy, but I don't care. I wind my way through the streets and down alleys, carefully avoiding the Roamers' patrol areas. Even during Welcoming Parties, there are always guards monitoring the Upper District, and cameras and sensors everywhere. The Roamers are always bitter about their role, since they're beneath the Raiders, and they're constantly looking for opportunities to prove themselves so they can achieve the status of a true Raider.

But I know how to avoid them.

Perhaps that is one of the perks of never leaving this place.

I kick my shoes off, the heels too difficult to manage on the unpaved gravel streets further from the Upper District. The stones dig into my feet, but I almost welcome the pain. And the distraction it gives me from my tormented thoughts.

I hesitate at a crossroads. Right will lead me to the Lower District, where I might find Sienna and the little girl. Her warm, light brown skin and dark curly hair throb in my mind.

Perhaps I could find them, help care for the child or bring her some food. Ease her fears.

Or I can go left, into the forest. Away from this nightmare.

I'll cause a scene if I go to the Lower District so late, and Grandfather would doubtless find out, which would be dangerous for me. The best way to handle him is to appear to do as he says and keep him happy. Most of the time.

I'll bring food and blankets tomorrow.

Plus, I need time to think. And there's one place where I can do so better than any other.

Night has fully fallen, but I could find my way there with my eyes closed. I go left.

The walls of the compound extend beyond the housing

areas and encompass parts of a forest, and the place I love, a small cove at the foot of a waterfall.

The grass is cool and slightly damp beneath my bare feet, and each step away from the Welcoming Party eases more of my anxiety and frustration.

Once, a few years ago, when I was about fifteen, I attempted to run away after a particularly frustrating conversation with Grandfather. I was sure the cove would lead to my freedom, and it had, but I'd realized that I had nowhere to go. So I returned to my grandfather, who was sick with worry, and we moved on.

Ever since, this space has been my sanctuary.

The compound is secure, locked up, impregnable. But I know the way out. And the way back in. I'd lied to Grandfather, told him I'd been hiding in the forest and somehow avoided being found by the dozens of Raiders searching for me. And I never told anyone of the way in and out of the compound.

It was there for me to use if I wanted it.

I considered leaving more and more often, but now the captives in the Lower District called to me. Miriam. Others I considered my friends. And now the little girl.

I duck under the branch of a tree and make my way deeper into the forest. Yes, I need to go to my special place and *think*.

Before long, I approach the cliff. I dig under a large bush until I find the rope ladder, and unroll it over the edge of the cliff. The distant sound of the waterfall echoes through the air, but there's a peaceful stillness to this glen that's undeniable. Less than a mile away, the river churns angrily before it launches itself over the edge of the cliff like thousands of wild horses. But by the time it arrives here, it's calmed. Like a child napping after her tantrum.

I descend the ladder and make my way to my bench. Or, rather, the log I use as my bench. A light breeze whispers through the air, playing with the edges of my hair. Even in the duskiness of the late evening, there's a peacefulness that instantly steals over me. I settle on my log and bury my toes in the lush grass.

My gown will be ruined after this, but I don't care. Grandfather's disapproving scowl comes to mind. I shake it off. I'll bake him some of his favorite cookies and go to all my lessons this week.

A sigh escapes my lungs. All the things I need to think about pounding at the door of my mind, demanding release and answers to questions that plague me more than I know how to put into words.

Miriam's words to me.

Grandfather's anger.

The child who has already, undoubtedly, experienced horrors her young eyes should never have witnessed.

And I'm trapped here, in the middle of it all.

*God, what do I do?* The prayer cries from my heart for the second time in mere hours.

Grandfather has always insisted those who believe in a god are weak. But Miriam, though old, is the strongest person I know. And the God she introduced me to has given me hope and peace.

Still, she has something in her faith that I don't yet. Something I can't quite put a finger on.

"Uhhahha." The moaning to my left jolts me out of my seat.

Someone else is here.

I grab a stick and squint into the murkiness of the deepening darkness. My heart pounds in my chest, and I hold my breath, searching for the person who made the noise.

But I don't see anything.

I take a tentative step toward the river, my senses alert. I've never been very good at the daily exercises and fight-training all Raider children receive. Partially because Grandfather insists on me having private tutoring each day that starts in the middle of those lessons. But now I find myself thankful that I at least know *some* techniques.

I strain my ears, but there's no other sound. My heartbeat slows. Maybe it was a night owl, or I'm just hearing things. I lower the stick.

"Ahh." Another moan to my left.

In a swift motion, I raise the stick to an attack position and creep toward the sound. Moonlight trickles through the trees, illuminating my path. I round a bush and stop.

There he is. The source of the groans.

A young man lies on the bank of the river, his body half in the water. He's unconscious, which makes him less of a threat, but I don't recognize him and he's not wearing Raider leathers or Welcoming Party dress clothes. Which means he's not one of my grandfather's men.

But I've never seen him in the Lower District among the captives. Not to mention, he's too muscular and healthy to be a captive. None of the Raiders would have dared taken someone like him. He'd present too much of a threat inside the compound.

I don't want to consider *what* they would do to someone like this stranger.

Maybe he's one of the hated Eryndale scouts. But a quick assessment doesn't show any weapons, so that's unlikely.

I stare at him for a long moment and make a decision. I can't leave him half in the water. Setting my stick aside, I drag him so he's fully on the bank of the river.

The man stirs, his eyelids fluttering.

I freeze.

The stranger's eyes open and catch mine. A breath hitches in my throat. I should be terrified. He's clearly stronger than I am, and I've set aside my weapon. But there's a gentleness in his eyes that I've never seen in a man before, not in my grandfather or uncles or any of the Raiders.

"Hi." His voice is a low growl.

Goosebumps rise on my arms.

He scoots himself into a seated position, grimacing. He takes in his surroundings for an instant before his eyes find mine again. "Where am I?"

I step back. "How did you come here?" Sweat trickles down my back, despite the coolness of the night.

He quirks an eyebrow at me, then shrugs. "I was fishing,"—

he nods toward the waterfall—"up there. Slipped on a rock, and next thing I knew I was waking up down here."

He stands, and I immediately wish for the stick I discarded. He's at least seven inches taller than me, and his muscles have muscles. Not to mention, with his deep brown skin, chocolate eyes, and strong jawline with the light scruff of a beard, he's far more attractive than any man has a right to be.

I blink. Where did *that* thought come from?

"You shouldn't be here." The words are harsh, but I don't know how to interact with this stranger.

He crosses his arms over his chest, an amused look spreading across his face like the sun's rays over the sky. "Where exactly am I, Miss...?"

"Catori!" The distant shout echoes in the glen and jerks me around.

Carver.

A new sense of dread wafts over me. Whoever this man is, he doesn't deserve to be victim to Carver's cruelty.

"Leave *now.*" The words rush out of my mouth along with a strange protectiveness for this stranger. "Please."

He steps toward me. "Are you in danger?" His piercing gaze searches my face.

"Catori, where are you?" Carver's voice is closer now.

Of course he came looking for me. He would have wanted to see me at the Welcoming Party—even though I *never* want to see him.

I squeeze my eyes shut as every worst-case scenario rushes through my mind. It was foolish of me to come here, tonight of all nights. I should have *thought.* Why don't I ever think through these things?

The last thing I want is Carver invading my glen with his cruel arrogance. But even more, I don't want him seeing this man. His kind eyes and instant protectiveness both warm me and set me on edge.

"You have to hide. He'll kill you if he sees you."

The man comes closer. Water droplets cling to his short dark hair, and his perfect, thick eyebrows draw down.

Why am I noticing how he looks right now? This is not the time for such foolishness.

"Catori?"

My name on his lips sends a small jolt through me, but I nod to answer his unspoken question.

"Are you in danger?" He reaches a hand toward me, then drops it. "Let me help you."

"I'm fine." I squeeze my eyes shut, my mind racing for a solution to a problem that is far too big for this late at night.

I don't want Carver to see this man, but I also don't want him to see *me*. He thinks we're betrothed, destined for each other, and I don't want to deal with any of his advances today.

The stranger's massive hand touches my arm. I jump, and he immediately pulls back. "Sorry. Bu—"

Before he can finish, I grab his hand and pull him away from the cliff's edge and the ladder I came down and toward the waterfall.

"Hey, Carver, over here!" Leon's voice. Of course Carver's lackeys are with him. "There's a ladder."

The voices travel easily down to us as though projected. I only hope they can't hear us.

My feet move over the earth deftly. But the guy I've decided to hide isn't quite as agile. His large feet clomp over the ground and reverberate through me.

"Try to move a little quieter," I hiss.

His hand squeezes mine lightly, and I realize I'm still holding it. And that I don't want to let go. His massive hand swallows mine and makes me feel safe. Which is totally dumb.

We round a corner. The noise of the waterfall echoes around us. I tug him toward it, and he follows my lead. I'm not sure if that makes him more likable or just plain foolish.

Our jog toward the waterfall is peppered with him glancing behind and all around us, watching for any sign that danger might be approaching.

Who is this guy?

Maybe I'm wrong, and he *is* a scout. I swallow against the hesitation I feel at the thought. If every Raider thinks scouts are evil, they're probably not.

Spray from the waterfall coats me as I lead us to the place I've never brought another soul. Not even Gabby. I want to stop, think, decide if this is a good idea. But Carver is probably in my glen now, and I don't know how long until he searches this area.

I shove away any imaginings of what might happen if he finds us, and press on, heading right to the waterfall. And this stranger lets me lead him without a single question directed at me. I'm tempted to stop and ask him *why* he would do this, but now's not the time. I let go of his hand to climb onto a barely visible ledge, and shimmy myself along it until I'm at the hole that leads to the caves behind the waterfall. I slip inside, and a moment later, the man joins me.

I don't even know this guy's name, and now he knows about this secret place.

Perfect.

I crawl over the rocky ground until I'm directly behind the waterfall. It's impossible to see what's happening on the other side of the water. But I also know the caves are equally impossible to find unless you know exactly what to look for.

To this day, I don't know how I found them myself years ago, but I'm glad I did.

I settle into a place farther back where the ground is dry.

Leaning against the wall, I stare at the water cascading in torrents in front of me.

The man plops down next to me, his shoulder brushing mine. A shiver races up my spine and back down. I don't know this person at all. I could be in far more danger alone in this cave with him than I have ever been with Carver.

Little bits of moonlight filter past the water, but not enough to allow me to see him clearly. Yet his features are somehow starkly imprinted in my mind. His firm jaw, broad nose, dark brown skin, brown eyes, full lips. I squeeze my eyes shut, but it doesn't erase his handsome face from view.

Excellent. Just what I need. To dissolve into some blubbering, foolish girl. I make *fun* of the other women in the Upper District who swoon at the young Raiders. There is no way I'm going to be like them. No matter how gorgeous this guy may be.

"I'm Micah." His voice is low, a whisper I can barely hear over the roaring waterfall. He nudges me with his shoulder. "Not sure what just happened, but I think I should thank you. So thanks."

I turn toward him, his face cloaked in darkness. "You shouldn't be here. It's not safe. We'll wait for a while, until Carver tires of searching for me, and then I'll show you how to leave. And you can never come back."

He doesn't respond for a long while, and I release a breath I didn't know I was holding. Disappointment trickles over me like the droplets of water on my skin. I want him to respond, to argue with me maybe. But he's silent, just like every other man who's watched the injustice in this blasted compound and done nothing to stand against it.

Not that I have done much to stand against it, but still...

Micah doesn't know about the injustice. He has no clue there's a young girl who's been taken captive, who's scared and alone right now because of the viciousness of the Raider attacks. He's not part of the raids.

Yet I bristle at his silence.

He breathes in. I feel his shoulder rise, then fall as he exhales slowly. I didn't realize we were sitting so close. My cheeks warm, both with embarrassment from being this close and frustration with him. Which is not okay. I know logically I shouldn't be frustrated with a man I just met for not disagreeing with me.

"I don't know you." He shifts, and I can sense him facing me more fully. "But my mama would whip me into next week if I left a woman like you to fend for herself against a man she's afraid of."

"I'm not afraid of him," I snap.

"Sure. So you run and hide in caves just for fun? And it's, what, normal for you to think this Carver guy is going to kill a stranger?"

I gnaw on my lower lip, annoyed with Micah and myself. He's now doing what I wanted him to a moment ago, but I don't find myself appreciating his reasoning. "It's complicated."

"Things aren't always as complicated as we think. There's right and there's wrong. And it's wrong for a man to act in a way that makes a woman fear him." He says each word with a quiet conviction that leaves me wanting to know him more.

And that's completely impossible.

I stand. Micah follows suit, but ducks low to avoid the ceiling of the cave.

"It's been long enough now. I'll show you how to get out of here and back to wherever it is you came from."

Before I can walk two steps, his hand catches mine. His grasp is gentle, not forceful and insistent like the drunk men in the compound. Because of my grandfather, most of the men won't touch me like they do with the other women. The few who were drunk enough to think it was okay to grab me regretted it before much could happen. Yet their arrogant assumption that it was their right to do so still burned a mark on my skin. I struggled as soon as they touched me.

But I don't pull away from Micah.

"Come with me," he says. "I don't know what this place is or what trouble you're in, but I can protect you."

I tug my hand, and he immediately releases it. "I don't need protection. I'm fine here." I walk over to the small gap that leads to a series of tunnels and ledges out and to the top of the cliff on the other side of the river. Micah is broad, but I think he'll be able to make his way through. "Go through this opening—"

"I can't leave—"

"Yes. You can and you *must*. And never come back."

He doesn't respond, so I give him the instructions he needs to find his way out of the cave.

When I'm finished, he hesitates, but after a long moment, he steps toward the opening. He turns back to me. "I'm glad to have met you, Catori."

With that, he disappears.

# FOUR

I stare at the canopy above my bed as sunlight sneaks its early rays into my room. It was easy enough to slip in last night without Grandfather knowing. He'll probably be sleeping off his overconsumption of alcohol until this afternoon.

If only sleep came as easily to me. Instead, I spent the night tossing and turning, trying to sort through the events of the evening. Micah. The child at the Welcoming Party.

The face of the little girl throbs in my mind, and I can't shake it away.

I turn to my side. The shadows of my room lighten, revealing my desk, the discarded—and ruined—gown in front of my walk-in closet, and my small bookshelf, with books tossed on it haphazardly. I should really clean that up. If J walked in and saw the shelves, she'd be mortified.

But there's no time for cleaning now.

I throw the thick covers off, get out of bed, and head to my closet. Kicking the gown aside, I enter the small room within my room. I select my most comfortable leathers, slide on boots, and then quietly make my way out of the mansion I share with Grandfather.

Time for class.

As much as I want to skip it and head to the Lower District with food for my friends and to check on the newest wave of captives, self-preservation keeps walking in the opposite direction. Grandfather will be furious enough as it is that I left the Welcoming Party early. If I skip out on classes too, who knows the fury I'll unleash.

Better to do as I'm expected to this morning and check on the new captives and the little girl later today.

My boots crunch against the gravel as I weave down the streets to the school at the edge of the Upper District. Other than fellow students heading to class, it's quiet this morning. Shops won't open until later and even the captives in the Lower District won't be expected to go to the factories for work until mid-morning at least.

Not because anyone cares about their well-being, of course. Just because none of the men and women who oversee the labor will get out of bed earlier than mid-morning.

I grind my teeth together. Maybe I *should* go to the Lower District now.

"Catori!" Gabby calls from behind me.

I stop and turn to her with a wave, some of the tension easing from my shoulders. At least I'll be able to spend time with her this morning.

She jogs to catch up to me, and we continue toward the building that looms at the end of the street. The two of us are among the oldest still in school. Most teens train to become Raiders, Roamers, or Inventors once they turn sixteen. Grandfather and J wanted me and Gabby to receive the best education available in the compound. Usually, it's only for those who might become Advisors to the Chief.

If Grandfather has his way, the fourteen students in my class will be Advisors to *me* one day. And whoever I marry. A tremor twists my stomach into a knot.

"You made a quick exit last night," Gabby remarks, pulling me back to the moment.

Her tone is light, but there's a crease between her eyes that tells me she doesn't approve.

"I wasn't feeling well." It's not exactly a lie.

"Sure."

I can practically feel her eye-roll. "Ms. P. should be in interesting form today."

Gabby smirks. "She really got into things last night." She throws her elbows out, mimicking Ms. P.'s dance from the night before.

I laugh, happy to move beyond the tenuous reality that Gabby and I are going in different directions. Especially since I know she doesn't approve of my interactions in the Lower District. Today can be like old times.

We climb the steps to the schoolhouse. With a pang, I realize after this there will be less than ten more times Gabby and I make this trek together.

"Maybe we'll get out early today," I say to distract myself from the painful thought.

Gabby wiggles her eyebrows. "I'm banking on it. J will make me train after class, but let's do something together later."

I do a quick mental calculation. Her training should be at least three hours, which will give me enough time to bring leftovers from the party down to the Lower District. "Sounds good."

We enter our classroom with the other advanced students and slide into desks near the front.

Ms. P. slumps behind her desk at the head of the class,

fingers pinching the bridge of her nose. Most of my classmates look as bad as she does. Gabby and Aiden, her younger brother by one year, are the only other students who look even semi-alert. Probably because J won't allow anyone in her crew to drink during Welcoming Parties.

A bell chimes through the school, signaling the beginning of class, and there's a collective groan.

Ms. P. takes a swig of coffee, rolls her shoulders, stands, and begins droning on with her favorite post-Welcoming Party lecture. Gabby and I are convinced she does it so she doesn't have to think. We all know this speech by heart and it's hard to focus. I stare at the window that faces the Upper District and watch the streets come to life as men and women finally begin their day.

Gabby leans against me and starts whispering, word for word, Ms. P.'s speech using the same ridiculous tone she used last night. "...which is why it's vital for each of you to best understand how our illustrious compound fits within our world. In order to be the best Advisors you can be, you must know how and where to send out Raiders, which missions are worth risking a closer encounter with Eryndale, and what losses and casualties are acceptable."

A chuckle escapes as Gabby says the last word with as much flourish as Ms. P.

Everything goes silent. Gabby immediately pulls away from me and sits straight in her chair, lower lip clenched between her teeth.

*Oh no.*

Ms. P. strides down the aisle between desks, her heeled shoes clacking against the wooden floorboards. She stops next to us. Her piercing gaze focuses on Gabby.

"Gabrielle, stand up."

A pulse throbs in my throat. No one calls Gabby by her full name.

Gabby stands, every trace of humor washed from her face. She keeps her head lowered, hands clenched together.

"Congratulations. You've just been awarded your final demerit."

Gabby's head flies up.

"Pack your things," Ms. P. continues, looking down her sharply pointed nose at my friend. "And good luck finding a job in any respectable compound after this."

"Ms. P.—" Gabby's voice breaks—"I'm sorry."

Ms. P.'s hand slashes through the air. "Not good enough."

Silence, thick and heavy, descends on the room. Gabby regularly disrespects Ms. P., but neither of us expected the woman to go to these lengths.

Gabby's jaw trembles and her hands shake as she reaches down to grab her bag.

I stand abruptly. I can't let this happen. Not to my best friend. "The offense is mine, not Gabby's." The words rush from my mouth. "So the demerit is mine as well."

Ms. P.'s hawk-like stare zeros in on me, and Gabby's movements freeze.

Maybe this was a bad idea. Grandfather will *not* be pleased to hear I received a demerit. My first, but still.

"I heard Gabrielle. Not you." Ms. P.'s lower eyelid twitches.

I straighten my shoulders and tilt my chin upward. I've already started down this path. No sense stopping now. "You would question me, Rolinda?"

My use of her first name has her taking a step back. One of the other students releases a small gasp. But I maintain my stance, despite the fact that my insides are quaking. It's always been my right as Princess to call her whatever I want. I've never exercised it before now, since I didn't want to stand out. But I need all the power my position holds.

Ms. P. opens her mouth as though to argue, then ducks her head in a small bow. "Very well. Gabrielle, the demerit is cleared from your name." Her eyes flick to mine. "*Princess Catori*, you've received your first demerit." She marches back to the front of the class.

I slip back into my seat next to Gabby, still feeling the weight of the stares of the other students on me.

Gabby takes my hand and squeezes it so hard my knuckle cracks. I squeeze her's back, and swallow the bile rising in my throat. What did I just do?

It doesn't matter that a demerit for me holds far less weight than it would for any other student. The stain on my academic record will *not* go ignored by Grandfather. He's going to be furious.

<hr>

There are nods and whispers from shop owners as I head toward the poverty of the Lower District. I ignore them, hoping everyone decides today is a good day to mind their own business.

Although I know *that's* unlikely.

Oh well.

Between leaving the party early last night and receiving a demerit in class today, I know it's only a matter of time before I stand before Grandfather and feel the weight of his displeasure.

The thought twists my insides, but I maintain a steady pace, adjusting the heavy basket on my arm to a more comfortable position.

I might as well visit the newest wave of captives and bring

the leftovers like I promised Marsha I would. It'll be better to get all my infractions over with in one day, right?

Ms. P. ended class a few minutes after our conversation, and Gabby and I said quick goodbyes before she practically ran to train with J. I don't blame her. I'm just as eager to busy myself with other things rather than dwell on what happened. Gabby hates thinking about anything negative. Although I know she appreciates me taking the fall for her, I doubt she'll ever again want to discuss her display of fear and vulnerability. Or that she was seconds away from becoming as despised as the slaves I'm heading to visit now.

I round a bend and duck under a broken archway and into the Lower District. It's mid-morning, so the captives are now preparing to head to their shifts after the delayed start. I unfold the fabric napkin on top of my basket, and the scent of freshly baked bread wafts out.

As I press deeper into the Lower District, I pass out still-warm rolls and containers of leftover food to any of the captives who will approach me. I smile whenever one dares to make eye contact. I know many of them, but they almost flinch when I call them by name. It's better when I do this with Miriam, but it's early, and my elderly friend is likely still in her home.

Can't they see that I'm different? The blood of my family might run through my veins, but I'm not like them.

I'll *never* be like them.

I pick up my pace, my basket lighter than it was a few moments ago. At least I'm trusted enough now that they'll take the food I offer. It's far better than the measly rations appointed to the captives.

My eyes scan the dilapidated buildings, hunting for a glimpse of the child from last night. She's nowhere to be seen. She has to be here *somewhere*, right?

I round a bend and almost plow into Sienna. Her eyes are wide, nearly frantic.

"Are you okay?" I ask.

She doesn't even look at me, her gaze desperately scanning every corner of the alley we're in.

"I can't find Jordyn," she says, the panic in her face reflected in her words.

"The little girl?" I ask, already knowing the answer.

Still, when Sienna nods her agreement, my heart seizes.

"I'll help you look." Typically, when I offer to help Sienna, she turns me down. She fears any repercussions of closely associating with me. It hurts, but I understand. At least a little.

Today, she just nods, and together we split up to search for the child.

Jordyn.

CHAPTER

# FIVE

I half-jog through the streets, gaining many startled stares. The sun warms my skin and causes sweat to trickle down my back. With every passing moment, I become more frantic. Where is she? She's been here less than twenty-four hours.

Maybe she tried to run away.

If a Roamer or one of the Raiders finds her...

I shove the thoughts aside and race down another alley, crammed full of debris and castoff supplies from the clothing warehouse.

Blood pounds in my ears. Maybe Sienna found her. It's been at least a half-hour of searching. I should find Sienna, and if she doesn't have Jordyn, we can regroup.

A muffled sob echoes from behind a discarded table with one leg missing.

I duck low to peer under it and breath whooshes from my lungs. I found her.

"Jordyn?" I drop to my knees so we're eye-level.

Her head snaps up from where it rested on her knees, and her striking grey eyes widen. Her tiny body shakes.

"It's okay," I say, trying to keep my voice calm, even as anger pulses through my veins. A child should never know the fear I see reflected in her beautiful eyes. "I'm Catori. I'll keep you safe."

I ease my hand toward her, trying not to scare her more.

She hesitates, chewing on her lip. Then she uncurls herself, grasps my hand, and comes out. Her brown skin is caked in dirt, and tear tracks mar her face.

"Why are you hiding here, little one?"

She releases my hand and buries herself in my stomach. I freeze for an instant, then scoop her into my arms and stand up.

I rock back and forth, her little body shuddering in fear and tears.

"There she is. I couldn't find the kid anywhere."

I spin to face Carver, as Jordyn's arms wrap around my neck so tight I almost can't breathe. "What do you want?"

He steps closer. "I want the girl. She's supposed to be working. I didn't bring her here to live a luxurious life." He reaches for her, and I step back.

"No. She's a baby."

His eyes harden. "She's six. Old enough to make herself useful. And she needs to learn her place here. The Lower District serves the Upper District. That is the way things are. And the brat was brought here for a purpose. Don't get in my way, Catori."

I shift so I'm shielding the little girl more, her entire body clinging to me. "She's scared, Carver. Have some decency." My tone is almost pleading, which I hate. But I know, when it comes down to it, if Carver wants to take the child from me, he can. And there's nothing I can do. I bow my head. "Please."

He sighs. "Fine. You play with your new toy for now." His hand cups my cheek, and it takes everything in me not to pull away.

I look up at him, hoping my hatred doesn't show in my gaze. Not this time.

He smiles, his thumb stroking my cheek. "I can't deny you anything."

With that, he turns and walks away. A moment later, I hear him screaming at someone else. But at least he left me with Jordyn.

"Shh, it's okay. He's gone," I whisper into Jordyn's ear. "I won't let him hurt you." I only hope I can keep my promise.

"He scares me," Jordyn says, her voice small. "He killed my mommy and daddy."

My eyes slide close. She witnessed the murder of her parents?

I don't know what to say, so I start walking. I need to find Sienna and let her know Jordyn is safe.

Jordyn lays her head on my shoulder, and my chest tightens at her trust. I rub her back. I'll do everything in my power to be worthy of that trust.

After a few minutes, I find Sienna. As soon as she sees Jordyn, a sigh escapes her, and she swallows hard.

"Let's get her something to eat," Sienna says. She leads me to her house.

Jordyn refuses to let me put her down, and I find I don't mind. I sit on a rickety chair at Sienna's table and settle Jordyn on my lap, while Sienna puts together a small bowl of oatmeal. The meager portions in her cabinet gnaw at me. Once Jordyn is settled, I'll go back to the Upper District and gather supplies for Sienna and Jordyn, since I abandoned my basket somewhere in my search for the child.

Now that the little girl is here with her, Sienna can't deny my help, right?

I haven't spent much time with kids, so when Sienna makes light conversation with Jordyn, I can't help but feel relief. Jordyn relaxes more and more with Sienna, and soon she seems almost at ease.

She eats her oatmeal, and Sienna focuses on me.

She opens her mouth, but before she can say a word, there's a knock at the door.

Sienna winces, and Jordyn stops eating.

"Catori, I know you're in there." J? What is she doing here?

I move to get up, but Jordyn spins and wraps her arms around my neck.

Sienna opens the door, and J glides into the room. How the woman moves without ever making a sound is beyond me.

Her gaze flicks from me to Jordyn to Sienna, who presses herself against the wall, head bowed. "Looks like a party." Her tone is dry. "Your grandfather wants to see you. Now."

I tuck a piece of hair behind Jordyn's ear. "I'm in the middle of something."

J's eyebrow arches. "Excellent. I'm sure that tidbit of information will be more than enough for your grandfather." The sarcasm wafts out of her, and she rolls her eyes. "Let's go." She waves a hand toward the door.

I press my lips together. There's no sense in arguing with J. Everyone knows that. Plus, she's right. Grandfather would never take *any* excuse for me not instantly obeying him. Especially if that excuse involves the captives of the Lower District.

J focuses on Sienna, whose gaze is still trained on the floor. "Take the kid."

Sienna instantly moves to obey, and Jordyn goes to her when she reaches for her. I stand from my chair and follow J from the house.

I grit my teeth, annoyed at J *and* myself because I'm leaving Jordyn behind.

"Don't be mad at me," J says, as though she can read my thoughts. "This is on you. You know your grandfather wants everyone at the Welcoming Party, and you left during his speech. Novice mistake, Tor." She shoots me a sideways glance. "You know better than that."

My cheeks warm. She's right. "I needed air."

J grunts.

She mentions nothing about the demerit, and I hold on to a twinge of hope that maybe Ms. P. decided not to tell Grandfather about class this morning. Which is almost as foolish of a thought as leaving during Grandfather's speech.

We make our way toward the Upper District. Every time we pass someone—whether they're a captive, Roamer, or Raider—they practically leap out of our way. J's crew must be on a training exercise because we don't see any of them. I think they're the only ones *not* afraid of her.

She is intimidating, but growing up with Gabby has given me a glimpse of a side of her not everyone else sees.

J stops and I suddenly realize we're at the Central Quarters. The family mansion dominating the very center of the compound looms before me. Grandfather's domain. My shoulders tense.

J sweeps her hand toward the door. "After you."

I slip past J, and into my family home.

"This will be fun," she murmurs, just loud enough for me to hear.

I want to roll my eyes, but Grandfather stands before me, arms crossed and jaw set.

Excellent.

Uncle Briggs marches into the entry from the sitting room.

I freeze just inside the door. Our entry way is spacious with high ceilings and a sprawling foyer that spills into the rest of the mansion. But with the two men glowering at me, it feels way too small.

J prods me in the back, and I stumble a step forward. Part of me wants to glare at her for the shove, but despite the fact that her sister and I are best friends, she still intimidates me. Her mouth twitches like she knows it.

Grandfather clears his throat, drawing my attention. "What is *wrong* with you?" His tone is grating.

Like what he uses when he's about to punish one of his men.

I bow my head and clasp my shaking hands together. "I'm sorry, Grandfather."

Leaving last night was a terrible idea, and unless I want to incur the fullness of his wrath, I need to make this right.

"Sorry?" Uncle Briggs scoffs. "You shamed all of us when you left the Welcoming Party early last night."

The floor rumbles, and my head snaps up to find Grandfather stalking toward me. His eyebrows draw down, and a vein throbs on his forehead. I take a small step back. He reaches me and grabs my upper arm in a painful grip.

I wince, but suppress a cry.

He shakes me. "I let you get away with just about everything, but this is unacceptable. We *must* show control, Catori. If you're going to lead this compound one day, you can't leave a Welcoming Party! You know that." He shakes me again. "And a demerit?" He practically spits the word.

Out of the corner of my eye, I notice J's eyes narrow.

"You finish your final term in a matter of days." His nostrils flare. "Show some maturity and stop acting like a worthless kid."

Jordyn's tear-stained face fills my vision.

"Why did they take a *child?*" The question spills past my

lips and warmth burns in my chest. Somehow, the answer to this question matters more to me than Grandfather's fury.

I meet his gaze. His eyes are narrowed into slits as he studies me.

He leans closer, and I want to shrink away. This is the man who raised me. If I do exactly what he wants, he shows his own version of affection and care for me. But I haven't done what he wants.

"It doesn't matter why." His words bite at me. Right now, he is Chief Jehoram, Founder of the Raiders. Not my grandfather. "The Raiders bring in captives to serve us. Age doesn't matter. Gender doesn't matter. Race doesn't matter. They are here for one purpose—to improve our lives because we are more powerful than they are." His grip on my arm tightens, and this time a small whimper escapes me. His lips twitch in the flash of a smile. Like he's feeding on my pain.

I close my eyes against the hurt echoing through me. But I can't pull my mind from Jordyn. Her fear. A sense—a *need*—for justice opens my eyes.

"But she's a child. It's not *right*, Grandfather."

He pulls back, like I slapped him. Then he lifts me off my feet and throws me to the floor. I skid across the marble for a few feet, pain exploding through my hip.

*Oh, Catori. What were you thinking?*

Grandfather's rage is notorious. And now it's directed at me.

J steps between Grandfather and me. I blink. What is she doing?

"Out of my way, Captain," Grandfather says. "I need to deal with this insubordination."

J inclines her head, but doesn't move. "Agreed. But I think Catori misspoke." She turns toward me. "Didn't you?" Her eyes flash a warning that I know I must heed.

I bow toward the floor, adopting the subservient pose my grandfather expects. "I did. A thousand apologies, Grandfather. You are wiser than I." The words taste bitter, but I have to say them. Appease him for now. And later I'll find a way to make things better for the captives. For Jordyn.

Grandfather crouches before me, his anger abated. Slightly. "You're my granddaughter, and I love you, Catori. But you need to watch your mouth. Understood?"

I nod.

"Good, girl." He pats my cheek with his calloused hand. It should be a tender gesture, but it feels harsher than necessary. Like a warning.

If I cross him again, I won't get away so easily.

"What will her punishment be?" Uncle Briggs asks.

My gaze swings to him. I forgot he was even here.

Grandfather stands to his full height. "She knows what she did wrong."

Uncle Briggs opens his mouth.

"Am I still Chief, or not?" Grandfather shouts the words, and they echo in the high ceilings of the foyer.

Briggs inclines his head. "Of course, sir." He straightens his shoulders. "Since this incident is settled"—he spears me with a poisonous glare—"perhaps we should discuss the other matter?"

Grandfather gestures to the left wing, where his office is, and Briggs turns on his heel and marches toward it.

I get to my feet.

Grandfather faces me and rests a hand on my shoulder. He smiles, but his eyes are hard. "Behave, Catori."

With that, he turns and leaves.

"Guess that means the Lower District is off limits for the rest of today," J remarks, her tone wry.

I roll my eyes at her, and she grins. I want to ask her why

she stood up for me, but questioning J isn't something I'm feeling brave enough to do right now.

"Come on." J heads to the door.

"Where are we going?" I ask, even as I trail after her.

"My house. Gabby wasn't herself during training this morning, and something tells me your demerit holds the reason."

I still, eyes wide.

J opens the door and gestures for me to exit. "Let's go."

J's intuition is legendary, and the last thing I want is to get Gabby into trouble with her sister.

"Now, Catori."

J's sharp words snap me into motion, and I exit the mansion.

I need a distraction, but this wasn't what I had in mind.

CHAPTER

# SIX

"A *fifth* demerit, Gabby?" J paces in front of where Gabby and I sit on her couch in the midst of her expansive library.

After a handful of vague threats, which Gabby and I didn't give into—partially because we both know J wouldn't hurt us—J went and dragged Aiden into the room.

One look from his oldest sister, and Aiden gave a rundown of the morning's events, then made as fast of an exit as I've ever seen from him.

J stops her pacing, her eyes flicking between the two of us. "Do you understand what could have happened to you? To Aiden?"

Gabby hunches deeper into the cushions of the couch, arms crossed over her chest. One shoulder rises in a half-hearted shrug, but she doesn't lift her gaze to meet J's.

I shift forward. "It's okay—"

"No." J's hand slashes in the air. "It's not okay. I've worked my butt off so that you and Aiden could dual train as Raiders and Advisors. I can count on one hand the amount of people who've been able to do that." She taps Gabby's boot with her own. "Look at me, child."

That brings Gabby's head up. "I'm not a child."

"Then stop acting like one."

"You're not Mom," Gabby says through clenched teeth.

The sisters glare at each other for a long moment. Since their parents died ten years ago, J has raised Gabby and Aiden. Mostly, Gabby has appreciated her sister's care. But she's confided in me that she misses just being sisters.

I ease toward the edge of the couch. "I can leave…"

"No." J blows out a long breath and shakes her head. "You saved our family from ridicule. Kept my dumb sister from getting expelled from the compound, ruining her life, and tarnishing Aiden's and my reputation."

Gabby scoffs, but J's penetrating gaze remains fixed on me

"And destroying all I've worked for for this family." J pauses, and for an instant I see behind her hardened warrior mask to the sister desperate to care for and protect her younger siblings. "I owe you for that."

"You don't owe me." My gaze shifts between her and Gabby. "She's my best friend. What else was I supposed to do?"

Gabby shifts next to me, and I know she's uncomfortable. I search my mind for a way to change the subject.

J sits on the coffee table across from us and rests her forearms on her thighs. "And that's why I am indebted to you, even if Gabby doesn't want to realize the full impact of what could have happened. You didn't do it for a favor, which is why I owe you one. One as life-altering as what you did for Gabby."

Every argument dies in my throat. Gabby may be fine with arguing with J, but I'm not. So I give a slight nod.

J gets to her feet. "Now get out of here. Both of you. I want to read."

Gabby springs to her feet and I follow.

"Go for a ride," J remarks from where she stands gazing at one of her bookshelves. "Gabby needs more practice, and Catori is one of the best riders I know."

Gabby clenches her teeth, and I nod toward the door before she snaps at J. It's barely noon and I've hit my quota for confrontation today.

Once we're outside, Gabby picks up a stone and chucks it through the air. "She makes me so mad sometimes! It was just a joke."

"Wanna go for a ride?" I ask, hoping she says yes.

After J's suggestion, all I want to do is get on a metallic horse and race. Plus, I know Gabby understands the weight of what could have happened. She needs a distraction as much as I do.

"Fine," she says. "But it's *not* a training session. Your obsession with the horses is ridiculous and I'm not in the mood for another lecture."

I bite back a smile, and we make our way to the charging stables.

***

GABBY WAVES HER HAND IN FRONT OF MY FACE. "CATORI, HELLO!" The beads woven into her many braids clatter together.

I blink. "What?"

"You've been staring off into the forest for like a solid minute." She lifts her eyebrows. "What is going on?"

I give my head a subtle shake and finish pulling on my riding boots. "Nothing. Sorry. I was just lost in thought."

We've gone riding each day after class is over for the past four days. J wants Gabby to become more comfortable on the mechanical horses, and Gabby's convinced J's still punishing her for the almost demerit.

I haven't told Gabby about what happened with Grandfather four days ago, and J hasn't either.

But I'm just as glad. Gabby doesn't understand my obsession with the Lower District, and she already thinks it's crazy that I left the Welcoming Party early.

She rolls her eyes. "You've been getting lost in thought a lot lately. If I didn't know any better, I'd think you met a guy who turned your head. Finally."

Micah's face immediately comes to mind. "No. I haven't," I snap. And instantly regret it.

Gabby's been a little on edge with me since the demerit situation, but she's now found a new topic.

One I'm not at all eager to dig into.

A smile spreads itself over Gabby's face like softened butter over a piece of warm toast. "You *have* found a guy. Who is it? Did Carver finally win you over?"

I spear Gabby with a scathing look. At least I hope it's scathing. "I will *never* be with Carver."

Gabby holds up her hands, one with a glove on, the other with a glove almost falling off. "Okay, okay. Sorry." She adjusts her one glove, focusing on it intently. "I mean, the guy can be a jerk, but he's cute. You gotta give him that."

"I don't have to give him anything." I stride toward the metallic horses, and Gabby jogs to catch up with me.

I'm about to walk around it and make sure everything is ready to go when she places her hand on my arm.

I turn to her, eyebrow lifted.

"Don't give me that look." She squints at me. "Fine. It's not Carver. But there's a guy. I know I'm right."

Micah's face flashes in my mind again, and my cheeks warm. Although my skin isn't the same caramel brown as Gabby and J, I'm thankful I'm tan enough with the summer sun to hide a blush. Because I'm sure if I was any lighter, I'd be lit up like a red rose in spring right now. And that would give me away.

Not that there's anything to give away. I'm not interested in Micah. He hasn't caught my attention. It was one moment with him a few days ago.

Gabby clears her throat.

"There's no one." I busy myself inspecting the metallic horse I ride every chance I get.

"Whatever," Gabby mutters. "But I know I'm right." She does her own inspection of her horse, and we both fall silent.

They're shaped like real horses, and even move like one, with joints in their knees and hips to mimic the motion, allowing Raiders to travel all types of terrain. Mine is painted black, with a star-shaped white mark on his nose. Just like the actual horse I rode when I was a child.

I check gages to make sure all the fluids are filled, confirm he's been fully charged, and then give him a pat on his back flank.

In one swift motion, I place my foot in the stirrup and mount the metallic steed. The coolness of the metal centers me.

I need this ride today. I've missed going to the Lower District the past couple of days, but I haven't wanted to further risk Grandfather's wrath. We're settling back into our normal, and it's best that way.

But I miss Miriam and I need her wisdom. And I want to check on Jordyn.

Maybe I'll go after my ride.

I prime the engine by pushing the button in the center of the horse's head, pull the metal bars up and into position, then kick my right heel back to start the horse up. It roars to life, and though I've only been on a real horse once in my life, I feel the power of the metallic horse beneath me like a steed ready to gallop for miles. A thrill of excitement zips through me, in tandem with the pulsing might of the horse. I love riding, but I love racing even more.

There's nothing quite like pushing the metal horse as fast as it will go until everything passes in a blur and the danger of death from a fall is as high as the exhilaration of being invincible.

Grandfather hates it when I race. It's probably not the best thing to do something *else* to displease him, but I need the distraction. Plus, he's happier with me now.

Carver always tells him when I race. Another strike against the loathsome man.

I wonder what Micah would think.

I clench my jaw. I met the man *once*. Who cares what he would think? He won't come back. I just need to move forward in my life.

Gabby's horse roars to life. "Ready?" she shouts.

"Let's do this!" I let out a whoop and yank my hands back, raising the horse on its hind legs as I rev the engine. I drop him down, and we race forward.

My hair flies out behind me, whipping in the wind. The Inventors will be furious if they learn I went riding without my helmet, but I don't care. I need the wind to clear my head, since nothing else has worked.

Without communicating, Gabby and I take the route out of the Upper District—breaking every speed limit posted—and head toward the rim of the compound where races take place. The track is vacant today. Just like I hoped. I open the throttle, shift to a higher gear, and let my horse kick up speed.

Its legs pound the earth beneath me, faster than a thousand horses combined. Well, at least five times faster than an actual horse.

My body moves in practiced rhythm as I bend low. The

distinct whir of the gears of the horse is one I barely notice. The Inventors can make the horses soundless, but they've chosen to leave the whir to instill fear in all who hear it.

Gabby is far behind me now. She's never willing to push her horse as fast as me. Partly because she's afraid of what it will do to her hair, and also because the Inventors have a soft spot for me and will do just about anything I ask. Including teaching me how to add in upgrades to my horse that only the top Raiders get for their missions.

Time seems to slow as I round a bend in the track, the wall to my right rising high. Something gnaws at me.

The past couple of days have been too much.

First Jordyn. Then Micah. Grandfather's attack. The demerit. My mind swirls as I try to process emotions I don't understand.

From the time I discovered the Lower District at sixteen, I've struggled with the fact that Raiders bring in men and women as captives from any town or village they could conquer. I'd seen the captives brought in during Welcoming Parties many times before discovering the Lower District. Thought nothing of the servants who made my life comfortable. Like every other Raider I knew, I assumed it was my right to be served, since my family was the strongest.

But the Welcoming Party where Miriam was brought in changed everything. She was the only captive I ever witnessed who didn't cower in fear. Although she wore many decades on her fragile frame, she stood tall. When her eyes caught mine that night, she smiled with a sadness in her gaze. For me.

Somehow, I knew she pitied me.

The next day I went in search of her and discovered the Lower District. Witnessed for myself how the captives were treated. Saw the factories they labored in—textiles, woodworking shops, masonry, food prep. The working conditions horrendous in every place. And I met Miriam.

Her kindness, compassion, and strength called to me, and that's when I began my secret lessons with her. She opened my eyes to the truth of who my people are. What they do.

And she showed me a new way. God's way.

I thought my changes, how I bring food and blankets and necessities to the captives, would be enough.

But now there's Jordyn. She's so little. Why would they take *her?*

I grind my teeth and push the horse faster, the power of the engine beneath me warming with the speed.

For a moment, I let myself consider what it would be like to ride into the Lower District, pick the girl up, and race out of the compound. Leave this life.

But what about Grandfather? My family and friends? I couldn't actually leave them.

Not to mention my horse has a kill switch. The Inventors set up every horse other than the men and women who are sent out on missions so that they can't leave the compound without dying. It's the one thing they haven't taught me how to change.

And then there's Micah.

I spent less than an hour with the man, and he's haunted me ever since. I almost wish I could just be the princess everyone expects me to be. Forget the Lower District. Forget Micah—especially since I won't ever see him again and just—

A figure stands in the path ahead of me, blocking my way. I'm going too fast to change direction, and if I don't stop, I'm going to plow right into him. I use the hand break, squeezing my knees into the sides of the horse, and yanking the handlebars back as I pull myself upright.

Everything locks up, the legs of the horse freezing, and I

skid toward the figure. There's won't be enough room. And the idiot isn't moving out of the way.

I pull harder, every muscle gripped with the need to stop myself from killing the man. The back end of the horse skids hard to the left, then whips around to the right. And stops. Inches from the guy.

Carver.

"What is *wrong* with you?" I screech. "I could have killed you! And I have no idea what kind of damage I just did to my horse." I flick open the diagnostic panel above the power button and scan the numbers.

"Come now. Is that any way to speak to your future husband, Catori, my dear?" Carver's voice is sultry smooth. Like the liquid mercury they use to kill mechanical horses that have been tampered with.

I bring my gaze up from the panel to meet his.

A smile plays around his mouth. "You shouldn't have been going so fast, darling. You know that." He makes a tsk sound. "I'll just have to have the Inventors change your speed parameters once we're married."

"I'll never marry you." I spew the words at him, even as a sense of foreboding wraps its smothering arms around me.

Carver's grin widens. "Your grandfather thinks it's a wonderful match. You, the princess of the Raiders, and me, the strongest warrior of our clan." He stalks closer, his gaze predatory. "We're made for each other."

He rests his hand on my thigh.

I slap it away. "Don't. Touch. Me."

His mouth compresses, eyes narrow. He lifts his hand, and for a moment, I wonder if he'll strike me. But he exhales slowly. "You'll learn to love me."

"Never. I will never marry you, and I will never love you."

I want to ride away, but the sudden stop has frozen the horse, and it needs another three minutes to recalibrate.

Three interminable minutes.

*God, make this man leave. Please.*

Carver's face hardens into the ruthless man I know him to be. "Then you'll learn to fear and obey me, you wretch. The quality of your life is up to you." He grabs my arm and jerks me forward so that I almost fall off the horse. My face is inches from his. "But you will marry me. Soon."

I spit in his face.

His lip curls, and I know he's about to strike me. The sound of a horse draws our attention.

"What's going on here?" Gabby's voice is light, but I hear the hard edge beneath it. "We're not finished our ride already, are we, Catori?"

I yank my arm free from Carver and settle myself in my saddle. "No. My horse just needs to finish recalibrating." I almost gasp in relief when I see that it's in its last thirty seconds.

"Everything okay, Carver? I thought you were readying for a mission?" Gabby keeps her voice innocent and sweet, but there's a challenge in her eyes. Her training for missions has been a source of contention between the two of us. But one benefit is that she knows the officers who could discipline Carver if they knew he wasn't doing all he was supposed to.

Carver gives a curt nod. He turns to walk away, but pauses and glares at me. "This conversation isn't over."

With that threat and promise, he strides away.

"What was that all about?" Gabby asks.

I turn my horse back on and let it warm up. "Nothing." I can't bring myself to share what Carver just said. If I do, I'm afraid it will make it too real.

"Yeah. Right. Because I'm an idiot and can't tell when something isn't okay with my best friend."

I sigh and focus on her. "He said he's going to marry me."

Gabby pulls her lip into her teeth, the way she does when she's about to say something she doesn't think I'll like.

"What?" The word is harsher than I intended, but I can't help it.

"It's not the worst match. He's respected, wealthy, handsome—"

"Are you serious?" I shake my head. "He's a monster." Before she can respond, I kick my horse into gear and ride away. There's no way the two of us will agree.

"Catori!" she shouts after me, but I ignore her.

As much as I love my friend, Gabby is becoming more and more like the other Raiders: believing that the most important work any Raider can do is further the power and prestige of their compound.

I push the horse faster.

I need to think, to prepare for a conversation with my grandfather. He couldn't have agreed to Carver's proposal. Not without speaking to me first. Right?

I ride aimlessly for another hour, my thoughts a chaotic vortex, and find myself in the forest, riding toward my glen. I haven't been back since the day I met Micah four days ago, but the peace and tranquility beckons me.

When I reach the cliff, I power down my horse, open its solar recharging panel and dismount. It was getting low on battery, anyway.

I make my way to the ladder and down into the glen, inhaling deeply. The freshness in the air, the pine and evergreen scent—it cocoons me. I wander to the water, my gaze drawn to the place where I first saw Micah. Even though it was only days ago, it feels like a dream.

I crouch by the river and run my hand through the water. Although I don't want to admit it, a part of me knows Grandfather is going to insist I marry Carver. According to all the laws of the Raiders, he's perfect for me.

But he's also the reason Jordyn is here.

"I wondered when you'd come back," the hot cocoa-like voice of Micah wafts through the air.

My eyes slide shut, and I swallow hard. A battle wars within me. I both *want* to see this man I rescued and fear the strange emotions welling within me. I stand and face him.

He's even more handsome in daylight. The kindness in his eyes, the smile on his face—why are they so comforting? I want to run to him and let him hold me.

Which is probably the *dumbest* inclination I've had all day.

"What are you doing here?" I ask. "I told you never to come back."

He shrugs one of his broad and muscular shoulders. "I've never been that good at listening."

CHAPTER

# SEVEN

I stare at Micah, annoyed at the war within me. I want to be angry that he's here, but I'm actually happy to see him.

Especially after the week I've had.

I don't know him at all. Logic would dictate that I not trust him. Maybe even report him to the Roamers and let them know he got into the compound. But doing so would inevitably lead them to discovering my secret exit. I can't let that happen.

Micah flashes a grin, his white teeth a striking contrast to his dark skin. "Does your silence mean you're happy to see me?"

"No," I snap. Then clench my teeth. I didn't mean to sound quite that harsh, but the encounter with Carver left me on edge. "Sorry. It's just been…" I shake my head. "You shouldn't be here."

He quirks an eyebrow. "Wanna walk?"

I gaze over at the cliff. I should tell him no. To be on his way. I should make it *very* clear that he can never come back here. But I turn back to him and nod. "Sure."

His grin widens and something flips in my stomach, an emotion I've never felt before. And it's unnerving.

Before I can change my answer, he grabs my hand and leads me downstream, away from the waterfall. "Great. I want to show you something."

His hand is twice the size of mine, and it's warm, reassuring, comforting. There's a confidence in the way he holds onto me that makes me feel protected. No man has ever made me feel like that. Not even my grandfather.

I tighten my grip. He doesn't show signs of letting go, but I find I don't want him to.

"When I was here yesterday, I decided to hike along the river for a bit, see what I could discover."

I stop walking and he stops with me, eyebrows raised in question. "You were here yesterday?"

"Course. I've been here every day since you saved me."

I tug my hand from his, immediately missing the warmth. "I told you not to come back. It's not safe here." I glance back at the cliff wall.

"I know exactly where I am. I know this is the main Raider compound. And I know what they'll do if they find me here... especially if I'm with you."

My blood seems to freeze in my veins, and goosebumps rise on my skin. A bird whistles its tune. A breeze blows, rustling the leaves on the trees. And it all stands in stark contrast to the growing horror I feel.

Micah seems to sense my unease. He steps forward. "I'm not going to hurt you. I give you my word." He hesitates. "I want to take you away from here."

"What?" The word is a screech that sends a nearby bird squawking into the air. "There's no way..." My voice trails off before I can protest more. "I don't even know you. And you don't know me."

His lips part, then close. He tilts his head, studying me. "Let me show you what I found. Okay?"

Carver's smug face flashes through my mind. His demands, his threats. I *know* what an evil man looks like. As much as I love my grandfather, I know he will do what he wants and what he thinks is best for himself before considering me and my needs. But Micah...he's different.

And some dumb part of me wants to trust him.

So I nod.

"This way." He gestures downriver, and I follow him.

I've explored this stretch of river dozens, maybe hundreds, of times over the years. There's nothing he'll show me I haven't already seen. Yet the excitement on his face, in the way each step seems to be filled with anticipation, makes *me* feel excited to see whatever it is he's discovered.

We don't talk as we hike. Some of my anxiety eases.

After a few moments, he pauses at the edge of the river. There are stepping stones across it, which is a new development.

"Did you...?" I nod at the stones.

"Yep. Come on."

He walks across the river, and each of the stones remains firmly in place. I can't help but be a little impressed. The one time I attempted to set up stepping stones across the river, it didn't go so well.

I follow his lead, and soon we are on the other side. We hike for another few minutes through the thick grove of trees, then round a corner.

I stop.

Before me is an open, grassy meadow peppered with wild-flowers, their colorful faces grinning up at the sun. I've seen this place before, and I've always enjoyed the beauty. But what has me gaping is the picnic sprawled out on a well-loved blanket.

"What..." My voice trails away and I stare at Micah as he plops himself on the blanket and pats the ground next to him.

"Come on."

I slowly inch over and settle myself across from him on the edge of the blanket. I stare at him, unsure what to make of the fact that he's been here every day since I found him. Part of me thinks I should feel creeped out by it. But I don't.

Which unnerves me.

He busies himself opening a cooler and pulling out a variety of dishes. I barely notice as I gawk at him.

Who is this guy?

As though he can feel me staring, he looks up and flashes me a smile. "I know you don't know me well, so I figured we could get to know each other over a meal." He waves at the many containers he just produced from his cooler. Then he ducks his head sheepishly.

Which is ridiculously endearing. "It looks lovely."

I'm rewarded with a dazzling smile that sends a shiver over me despite the warmth of the day.

"I'm not the best cook, so I enlisted some help."

I tense, ready to stand. "What do you mean? Is there someone else here?"

He waves his hands in front of himself. "No, no, no. Sorry. I just meant I had my galley chef prep the food. Each day I came. Maybe today the guys won't laugh at me since I'll be bringing less food back."

He chomps on a carrot stick, but I'm not interested in the food. His statement has left me with *way* more questions.

I stare at him for a long moment, and he lifts a perfectly formed eyebrow. His dark brown eyes seem to laugh.

"Yes?"

I gnaw on my lip and cross my arms. "Where do you come from?"

"I'm a riverboat captain," he says, leaning back on his hands. "I sail the river, do some fishing when I can. But mostly my crew and I deliver supplies to villages along the river. We're traders."

I nod. I've heard of these kinds of enterprises. Mainly because I overheard a meeting a few weeks ago about some Raiders forming their own crew and getting a ship to pillage those traversing the river.

When I heard them talking about it, I knew it was wrong. But now, sitting across from Micah, I'm actually afraid of what it might look like for someone like Carver or Uncle Briggs to sail the same river as Micah and his crew.

"You get quiet a lot." Micah breaks into my thoughts.

"Just...thinking."

He grins. "I figured." His grin fades, and he leans forward. "You're not how I imagined you'd be. Always thought the princess of the Raiders would be, well, mean."

I inhale sharply. "You know who I am." It's a statement. Not a question.

He nods.

The smartest reaction to this would be to get up and run back home. But I stay still.

"And you came back." Why I'm stating the most obvious reality is beyond me.

Another nod from Micah. "You're younger than I would have expected. Considering how old Jehoram is."

"He's my grandfather. My parents died before I can remember. In a raid from Eryndale scouts that killed my grandmother and aunt, as well as dozens of other Raiders." The words rush out of my mouth in a torrent, like the nearby waterfall gushing over the cliff. I clamp my lips shut.

Spewing my family history to a man I don't even know is foolish.

A line forms between Micah's eyes. "That doesn't sound like something the scouts would do." His quick defense of those Grandfather considers his mortal enemies surprises me.

Then again, maybe it shouldn't. Grandfather has lied to me many times before. Maybe his recounting of what happened to my parents is a lie, too.

I pick at a piece of grass, mind spinning. Why am I more ready to believe Micah than Grandfather? I focus on the wildflowers in the meadow, but feel Micah watching me.

Silence stretches between us.

"Do you want to stay here?" His words are soft, like a rose petal brushed against my cheek.

I focus on him. "What?"

He licks his lips. "You could come with me. I'll keep you safe."

I straighten. "No. This is my home." The answer comes immediately. But a part of my heart stirs at the thought of leaving.

What if I could just run away? Escape before Grandfather and Carver strike a deal that leaves me married to a man I hate?

Micah grins. "Well, it was worth a shot, right?" He winks. "Don't worry. I don't give up easily."

Heat warms my cheeks, and I press my lips together. He didn't get his way, but it didn't end in him yelling and screaming at me.

He picks up a sandwich and offers it to me. "Eat. Please."

I take it, the fresh bread soft in my hands. "Thank you." The two words hold a weight I can't express, but Micah seems to understand.

How can he understand when *I* barely understand?

He flashes me his heart-stopping smile and picks up his own sandwich and takes a massive bite. I follow his lead, and I'm shocked at how tasty the turkey and cheese sandwich is.

We eat in silence for a few minutes, and I relax. It's a gorgeous day, the sun is shining; the air is fresh and clear. And I feel strangely safe with Micah. I could almost forget my encounter earlier with Carver. The argument with Grandfather. My fears for Jordyn.

"So," Micah interrupts my thoughts. "Wanna hear about my crew?"

I swallow my bite and shrug. "Sure."

A roguish—and boyish—grin captures his face, and I can't help but smile in return. He launches into tales of a group of men that are almost unbelievable, but leave me laughing until my side hurts.

Time seems to slow while we're together, but soon the meal is finished, and the sun has sunken lower in the sky.

"I should go," I say, getting to my feet. "Thank you for the food."

Micah stands as well. "Thanks for joining me."

I turn to leave, then pause. "You really shouldn't come back, Micah." An ache at the thought of never seeing him again blossoms in my chest, surprising me. But I press on. "It's not safe. If they find you…"

"I know what the Raiders do. I've seen firsthand the devastation they leave in their wake." His face darkens, and he exhales a low sigh. "But Catori, I'll keep coming back." A ghost of a smile flits across his face. "Until I can convince you to leave with me."

A cloud drifts over the sun, sending the meadow into shadows, and fears darken my thoughts. An image of Micah injured or killed flashes vividly in my mind. The thought of his amiable smile, carefree manner, and strength forever extinguished feels like a blow to my gut.

"I'll never leave with you." I turn and almost run from the clearing before I can change my mind.

He doesn't run after me or call for me or yell at me, and for the second time in as many meetings with him, I'm almost disappointed. I look back to find him staring after me. His hand lifts in a wave, and I turn away.

Maybe he'll ignore me and come back.

Hope blossoms in me, followed quickly by shame. If Micah comes back, he'll be putting himself in danger once again. And if he's caught, Carver will kill him.

So why does the thought of never seeing him again bother me?

CHAPTER

# EIGHT

I wander down the alleys of the Lower District, cutting through passageways and avoiding the Roamers. It's well known that I spend time down here, but I don't want to draw any attention today. Mainly because I want to spend more time with Miriam. I need her advice, but first I plan to stop and check on Jordyn.

Things have settled into a rhythm the past few months. Two days after he stopped me on the racetrack, Carver was sent out on an extended mission. Which has been a relief. The Inventors need items they suspect will be found further East, so Carver and his crew were sent to find and retrieve them. Although I spend time learning from the Inventors weekly, I'm not sure what the items are. And asking hasn't proven to be successful, so I've given up. I'll find out eventually, and for now I'm just happy Carver is gone.

Grandfather and I are back to our usual balance of me being careful to not upset him and him being pleased with me. Which means attending the political functions he wants me to in order to observe how to rule as a Raider Chief, now that my classes have ended. Many of my fellow students have seats in the Advisor Meetings, and Gabby and Aiden come when they're not out on a mission with J.

It's one of the few times I see Gabby anymore. She's changing. But I guess so am I.

Since I'm doing what Grandfather wants mostly, I've been able to divide my remaining time between the Lower District and Micah. No matter how many times I tell him not to, he comes back to the glen whenever he can. There's a settledness about him. An unshakable quality to his faith and character that draws me to him and reminds me of Miriam's faith. Something I envy and admire at the same time.

He and his crew have had to run their trade route twice in the past month, but he comes to the glen the day they're back in the area. It's not safe for their boat to dock so close to the compound—which I've told him—but he doesn't seem concerned. And I feel like a terrible person because I'm *happy* that he doesn't listen to me.

I can talk with Micah in a way I've never been able to talk to any other man. He listens to me, encourages me.

Me. Catori, granddaughter of Chief Jehoram. *Princess* of the Raiders.

Never before have I hated my family connection more than when I'm with Micah. What would it be like if I was just a lowly captive and could run away with him? A longing I'm fighting more and more every time I'm with him.

Each time he visits, he invites me to leave with him. It's become almost a tradition now. He asks. I say no. He changes the subject.

The trouble is, every time he asks, it's becoming harder to say no.

I pull the scarf covering my black hair tighter to my face and duck under a low beam.

I give myself a subtle shake. He's become a trustworthy friend, which is a rich blessing. But today I need to tell Miriam about him, because I'm afraid he's starting to mean *more* to me than just my friend. And I'm not sure what to do about that.

I stop at the doorway of Sienna's house, knock three times, and wait. I know I'm delaying talking to Miriam, but I want the distraction of seeing Jordyn first.

The door opens and Sienna's eyes widen, but she steps aside and allows me to enter. I walk inside, close the door behind me, and smile.

Jordyn is sitting at the table eating breakfast. She grins at me and waves. "Hi, Catori!"

"*Miss* Catori," Sienna corrects the girl gently.

Jordyn ducks her head, lower lip trembling. "S-sorry."

Sienna pats the little girl's head. "It's okay, little one."

"She can call me Catori," I say. My heart aches for the horrors this child has experienced, and I find I'm *glad* she's grown comfortable enough to call me by my first name.

Sienna's gentleness toward Jordyn melts away as she spears me with a fierce look. "No. She can't." She nods toward the kitchen. With another tender touch on Jordyn's shoulder, strides that way, clearly expecting me to follow.

And I do, because there's something about Sienna that almost scares me.

When I enter the kitchen, Sienna rounds on me. "You can't let her address you so casually," her words are a harsh whisper, but I hear the fear lacing them. "Do you know what they'll do to her if they think she doesn't respect those of the Upper District? Especially you."

"I didn't think—"

"No. You clearly didn't think. You come here, and they let you because you're their *princess*," she almost spits the word.

"But if we act like we're your friends or anything close to that, we're in trouble. Don't you get that?"

"Sienna, I'm sorry," I say, but the words feel empty.

Sienna ducks her head and inhales, then exhales slowly. Her eyes find mine. "I know you aren't the same as the rest of them. But you have to understand, they'll do whatever they want to us. We're their slaves, nothing more. And as soon as they suspect we might start thinking we're anything more, we're in trouble."

Pounding begins in my ears as dread coats me like mud on my shoes during the rainy seasons. "What did they do to you?"

She gazes out the window and doesn't answer me.

"Please. Tell me."

"It doesn't matter. What's done is done." She looks at me now. "But I fought to get that baby girl placed with me, and I'll die before I let them touch her."

I want to push her, make her tell me what happened and who hurt her. But another part of me doesn't even want to know.

"Why are you here?" She goes to the sink and begins washing the breakfast dishes. "I need to leave for work soon."

"Who watches Jordyn while you're working?" I ask, avoiding her question. Now is clearly not the right time to mention that I just wanted to spend some time with the little girl.

"She works with me."

My mouth falls open. "What? At the textile factory with all those dangerous machines? She's just a child. They can't expect—"

Sienna spins around. "Catori, you have to get your head out of the sand and realize who these people are. Who *you* are. Yes, they *do* expect her to work. And they'll beat her if she doesn't. You can keep walking around this place as though you're some angel of mercy for the slaves in the Lower District —and hey, some around here may even agree with you. But every night you go back to your palace and sleep in a warm bed, eat good food. And get to do whatever you want. While the rest of us are left rotting down here, never to see our loved ones again." Her voice hitches. "Our lives reduced to slavery until we die."

Heat spreads over my body in waves, and words escape me. I gape at the young woman who I consider a friend but who doesn't trust me or want me around.

She squeezes the bridge of her nose for a moment. "Look. I know you don't want to see how things really are. I probably wouldn't either if I were you. But, girl, one of these days you're gonna have to wake up and decide what side you're gonna be on and learn to live there, no matter what the consequences are."

Sienna's words reverberate in my mind as I say a quick goodbye to Jordyn and head to Miriam's home. Although, after my...conversation...with Sienna, I'm not sure it's safe for me to be with Miriam. Has she gotten in trouble because of me?

I thought I was helping, but am I really making things worse for those I care about in the Lower District?

I hesitate in the alley by Miriam's home. Maybe it's better for her, for everyone, if I just leave. Indecision freezes me in place. Miriam's door opens. Her weathered face softens into a smile, and her eyes search my face.

"Come in, child. I'll make some tea."

I nod and enter her home. It's selfish maybe, but I need to speak with her today. Need her wisdom.

The one-room apartment of Miriam's home is cramped, but the most welcoming place I know. I settle onto one of the two rickety chairs at her battered table while she bustles about the kitchen, warming a dented pot of water on her stove. She doesn't say a word, and I know from experience that she'll wait for me to talk when I'm ready.

I lean back in the chair, memories rushing over me. I've sat here dozens of times and talked with Miriam over the past few years. She's the reason I came to understand that there is a God, and that He loves me. Her faith, so deep and pure despite all she's been through, pulled at me, and the more I learned of her God, of Jesus, the more I wanted what she had. My interactions with her changed my life.

And I thought I'd helped her in return. Grandfather was furious when I first suggested Miriam's hours be shortened to half-day shifts in the factory. But when I explained it would decrease productivity greatly if she died while working, Grandfather relented.

Could it be that she's suffered more than I realized by caring for me? Befriending me?

Miriam sets a worn mug on the table in front of me, breaking me from my memories. The scent of raspberry infused tea wafts through the air. My favorite. I stare into the steaming mug.

"Do they hurt you?" The question is a broken whisper, but all I can manage. "For being my friend?"

Miriam places a weathered hand on my arm and squeezes gently. "Now, where is that question coming from?"

I pull my gaze to her, eyes searching her face. "You didn't answer."

She gives me a soft smile, and pain shoots through me because the answer is far too clear. My friendship with her has cost her, but never once did she send me away.

"Why?" My voice trembles as the word slips past my lips.

A smile lifts the corners of her mouth. "Love costs something, sweet girl. It is never free, but the price is worth it. For a life without love is no life at all."

My eyes burn and I swallow past the sudden thickness in my throat. "I should go." I move to lean back, but Miriam's grip on my arm tightens, holding me in place.

"No." The word is a command. "Drink your tea and tell me why you're here."

A part of me knows I should just go, but most of me *wants* to do what Miriam is telling me to. So I do. My conversation with Sienna spills out of me, along with mismatched information about Micah, and my confusion about who I am and the life I live. The words tumble around, confusing even to me, but Miriam just sips her tea, nods occasionally, and lets me talk. And talk.

I suck in a deep breath. "All I wanted to do was make things better for you, Jordyn, Marsha, Sienna..." My voice trails off. "I just want to make things better."

Miriam leans forward, her gaze locked on mine. Depths of ancient wisdom echo in her eyes, along with a love for me. "There are times when God calls us to moments of great courage, my daughter. Courage to step out and do what we most fear. Courage to forsake our own comfort in order to do what is right. Courage to love like our Savior...even when it means painful sacrifice. Especially then." Her gaze flicks back and forth between my eyes. "In those moments, our lives are defined by what we choose to do. That choice will impact not just our own lives, but others as well." She reaches across the table to brush a tear from my cheek.

A tear I hadn't even realized had fallen.

"One day soon, you will face such a choice. It will be a crossroads that will change the destiny of your life. Make the courageous decision, Catori. For it is on that path, no matter how terrifying it may seem, that God will be with you."

# CHAPTER
# NINE

The Advisor Meeting buzzes as men and women argue over what to do about a village fifty miles away. They've been putting up more and more of a fight with every Raider attack, and no one seems to know why.

I glance to the left, where Advisors in training sit in the cavernous meeting room. Gabby's here, and I give a small wave with the tips of my fingers. One side of her mouth quirks and her eyes widen ever so slightly. She hates these meetings as much as I do. But for a different reason.

Gabby thinks they're tedious and keep her from the more important work of being a Raider. I hate them because the more I learn of the depths of who my people are, the more sickened I feel.

Briggs pounds the table in front of him so hard my glass shudders, sloshing water. The room quiets.

"Wipe them out." Briggs's voice grates over the air like a thousand wasps ready to sting an intruder. "If they're going to be so difficult, they don't deserve to continue drawing breath."

I press deeper into the scratchy, cushioned chair next to

Grandfather. Why is murder always the option Briggs and so many other Advisors settle on?

"We need their produce," an older Advisor says. "If we kill them, we won't get that." He speaks as though he's talking to a young child, and Briggs's lips curl into a snarl.

Before he can respond, Grandfather interjects. "Phos has a point. Just send in more Raiders next time. If they put up a fight again, make a few...examples." The pleasure in his voice and on his face as he says *examples* turns my stomach.

But I stay silent.

Silence is the only role expected of me in Advisor Meetings, and the last thing I need is to cause a scene when all I really want is to get out of here. As soon as possible.

I tried to skip out on today's meeting by working with the Inventors, but it wasn't an option. Briggs found me and escorted me himself.

I'm expected at every meeting to better prepare myself to take my position. I don't *want* to take my position. Ever. But for now, I'll do everything I need to in order to keep Grandfather's anger toward me at bay. Miriam's words from yesterday about courage tug at my heart, but I push them aside. I can't focus on that now.

Courage in this place would be life-threatening.

The meeting moves on to cover the increased force and resistance of Eryndale Scouts. Just the mention of the refuge city to the east brings raised volume and a palpable anger to the room. I pick at the cushion on my chair, bowing my head to hide any sign of my feelings. Micah has shared more with me about Eryndale, and I'm confident they're nothing like how the Raiders see them.

In fact, the more he tells me, the more I long to experience life the way *they* live it.

Grandfather raps his gavel three times, signaling the end of the meeting.

Finally.

I slip outside and drink in gulps of air, but my chest still feels tight. *God, I hate it here.*

Gabby strides over with a grin. "Glad we're finished that. What a waste of time."

My gaze darts around. "You can't say that."

She shrugs. "Whatever. You free? Want to come over for a bit?"

It's the first invitations she's extended in weeks, so I nod. Micah's crew shouldn't be back for a few more days, and I'm hesitant to return to the Lower District after Sienna's harsh words yesterday.

Before long, I'm leaning back on the plush sectional sofa in J's expansive library, not listening as Gabby jabbers on and on about her latest training with J's crew.

My gaze roams, scanning the floor to ceiling shelves lining every wall in the library, save the one with J's bay window and bench seat. Where she's currently perched, reading a novel. She has more titles than any person I know. Most procured during her missions for Grandfather.

She's feared by everyone. Captive and Raider alike. Yet here I sit, comfortable in her home.

Could Sienna be right? Am I all the things I hate about the Raiders because I'm one of them? I don't do what they do. But is my silence, my acceptance of all the luxuries afforded to me because of who my grandfather is—does that make me a conspirator with them? With evil men like Carver?

And then there's my conversation with Miriam. I wasn't sure how to respond to her passionate speech, and she seemed to know that. After letting her words sink in, she shifted the conversation to Micah. She asked me more about him, and giggled with me like we were the silly girls fawning over the most attractive young Raiders.

Ridiculous.

But also far more fun than I expected.

It eased the tension growing in me, and I left her house with a smile on my face that I couldn't shake. If only there was a way for Micah and Miriam to meet. If they did, I have no doubt they would get along fabulously.

Gabby shakes my foot. "Catori. Have you heard a word I said?" Her eyebrows are raised, and there's a hardness in her eyes as she stares at me that takes me aback.

"Uhh..." I bite my lip, wracking my brain for *something* to say.

"She ain't listening to you," Aiden says, strolling into the room. "You're more boring than Ms. P's lectures." He collapses his long body onto the far end of the couch, making the entire thing shudder.

"Don't you dare break my couch, Aiden," J says without glancing up from her book.

Aiden rolls his eyes dramatically. "Sure, sure. Whatever you say, dear sister."

J glowers at him, clearly the older sister in charge, but Aiden just winks. His antics have been part of both annoying and entertaining me and Gabby for as long as I can remember.

Gabby's frowning at him. "I'm *not* boring."

Aiden leans toward me and drops his voice into an overly-loud whisper. "She's totally boring."

I can't help but smile.

Gabby chucks a pillow at him, and he snatches it out of the air and props it behind his head. "Ah, just want I needed."

My grin widens.

"Don't encourage him," Gabby says through clenched teeth.

Aiden wiggles his eyebrows. "Sorry, sis. I'm just that funny. Plus—" he props his feet up on the couch—"I know what's distracting her."

My grin vanishes, but before I can find a word to respond, J is behind Aiden, flicking him in the ear. I blink. How does she move so *silently?*

"Feet. Off. My. Couch," J says.

Aiden rubs his ear but complies, and J slips out of the room.

"You think you know my best friend better than I do?" Gabby asks, crossing her arms.

Aiden lifts one shoulder. "Nah. But I *do* think I heard rumors she hasn't shared. Or you wouldn't be talking about your stupid horse upgrade. Everyone else already *has* that upgrade." Aiden adds the last part in a rush of words, then smirks.

Gabby frowns, but even I can see the curiosity in her eyes. "What are you talking about?"

I'm not sure I want to know, but I can't find words to stop Aiden from sharing whatever he's about to.

"Seems like congratulations are in order. Or will be soon," Aiden says. He pauses, watching the two of us.

"Spit. It. Out." Gabby glares at her brother, which only seems to make him *happy*.

But at the moment, the interaction between the siblings is the last thing I care about. Dread pulses in my throat, threatening to choke me.

"Catori, do you want to share?" Aiden asks. "I hate to be the one to share news before I should." The glint of laughter in his eyes says otherwise.

I clear my throat. "I don't know what you're talking about." Good. I sound normal. Not like I'm about to be sick.

Aiden's brows draw together. "Huh. Really?"

Gabby whacks Aiden on the side of the head with a pillow. "Aiden. Either say what you think is such big news, or leave us alone."

"Ow." Aiden rubs his head. "I might need to get ice. Test for a concussion."

Gabby lets out a frustrated growl and lifts her pillow again.

Aiden holds up his hands. "Okay. Okay." He leans toward us, elbows propped on his knees. "Word is Catori's getting married soon. To Carver."

I jerk to my feet, knocking over a stack of books on the table in front of me.

"I need some air." With that, I exit the room and almost run from the building, ignoring Aiden's shocked expression and Gabby's calls after me.

I burst out into the sunshine and gulp in air. No. This can't be happening. There's no way I would ever marry Carver.

But, as much of a goofball as Aiden is, deep down I know he's not making up what he heard. I look back toward J's house, but Gabby didn't follow me. Which is what I expected. She'll stay and drill Aiden until he gives her every shred of information he has.

I don't want any of the information. Right now, I just need to think.

I race through the Upper District, every bit of opulence mocking me. Each invention for our protection feeling like prison bars, restricting me. When I finally reach the forest, my breath comes in short bursts. I slow down and lean against a tree, the bark rough against my cheek.

But the reality closing in on me is even rougher.

What am I to do? This is my life. The Raiders are my family. I know they're cruel. I've heard of the things they've done. Is Sienna right? Have I just buried my head in the sand?

"I've been looking for you."

I leap back from the tree and spin to find Carver much closer than I ever want him to be.

A menacing smile washes over his features, and he tucks a piece of hair behind my ear. I smack his hand away, and in an instant his smile is gone, and a snarl has marred his face.

He grabs me by the throat and shoves me against the tree, his face inches from mine.

I gasp, my lungs burning, and try to pull away, but he's too strong.

"You will learn respect once we're married, woman. I promise you that."

Rage pulses through me, blinding me to the reason and cool-headedness a small part of my brain knows I need right now. I spit in Carver's face.

His eyes widen maniacally. He whips me across the face with the back of his hand. The ring he always wears punctures my cheek. Warm blood bubbles to the surface, and my skin burns. He drops his hold on me and steps back, a cool, calculating look replacing his anger.

Fear washes over me.

What was I thinking?

Angering Carver is worse than a bad idea. It's foolish. He's known for his anger, his revenge. His ruthlessness.

My fingers shake as I reach for my cheek, the sticky blood coating them. I should apologize, beg his forgiveness. "My grandfather will not be pleased."

His eyes narrow, and an insidious grin smears his face. "If you utter one word of this...encounter...to anyone, the girl you're so fond of will have an accident. A *fatal* accident. Understand?"

My breath hitches in my throat. No. Not Jordyn. I incline my head in agreement.

"Good," he says. He withdraws a handkerchief from his pocket and hands it to me. "Clean yourself up, then go see the medics and have them heal you as much as possible. And find a reason for the injury that they'll believe." He reaches out and tucks a piece of hair behind my ear again and I will myself to stay still. "I don't want anything interrupting our wedding tomorrow."

He moves to leave.

"What?" I choke out the word. "We're not getting married tomorrow?" What I meant to be a statement comes out like a pathetic question.

"Oh yes, my dear Catori. We are. Your grandfather was very pleased with my recent endeavors and my success. He's agreed to allow us to be bound for eternity tomorrow." With that, he strides away, and I let him.

There's no use arguing.

Aiden's rumors were true.

I drop the handkerchief as though it's burning coals and stumble toward the glen, tears blurring my gaze. As much as I want to believe my grandfather wouldn't force me to marry Carver, I know every word he just spoke is true. Grandfather believes in power, control, and revenge. I think he loves me in his own way, but that love is wholly conditional. He will expect my full obedience to his wishes.

Carver wants me, and he's one of Grandfather's most vile and ruthless men. If Grandfather gives him me, Carver will be indebted to him, even more loyal.

If I argue with my grandfather or indicate at all my unwillingness to yield to this marriage, nothing good will come of it.

Sienna is wrong.

I may live in opulence, seem to receive whatever I desire. But at the end of the day, I'm as much a captive in this place as she is.

I swipe my arm over my eyes and quicken my pace, desperate for my glen. Although there's a part of me that knows it's foolish to think a place will help me now.

I drop the ladder over the edge of the cliff and climb down, gritting my teeth against the tears that want to continue to fall. I need a plan. Help. A way out of this mess.

The last few rungs of the ladder dangle below me, and I jump to the ground. *Think Catori. What can you do?*

"Good. You're back."

I spin to the warm, comforting sound of Micah's voice. A man I've only known for a few short months. Who I should probably fear as much as the men of the compound.

"Why do you keep coming back?" The words sound harsh, even to my own ears, but I don't apologize.

Micah's eyes narrow, and his probing gaze lands on my cheek. In three quick strides, he's inches from me, concern and something else washing over his features.

"Who did this to you?" His voice is lower than usual, as though he's trying to keep himself calm.

"I fell—"

"Don't lie to me, Catori. Please."

I look away, towards the river. Because there's no way I can continue to look into his eyes. "It's nothing."

A strange protectiveness fills me for this man. Somehow I know that if *he* knows about Carver, what's coming for me, he'll do something rash. And I don't want to see him risk his life any more than he already has in coming here. Plus, Carver will hurt Jordyn if he thinks it will help him. I can't—

Micah's hand captures my chin, his calloused fingers as gentle as if he was holding a baby bird. I don't pull away, but allow him to turn me to face him. A thousand words seem to fill his eyes, but all he says is, "Come with me."

We go to the river. He removes his jacket and sets it on the ground for me to sit on while he soaks a handkerchief in the water. I study him, neither of us saying anything. His shoulders are tense, yet, when he turns to me, his eyes are tender.

"May I?" He holds up the wet handkerchief and nods at my face.

And I find myself saying, "Yes."

He gently dabs at my cheek, pausing when I suck in a painful breath. When I stay still, he continues.

I want to believe all men are vicious, filled with rage that will boil over at any moment. No self-control. Each one bent on revenge. But Micah shatters that belief a little more every time I'm with him.

"Why do you keep coming back?" I ask the question that plagues me, haunts me. "You know who the Raiders are...who I am. Why...?"

He finishes wiping my cheek, and leans back to study me. "Because I know you're not who everyone thinks you are. I know you don't want to be here. And I figure, one of these days, I'll convince you to leave with me." He gives me a half smile.

"I'm the princess of the Raiders. Why would you think any of that?" Even as I say the words, my heart lifts at the possibility of leaving with Micah, escaping Carver. My imminent marriage.

"Because you hid me and protected me from capture, even when that very choice put you at risk."

I study him for a moment. Jordyn's precious face comes to mind, along with Carver's threat. But how would he ever know I told Micah?

"The man who did this is the man I'm to marry tomorrow. My grandfather has given his blessing, and there's no stopping the union." I watch Micah tense more with every word I speak.

"Leave with me now. I'll protect you, and you never have to experience this cruelty again." His eyes plead with me to agree, to leave.

Can I do it? Can I walk away from the life I've always known?

"Okay," I say the one word, and know that my entire life is about to change.

The ecstatic smile that covers Micah's face almost comforts me. But then I think of Jordyn.

"Let's go now. The more daylight we have, the better." He springs to his feet.

I stand slowly, torn. What will Carver do to the little girl when he can't find me? I gaze back at the cliff, my ladder swaying gently in the breeze.

"I can't."

Micah's face falls. "What?"

"I'm sorry...there's a child. If I leave, I'll only be endangering her." And Miriam and Sienna and every other person I know and care about in the Lower District.

He places his hands on my shoulders. "We'll bring her too."

My heart lifts at the thought, even as my mind immediately begins calculating how impossible this will be. But I have to try. I can't leave Jordyn behind.

I chew on my lip, eyebrows scrunching together. "Okay, we

can try. But you can't come with me." He begins shaking his head no, so I rush the rest of my thoughts out of my mouth. "You'll be noticed and killed if you try. I'll go get Jordyn, bring her back here. You wait behind the waterfall, and I'll meet you there. Then we'll leave."

"I don't like it. What if you can't make it back here?"

His question is the one I didn't want to allow space in my mind. But the reality is, I probably *won't* make it back here. Not unless, by some miracle, God can keep me from being seen. If I was by myself, it would be possible. But I'll have Jordyn with me.

"If I'm not back by dusk, leave."

Before he can argue, I turn and march toward the ladder.

<hr />

IT'S BROAD DAYLIGHT, AND IT'S HARD FOR ME TO BELIEVE THAT JUST this morning I was in an Advisor's Meeting, going about my day as normal. Now, I'm striding back toward the Lower District, head held high. Desperately hoping no one thinks twice of it.

I come down here all the time. This is normal. It will all be fine.

The thoughts chant through my mind, sporadic and desperate, and bringing no comfort at all. This may be a normal occurrence for me, walking down to the Lower District, visiting with the captives. But it's *not* normal this time.

This time I'm about to act.

Could this be the act of courage Miriam spoke about?

Maybe. Then again, I feel like a coward.

And my actions could very well harm those who I consider friends.

I swallow hard and continue winding my way down the

streets and between buildings that are more rundown and crammed together than in the Upper District. I'm leaving everything I know, every person I care about. My friends in the Lower District. Gabby and Aiden. Miriam.

My heart beats an erratic rhythm in my chest and it takes all my willpower to not turn around and run back home. Back to Grandfather.

He's not perfect, but maybe I could reason with him, let him know how much I don't want to marry Carver.

If he's in a good mood and I've done everything he expects, sometimes he allows me to have my way. A pang shoots through my chest.

If all goes according to plan—not that there's *much* of a plan—I'll never see Grandfather again.

Unbidden, memories of the times I've defied him wash over me. His anger. Cruelty.

If he wants this marriage, that's what will happen.

This is the only option.

I stop in front of Sienna's door and clench my hands into fists. It's the middle of the day. She'll be at work right now.

I gnaw on my lip until it bleeds. Indecision freezes me in place as I stare at the weathered door before me, willing it to give me an answer to the questions plaguing my mind. A solution to a problem that I can only see leading to devastation.

It's rare that I visit any of my friends from the Lower District while they're working. The mangers at the factories hate it when their laborers are interrupted, but they don't yell at me because of who my grandfather is. Still, I know if I show up and cause any delays in production, my friends end up paying the price later.

And if I go, how will I take Jordyn without anyone noticing?

"Catori?"

I jump at the voice, my heart skipping a beat, and twirl around.

Miriam stands before me.

She cocks her head to the side, her astute gaze studying me and taking in everything. Her face hardens when she sees the cut and bruise forming on my cheek.

"What happened?" Her voice is low, protective.

She would do anything for me.

"I can't talk about it, but..." My voice trails off. Maybe... "I need to get Jordyn."

Miriam studies my face, reading everything. Somehow, she knows that I'm taking Jordyn from here. If I didn't know any better, I'd think she even knew about Micah waiting for me behind the waterfall.

Our earlier conversation about Micah comes to mind. It feels like weeks ago, but it was just yesterday. Maybe she *does* know he's waiting to take me from here.

Sweat trickles down my back.

"They have her working in the textiles facility," Miriam finally says. "But, child, if you're about to do what I think you're about to do, you can't waltz in there just looking like yourself."

I blink. "Why?"

She inches closer, her weathered cheeks folding into beautiful creases as she smiles. "Because you need them to think another captive took her to try to save her, so they look in the wrong direction while you get her out." A serious light fills her eyes. "And you do everything you can to get that baby girl out, you hear me?"

"Yes, ma'am." It never ceases to amaze me how Miriam can read me—read just about anyone. But a burden lifts off my shoulders from realizing the older woman knows and understands.

"Now you come with me," she says. And walks away at a faster pace than I've ever witnessed. As though the urgency of what I'm about to do, and all of the possible ramifications, is fueling her.

I follow her without question. Already, she seems to have more of a plan than me. Not that I had any plan at all other than grab Jordyn and pray that I could get her out of here.

Miriam leads me down back alleys and through nearly imperceptible doorways. There's not a camera or Roamer in sight for the few minutes of our journey. She stops and raps on a door: two knocks, pause, three knocks, pause, one knock.

The door opens, and we step into a nearly black room.

There's a clunk as the door shuts behind us, the strike of a match and the soft glow of lantern light. Although some Raider Compounds apparently don't have electricity according to my grandfather, ours does. Even in the Lower District. So the lantern light seems almost unreal.

But the space lightens, and my eyes connect with a very grouchy man's.

A man everyone thought was dead.

I gape at him. "You... you died. In that horrible accident at the chemical facility. A year ago." I didn't know him personally, but everyone in the compound knew about the accident.

"Clearly I didn't," he grumbles. His ornery gaze flicks to Miriam. "Why, pray tell, did you bring little miss princess here? You're risking everything."

"What...?" I can't find the rest of my question.

"Now Hosea, you know I wouldn't do this for no reason, and I do not appreciate your tone."

His nostrils flare, but when Miriam raises her eyebrows at him, he ducks his head. "Sorry. But she's—"

Miriam grabs Hosea's hand holding the lantern and lifts it higher and toward my face. "She's clearly in trouble."

Hosea's eyes widen almost imperceptibly and he grunts. "Fine. What'd you do to get a lashing like that?"

"I told Carver I wouldn't marry him." The truth spills out of my mouth, and I'm rewarded with what I assume is a nod of respect, or at least tolerance, from Hosea.

"And she's going to leave and take the baby girl with her." Miriam fills in gaps that I still don't understand how she knows, but I let her. "In order to do that, she needs our help getting Jordyn from the textile factory. So she'll be using the tunnels."

Hosea flashes a dark look at Miriam, clearly unhappy with what she just disclosed. "Fine. I'll do this for Jordyn. Lord knows a child shouldn't have to live like this. But I want something in return."

A million questions dance through my mind, but I cling to the mere possibility that this might work. That I might actually get Jordyn out of here and get back to Micah. And away from this place. The thought still feels far more bittersweet than I wish it did.

"Name it," I say.

"How you gonna get out of the compound? Seems like a near impossibility."

I hesitate for an instant, not sure I'm ready to disclose my secret.

And it's just long enough for Hosea to put his guard back up. "We can't trust her. You've already exposed far more of our operation than you should have and now—"

"No!" I interrupt, desperation clawing at my lungs. "You can trust me."

Before he can argue the point, I launch into an explanation of the secret passageways I found behind the waterfall. By the time I'm done, he grunts.

"Fine. If that's true, this all may prove more useful than anticipated."

"Just do me one favor," I say, even as the thoughts crystalize in my mind.

"What?" Hosea's eyes narrow.

There is clearly an organization among the captives and a hope and plan to escape. And Miriam trusted me enough to let me glimpse it. "Please wait to use the exit, at least for a few days. Let me get Jordyn free from here."

Hosea slams the lantern on a rickety table and crosses his arms.

"If you wait," I press on, "you can escape while they're searching for me." And it will give me a greater chance of getting away. I keep the thought to myself, ashamed of my cowardice, but unable to push beyond it.

"What if they find your so-called secret passage before we can use it? You want us to stay here and rot away as slaves for the rest of our lives?"

"No. Never." The words are emphatic. "They won't find it." I lift my shoulder. "They didn't the last time I left."

"That seems like a very reasonable request," Miriam interjects. "Now, we've wasted enough time. Let's get Jordyn out of here, shall we?"

Hosea lets out a grunt, retrieves the lantern, and leads me to the back of the room. He rolls back a tattered carpet, then pulls on a floorboard, opening up a trapdoor.

"Follow me," he says. He climbs down a ladder, disappearing.

I hesitate. This is it. I'm leaving.

Miriam places a hand on my arm. "I'm sure you're scared, dear girl, but I admire your bravery. It takes a great deal of courage to leave everything one has known. Even when much of that life is filled with evil." Her weathered hand caresses my cheek, and a tear escapes my eye. "My prayers will be with you. Now go."

I swallow the lump in my throat and wrap my arms around Miriam in a quick hug. The woman who is like a grandmother to me. And I'm leaving her too. I could bring her with me. Micah wouldn't mind. But if she comes, it will make my escape that much riskier.

She gives me a tight squeeze, then pats my back and lets go. Much sooner than I want to.

But it's time.

"I love you," Miriam says.

Her words almost break me. How can I leave her? But I must. "I love you, too."

My throat clogs, and I climb down the ladder before I start sobbing.

I reach the bottom and join Hosea in a network of underground tunnels that leaves me gaping. And provides a much needed distraction.

"Took you long enough," he mutters. "Let's go." With that, he leads me through concrete tunnels with old train tracks and discarded trash.

"What is this place?"

"I staged my death with Leroy's help, and the plan was for me to start digging, make a tunnel and get us out of here. No matter how long it took. When I started, I found this." He releases a bitter laugh as we duck under a hunk of concrete wedged precariously between the top of the tunnel and the old train track. "Thought it was my answer to prayer. Turned out none of the tunnels go farther than the Lower District. I think you people let us find them. Give us enough hope to lift our spirits, only to crush it when the tunnels don't lead anywhere at all."

"I'm not like them," I argue.

"You're their princess. And even though you may have some guts standing up to Carver, truth is that we're all risking our lives for this venture of yours. They find you, you get a marriage you don't want. They find out we helped you? Well then, we die."

A part of me wants to argue that a marriage with Carver would be worse than death, but I don't think Hosea would appreciate it. I keep my mouth shut and follow him in silence.

There's a musty dankness to the air, and Hosea steers clear of certain areas that are crumbling. We climb over rubble, and, at one point, go through an old train car. Hosea comes to a stop at the foot of stairs that are from an era long past.

"You go up these and you'll find a trap door, like the one at my house. Comes out right at Leroy's workstation in the Textile Facility. Knock three times, pause, knock twice. He'll open up when it's safe. Tell him I told him to send Jordyn to you."

"Why can't you tell him?"

"I can't risk anyone seeing me. They all need to believe I'm dead for as long as possible. Forever if I can help it. I'll wait here and take you through the tunnels. Get you as close to the forest as possible."

I ease my way up the steps, apprehension filling me. Every creak and grinding of rubble beneath my feet sets me more on edge. What am I doing? Am I really about to grab Jordyn and escape this place, leave behind everything I know?

The trapdoor looms above me, and I clench my hand into a fist, squeezing my eyes shut. The sound of shuffling and people walking comes through, muffled. I force myself to think of Carver, feel the ache in my cheek that's created a dull headache. Realize that, no matter how much I beg or how desperately I try to convince my grandfather, he'll force me to marry Carver.

It's an alliance he approves of.

Inhale. Exhale.

I knock, using the pattern Hosea told me to. Then I stand staring at the trap door for what feels like an eternity. Nothing happens. The door doesn't budge.

# CHAPTER
# ELEVEN

I turn to look back down at Hosea, and then there's a low grunt, a slight grinding. And the door cracks open.

The scrawny man whose face peeks through the opening stares at me with wide eyes, and I know he's about to slam the door in my face.

"Hosea sent me. I need you to bring Jordyn to me. I'm going to get her out." I spew the words in a hushed whisper.

The man presses his lips together and drops the door with a thud, sending dust cascading down into my face. I sneeze.

"Well, that could have gone better," I mutter.

I turn to walk back down the stairs and find Hosea planted in my way several feet from me.

"Where you going?" He grouches. "He'll be right back."

"Did you see the interaction we just had? I don't think he's coming back."

Hosea jabs a finger at the trapdoor. I roll my eyes, but remain where I am. Minutes tick by. Finally, the door opens again, and Jordyn scurries through the gap. The door closes.

I crouch down to Jordyn, placing my hands on her shoulders. "Hi, little one. I'm gonna get you out of here, okay?"

Her eyebrows knit together, and her lips tilt down. "It's scary down here."

I pull her in for a quick hug, and her little arms wrap tight around me. "We won't be down here long," I whisper into her hair. "Trust me."

"Let's get going," Hosea hisses up to us. "Longer we wait, more danger we're all in."

I bite back my retort that everyone thinks he's dead and I'm the one who's taking the risk, and take Jordyn's hand and follow the irritable man deeper into the tunnels.

We weave our way through corridors for several minutes in silence. Even Jordyn is quiet, but her little hand is fastened to mine.

"You sure you know where you're going?" I ask, more out of a need to interrupt the quiet than because I'm actually concerned.

I'm rewarded with a scowl. "We're almost there," Hosea says.

"Where are we going?" Jordyn asks, her voice trembling. "Why isn't Sienna coming?"

My breath catches in my throat and my eyes slide shut. Sienna. She's the one responsible for Jordyn.

What will they do to her when they can't find the little girl anywhere? I clench my jaw. Why didn't I think of her sooner?

We round a bend and Hosea says, "We're here," before I can find an answer for the girl.

I turn to Hosea, aware of Jordyn's full concentration on us. She's a smart kid, and far more aware of what's going on than most children her age. Maybe it's a result of the trauma she's experienced, maybe she was just born that way. Whatever it is,

I know she's going to fully understand every word I'm about to speak.

"I need you to do me a favor," I say.

Hosea's eyebrows droop, and his lips pull down into a deep scowl. "What exactly do you think this is?"

I ignore him and press on. "Get Leroy to stage Sienna's death, like you did."

"It's too risky," he huffs.

"They'll kill her if you don't. She's responsible for Jordyn."

The words hang in the air like weighted dust particles, almost suffocating us.

Finally, Hosea gives a curt nod. "I'll do what I can."

"Thank you!"

"But I ain't making any promises." He stalks to a pipe and twists it around and looks through it. "Route is clear. I'm gonna open up and you two scamper out and make a run for it. This door opens on the outskirts of the Lower District, about fifty yards from the forest. There ain't any Roamers out now, and I've worked with a few others to reposition the cameras and alarms, so there's a straight shot to the tree line. From there, I'd run as fast as you can to your little glen. Because it's gonna be a race from here on out. And you'd better be ready for it."

My heart pounds in my chest as I nod at him and I squeeze Jordyn's hand, hoping the gesture comforts her. "Okay. Thank you for everything. I hope we meet again under better circumstances."

"From your lips to God's ears. Now get ready. It's time."

The door opens slowly as Hosea cranks a well-oiled lever that doesn't make a sound. When it's opened wide enough, I scurry through, half-pulling Jordyn with me. My heart thunders in my ears like a hundred fully charged mechanical horses during a race, and my palm is slick with sweat. As soon as we've cleared the opening, I run, and Jordyn's little legs pump furiously to keep up with me.

There's no way she'll be able to maintain this pace. I could run faster with her on my back. The thoughts catapult through my mind and, as soon as the forest has swallowed us up, I stop, and she stops with me.

"Hop on my back," I say, hoping the words sound calm and not at all hysterical. The sun is setting. It's later than I realized.

*God, please help.*

Jordyn immediately does as I ask. She's lighter than she should be, the malnourishment of the Lower District evident in her thin frame. But right now, that's an advantage.

"Hold on to me. I'm gonna run. Okay?"

I feel her nodding even as she says, "Okay," and I start jogging.

I race through the forest as fast as I can, my feet nearly silent over the undergrowth. One thing I've learned is how to run without making a sound. Speed and silence have always been my allies in getting to the glen without being noticed, and today is no exception.

Today, it's more vital than ever.

Daylight is quickly dwindling, and Micah may have already left.

He should have left. If he listened to me. I told him to leave as soon as the sun began to set, and now it's clinging to the horizon, ready to drop. Trusting him seems almost foolish, but I don't know what I'll do without his help. I have no idea what's really beyond the walls of the compound.

Sweat drips down my back and my lungs burn, but we're almost there. The edge of the cliff comes into view. My ears pick up a sound.

I stop and carefully whisper "shh" to Jordyn. Again, I feel

her nod. I creep to the edge of the cliff, the little girl's legs wrapped around my waist.

Voices float up from down below.

"I don't know what she sees in this place." Carver.

My blood freezes in my veins, and I duck behind a bush. What is he doing here?

"I don't know what you see in *her*," the voice is low, seductive. And familiar.

Gabby.

They lapse into silence, and I don't even want to know what they're doing. My brain is short-circuiting more than when I pushed my metal horse to run harder and longer than it was programmed to. Gabby is my friend...I thought.

But she's also a Raider, training with her sister's unit. Spending more time with men like Carver. And she's changed over the past months. I just never expected...

"Let's get out of here," Carver says. "I've got one more night before I'm a married man."

Gabby laughs, and the ladder shakes as they begin to climb. There's no time to move or find a better hiding spot. I only hope that the dusky shadows of the forest and the bush Jordyn and I are crouched behind are enough to keep us hidden.

I squint through the branches of the dense bush, and make out the silhouette of Gabby cresting the edge of the cliff. Then Carver. He loops his arm around her, and they saunter off, back toward the Upper District. Never looking our way. Gabby laughs at something Carver whispers to her, and my stomach churns.

What could she possibly see in him?

They disappear into the forest.

Before I can allow myself the dark thoughts of what she

may have shared with the man I've considered my enemy for years, I tap Jordyn's arm.

"Okay, you can hop off my back."

Jordyn does as I say, and I stand and lead her to the ladder. "Follow me down, okay?"

"Uh huh," she says, her voice trembling. She looks over her shoulder in the direction Carver and Gabby went. There's a haunted look in her eyes when she faces me again.

"I will not let him hurt you again, okay?"

A sigh lifts her little shoulders high and then they fall. "Okay, Miss Catori."

I caress her smooth cheek. "It's just Catori now. Let's get out of here."

I climb a few rungs down the ladder and pause and wait for her to start descending. Together, we crawl down the ladder and into my glen.

Although now the space seems desecrated by Carver's presence. But that's okay. I'm leaving for good. He can have the glen, though he could never deserve such beauty.

I jump the last few feet to the ground, the night sounds around me and the growing shadows a reminder that I'm far later than I should be. Jordyn drops next to me and grabs my hand.

We run toward the river, the rushing of the waterfall drawing me, pulling me towards it.

Micah hasn't listened to my countless warnings about not returning to the compound. He's come back day after day, always offering to bring me out of here. I can't understand it, but, as much as I want to be angry at him for not listening, I can't be. I've *wanted* him to be here every time I've shown up at the glen these past months.

And he's never disappointed.

But this time his life is on the line in a way it wasn't before, and I've left him to think about the ramifications of helping me for a long time. He knows who the Raiders are, knows what my family is capable of. I'm sure he can imagine all the gruesome things they'll do to anyone who stands between them and me once they discover I'm missing.

So, the question pounding through my mind as ruthlessly as the water raging down the cliff and spilling to the ground, is: will I find him waiting for me now? Or will I be on my own with a little girl outside of the walls of this compound? In a world I don't know or understand at all.

We reach the waterfall, and water sprays at us as I help Jordyn climb up the small ledge and direct her behind the water. She doesn't hesitate to do as I instruct, and I'm both surprised and relieved by her bravery.

I should probably encourage her, say something comforting. But words fail me. Everything is about to change, and I don't know what deathtrap I'm leading this innocent child into. My only hope is that I won't have to do it all alone.

We duck behind the veil of water, the darkness so intense that it steals my breath. Jordyn grabs my hand, her grip vise-like. I give it a gentle squeeze, even though I'm shaking.

I pull a small pin-light from my pocket and turn it on, bathing the area directly in front of us with a soft glow. The light is dangerous to use, but I need to see. Her grip lessens slightly now that there's light, and I lead her further into the cavern.

"Micah?" I call softly. "Are you here?"

My heart pounds at my ribcage with bruising intensity as I hold my breath, desperate to hear a response.

But silence greets me.

CHAPTER

# TWELVE

He left.

I don't want it to be true, but as the hope I was desperately clinging to turns to bitterness in my gut, I can't help but acknowledge that it *is* true.

"Okay," I say to myself more than to Jordyn. "Guess we're on our own." The last word comes out on a high pitch.

I clear my throat. What now? We need to move, but my feet are welded to the floor. *He's gone.* The two words blare through my mind like the high-pitched whine of a broken engine. I'm on my own.

There's a scraping sound in the tunnels, and I immediately extinguish the pin-light.

"Catori?" Micah's voice echoes softly around us like the comforting embrace of Miriam.

I almost cry in relief, but hold it together.

"Yes." I lead Jordyn toward the tunnels.

Although it's dark, I'm used to navigating the space and I can soon sense Micah's presence.

"Where were you?" I don't mean for the question to come out like an accusation, but it does.

Micah turns on a low green light and gives me a crooked smile. "I could ask you the same question. What happened to leaving before it got dark?"

"There were...complications."

He gives me a smile that warms me, filling me with far more relief that it has any right to. He turns his attention to Jordyn.

"Hi. I'm Micah."

Jordyn shifts so she's slightly behind me, but offers a small, "Hi," in return.

He grins at her before straightening to his full height, his face transforming into a serious mask. "We need to get going. I'm guessing it won't be long until they discover you're missing."

I nod.

He leads the way through the dank tunnels.

I haven't gone through this passageway in a while, and this time feels different from the first time I did. The first time there was this sense of adventure, rebellion, and the thrill of knowing I had discovered something no one else in the compound had.

But this time, all I feel is dread, anxiety, and sadness.

We emerge on the other side into the darkness of night.

Micah flicks off his green light and turns to me. "I have my men waiting down the river in my boat. It's a good hike, maybe ten miles. And we'll need to move fast."

"Okay," I say, unsure what to add to the one pathetic word.

Emotions clog my throat. I've left everything behind. My family. Friends. The world I know and understand, even with all its flaws. I didn't even return to my room to pack anything before getting Jordyn.

"What's her name?" Micah's voice is a breath in my ear.

"Jordyn," I say.

"Jordyn, would you mind if I carried you? I don't want you to get tired, and we have to go really fast."

The little girl's hand tightens in mine for a moment, and I register her fear is as great as mine. She was finally understanding the new life she'd been forced into, and now I'm taking her away from that. It's for her own safety, but I can't help but feel a little bad.

I place my free hand on her head. "Micah is safe, little one. He's going to help us get away from bad men like Carver, okay?"

She nods beneath my hand, releases her grip on me and steps toward Micah.

"Okay, here we go." He scoops her up and situates her on his back. His hand grasps mine.

My breath comes a little easier with my hand in his.

There's no time to analyze why that is, as he guides us toward the riverbank.

I squint into the murky darkness as we travel the rocky terrain, but Micah leads us with a sure-footedness and confidence that is comforting. With all the times he's visited me over the past months, I guess he's grown used to the trail.

The trek along the river is uneventful, but also difficult enough to keep me from thinking too much about everything that just happened. We hike along the water for miles. After a few hours, sweat is dripping down my back and my eyes are drooping.

Jordyn falls asleep on Micah's back and we pause briefly to secure her to him by tying his jacket around her and his chest. She doesn't so much as peek open an eye while we do so. At least she's at ease enough to be sound asleep. I suppose that's the blissfulness of childhood...even when a child's life has been completely upended by someone like Carver.

The water in the river is deeper and appears calmer the further we go. There aren't many rapids as we distance ourselves more and more from the waterfall that leads to the compound, and the scent of the surrounding pine fills the air.

A boat looms in the distance, anchored not far offshore.

"There she is," Micah's voice is a rumble that rolls through me. "*The Fearless Lady.*"

It could be my exhaustion, or maybe it's the way he says the boat's name with so much pride, but a laugh squeaks out of me.

"What's that for?"

"I thought you said your crew is all men..." I let my voice trail off.

"So?"

"Why is it named 'The Fearless Lady' then?" Mirth bubbles in my voice.

"Because it's a good name," Micah mumbles, though with less pride and a bit of sheepishness.

We reach the shoreline across from a boat that's larger than I anticipated. The bow is exposed and there's a covered portion in the middle and a raised platform on the back. It's big enough that I'm sure there's a lower deck.

Micah whistles, and there's some scurrying aboard the vessel. Two men lower a rowboat off the side and into the water. One of the men hops down into it and makes his way over.

"Took ya long enough, bro," he says when he's close to shore, his back toward us as he rows the last few yards. "None of us particularly enjoy being this close to the Raider's compound, even if you do have a crush on a girl there."

Micah clears his throat, casting a furtive glance in my direction. "Shut up, Davey."

The rowboat scrapes the ground as it comes to shore.

"I'm just saying," Davey begins as he turns around. He freezes when he sees me.

"Uh, whoops." He's taller than me, but a few inches shorter than Micah, and his face is covered in a patchy beard. He offers me an incorrigible grin, which, along with his unkempt, curly hair, gives him a boyish appearance. "Well, I guess the big lug's weird charm must have won you over." He bows and the rowboat rocks precariously beneath him, but he doesn't seem to notice. "My lady, it is a *pleasure* to meet you." He straightens and hops off the boat, landing on the ground with a flourish. "And now upon seeing you, I find I can understand Micah's peculiar behavior of late, and his ridiculous need to place us all in danger as he attempted to woo you."

Micah reaches to shove him, but Davey easily glides away from the shove and continues. "If only he wasn't the clumsy oaf he is, and perhaps if he had a bit more of my charm and exquisite good looks—then maybe we would have had the great pleasure of meeting long before this."

I press my lips together to keep from laughing, but a small chuckle escapes, which brings a toothy grin to Davey's face.

"Nice to meet you," I manage.

"We don't have all day," Micah says, the smile in his voice contradicting the annoyed frown on his face. "We need to get some river between us and the compound."

With that, he eases himself into the rowboat, easing Jordyn, who's still sleeping, to his lap once he's settled on the bench.

Davey offers me his hand. "May I be of assistance?"

I could get into the boat easily enough by myself, but with Davey's ridiculous flirtations and charming manner, I find myself smiling. I take his proffered hand. Moments later, we are gliding over the short distance between us and the boat.

A couple of men await our arrival, and Micah passes Jordyn up to one of them. The girl sleeps through the entire process. Unease at Jordyn being passed to someone I don't know twists inside me.

"It's okay," Micah's voice is soft in my ear. "My men are good men."

I expel a slow breath and nod.

Davey scurries up the ladder while Micah ties the rope dangling from the side of the boat to the hooks on the rowboat.

I follow Davey's lead. As I crest the ladder and land on the deck of the ship, I find myself surrounded by half-a-dozen men with ridiculous grins plastered over their faces.

My cheeks warm, and I step back.

Micah climbs over the side and stands next to me. I instantly relax.

"What are you all doing? We've got work to do," Micah says.

They just keep grinning, their eyes flicking between me and Micah.

Micah claps his hands. "Alright, let's get a move on, boys!"

"Bossy, bossy, bossy," Davey mumbles, shaking his head.

But everyone moves off to work, except for a man that makes Micah look small. He's probably the largest man I've ever seen, and he's holding Jordyn. She looks even smaller and more fragile than before, with his beefy arms cradling her. There's a gentleness to this giant that's evident immediately, but he turns wide eyes on Micah.

"I don't want to break her," the man says, frozen in place.

Micah grins and retrieves Jordyn from his arms, and the relief that floods the giant's eyes is almost laughable. "I'll take her below deck and get her settled," Micah says. "Thanks, Vik."

Vik joins the rest of the crew as they prepare the ship to leave, and Micah leads me to the back of the vessel, where there's an enclosed portion. We go through a door, and, once we're inside, he turns to me.

"Sorry about the guys," he says. "They act like they've never seen a pretty girl before."

Micah thinks I'm pretty? My stomach flutters.

"They're a rough bunch," he continues, "and a little crazy, but they're great. You'll get used to them." The words sound like a desperate hope, more than a reassuring promise to me.

"They seem nice. And interesting." I smile, and he visibly relaxes.

"I'll show you where you two can bunk and get some sleep and privacy."

We go down a precariously steep set of stairs, and there's a tight hallway with what seems to be rooms on both sides. Micah's shoulders almost touch the wall on either side of him, and we pass two rooms on the left—one that appears to be a kitchen—and three smaller rooms on the right.

He doesn't stop until we're at the door at the very end of the hallway. He shifts Jordyn to one arm and opens the door to a room with two small beds and a desk cluttered with maps and notes. Clothes are strewn on the floor, and the covers on the one bed are crumbled into a ball. The other bed seems to have become a table of sorts, and there's an array of items situated on it.

Micah strides over to the bed and gently lowers Jordyn onto it, and covers her with the blanket. He scurries around the room, scooping clothes into his arms and tossing them out the door. After that, he turns to the other bed and fills his arms with the items on it.

"Sorry for the mess."

"It's fine," I say. Clearly, he's giving us his cabin. "Where will you sleep?"

"I'll just bunk with the guys." He grabs a jacket from its hook on the wall. "There's an extra bed in the one room, so it works out great."

A part of me fears being indebted to him as much as I already am, let alone adding this in. Perhaps I should insist he keep his room. Maybe I would if I didn't have Jordyn here.

Exhaustion washes over me. Suddenly, I don't care how messy the room is, or even if, in taking it, I increase my debt to Micah. At the moment, all I want to do is lie down and fall asleep. It doesn't even matter to me if there are still stacks of books on the bed.

I place my hand on his arm, and he pauses his frantic cleaning. "Really, Micah. The room is perfect. You've done more than enough for us already."

He turns his dark eyes to me. "I'll keep you safe. I'll get you away from them. Believe me, Catori. No one will hurt you again."

The passion in his voice makes my heart skip a beat. And I desperately want to trust him. Believe every word he says.

He grabs what looks to be his Bible from the desk, then leaves the room. I lock the door, turn off the light, and crawl beneath the covers of the empty bed.

But when I close my eyes, I can still see Micah's fierce and protective gaze. It's hours before I'm finally able to fall asleep.

# THIRTEEN

I wake the next morning to Jordyn curled up in a tight ball beside me. I have no recollection of her joining me in my bed, but I don't mind. My arm cradles her, and the events of yesterday flood my mind.

A torrent of emotions threatens to drown me.

I've escaped the compound. Abandoned everything I know. And now, I'm on a boat on a river with a group of men I *don't* know.

At least I have Micah. He's only ever shown me he will protect me and stand against what's evil. I think I can trust his character. But I've only known him a few months. What if he's just like Carver? Cunning, cruel, and vicious. Just better at hiding it.

I pull Jordyn tighter to myself, and she stirs, but doesn't wake up.

There's a light rap on the door. I tense.

"Catori?" Micah's muffled voice drifts into the room. "Are you awake?"

I hesitate a moment, trying to determine whether to ignore

him or see what he wants. But staying cloistered in this room, pretending I'm safe from every imaginable problem, is ridiculous. I slide out of the covers and re-wrap them around Jordyn before going to the door. I unlock it and open it a crack.

"Yes. Jordyn's still sleeping," I whisper. "Is everything okay?"

"Oh, yeah," Micah says quickly, keeping his voice low. "I just wanted to see if you'd like any breakfast."

My stomach growls in response.

His lips twitch. "Is that a yes?"

I look behind me as my face warms. "I don't want Jordyn to wake up and find no one here." My stomach rumbles again in protest, but I won't leave the little girl alone.

"Okay. Well, whenever she wakes, just head into the galley. Nate will fix you up with whatever you two are hungry for." He flashes a grin and moves to go.

"Micah."

He turns back to me.

"Thank you. For everything." The words feel feeble in light of the risks he took. The risks he's currently *taking*. But I have to say them.

He ducks his head. "I'd do anything to keep you safe."

With that, he leaves.

I glance back to the bed to find Jordyn still sound asleep. I'm no longer tired, and I feel a deep restlessness that I don't want to think too much about. So I busy myself tidying Micah's room as quietly as possible. Although, if I admit it to myself, I don't mind if Jordyn wakes because of the cleaning. Since Micah brought up the subject of breakfast, I find myself famished. I haven't eaten since breakfast yesterday, and now that the adrenaline and stress of the last twenty-four hours have worn off, I could eat just about anything.

The cabin is small, but not uncomfortably cramped. Micah

has a bookshelf that most of his books aren't on, so I start there, surprised by the wide variety of titles in his possession. Some are worn and old, clearly finds from the rubble of some pre-Demise city. While others are newer. A few have bookmarks in them. The collection is almost as varied as J's, though not as large.

Hopefully Micah isn't as touchy as she is where his books are concerned.

A soft whimpering snatches my attention, and I turn to see Jordyn sitting up and looking wildly around the room. I set the book on the floor and straighten. As soon as she sees me, she sails off the bed and races into my arms. I pick her up as shuddering breaths rock her tiny body.

"Shhh, shh, shhh," I whisper in her ear. "It's okay. You're safe."

Her cries ease, but her arms remain clamped around my neck.

My breath catches in my throat. How am I going to care for a *child*? Sienna's face filters into my thoughts. What must she be feeling right now?

Before I linger too long on *that* thought, I focus on Jordyn.

"Are you hungry?" Maybe a distraction will help both of us.

She leans back to look me in the eye, and her tear-stained face breaks my heart.

"What's gonna happen now?" Her voice wobbles, and her eyes hold far more understanding than a six-year-old ever should.

I hate that her question so closely echoes the one I haven't allowed my heart to fully voice. The uncertainty of the next *hour* weighs on me with a crushing intensity. But I refuse to drag this baby girl into my own fears.

So I offer the biggest smile I can. "Now we go eat breakfast. Have you ever eaten food on a boat before?"

She shakes her head no.

"Me either! Shall we go see what it's like?" I smile again and this time she gives me a small one in return as she nods her head yes.

We leave the room.

The boat rocks as we walk, but I don't find it difficult to maintain a steady pace down the cramped hall. Jordyn's small hand clings to mine, and I wish I didn't feel the enormous amount of comfort from it that I do. We pass two rooms with bunks, one with stores of food and supplies, and near the middle of the hall, we find the galley.

The smell of bacon wafts through the door, and my mouth waters as my stomach growls. Jordyn grins up at me when she hears the sound, and we enter the kitchen.

A few tables are crammed into the small area, separated from the rest of the room by a counter. Behind the counter, a slightly stocky chef with close-cut hair on the sides of his head and a bun on top is whistling while he fries bacon and cracks some eggs into a pan. The sizzling sound fills the room.

"Good morning, ladies," he says without turning around. "I'm Nate." He twists to give us a toothy grin, then returns to his focus on the food. "Micah said you's would be down here soon, so I've got your breakfast just about ready."

"Thank you," I say. "It smells wonderful."

The remark earns me another grin. "It does, dunnit?"

Jordyn and I sit at one of the tables and watch Nate as he finishes up cooking our breakfast. Moments later, he brings over two plates and sets them in front of us with a flourish. I thank him again, expecting him to leave, but he grabs a nearby chair, spins it backwards and plops down.

I stare at him for a moment, unsure of what to do, but Jordyn doesn't appear at all bothered by his presence. She dives into the eggs and bacon, which has Nate grinning widely.

So I do the same. The saltiness of the bacon sizzles on my tongue. It's cooked perfectly. Crispy but not burnt. The eggs are fluffy and delicious. A small groan escapes. I'm not sure what I expected when I boarded this ship, but it wasn't food that tasted *this* good.

"Nate, why do you always insist on staring at people while they eat your food? It's uncomfortable." Davey bustles into the room, shaking his head. He gives a sweeping bow, removing a hat that has seen far better days. "Good morning, lovely ladies," he says. "I hope my brother isn't being too weird."

A quick look at the two men and immediately note the resemblance. They're built differently, but they have the same straight nose and blue eyes.

Davey wiggles his eyebrows.

Jordyn giggles, and my heart warms at the sound.

He drops to his knees in front of her. "You must be the lovely Jordyn."

She nods, a shy smile on her face as she leans closer to me.

"We're gonna be mighty good friends." He winks. He turns his focus on me and offers me a smirk that I'm sure he *knows* is engaging. I can't help but smile in return. "And you, my dear lady, are even more beautiful in the daylight." He smirks. "No wonder Cap's all in a tizzy."

My cheeks heat, and I duck my head.

"You say I make people uncomfortable when I watch them eat my delectable cooking, but you're more awkward than a shark in fresh water around any pretty lady."

Nate and Davey swap jabs back and forth. I return to my food—in part because I'm hungry, but also because I feel ready to tell them to knock it off and I don't even know them yet.

Before I get three bites of food in, two more members of the crew enter and introduce themselves. Followed by another two moments later. The introductions and lighthearted teasing bring the volume in the room to a nearly deafening level as they practically fall over themselves trying to say something to me and Jordyn.

The little girl crowds closer to me until she's half on my lap, but she smiles as she watches them, and every once in a while, I hear a giggle. I can't blame her.

They're a rowdy, loud crew. But there is a clear affection and even protectiveness for one another that shines through it all. It's so different from what I've ever seen or known before. At home, the men don't joke—at least not in this lighthearted way. Their jokes are more cutting, less good-natured. And there's always an undertone of challenge. The strongest, most ruthless Raiders, the ones who are most feared, are the ones who advance in the ranks, take over compounds, and are praised among my people.

I've always hated it. But as I sit here, surrounded by the total opposite—men who seem like brothers, even though most don't look alike, who can joke and laugh and tease and have fun together—I feel completely out of place.

Their antics produce smiles from me, but it's more out of a need to be polite and not make Micah look like a fool for helping me. What I really want to do is sink through the floor and into the river below and swim away. The trouble is, I have no idea where I'd swim away to.

A sharp whistle cuts through the air, and the men stop and turn toward the door. Micah stands there with an *enormous* dog sitting at his feet.

"How exactly am I supposed to navigate the river in a boat this size on my own?" Micah asks, but there's an amused look on his face.

"You're not on your own. You have Shep!" one guy—Shax or maybe Antonio?—shouts, pointing at the brown and black dog still poised at Micah's feet.

"Yeah, we all know he's a better crew member than you, Shax," Micah says, and hoots of laughter spring up around the room. "Get back to work, you goofs. There's no need to overwhelm Catori and Jordyn with your stench and chatter."

There's some complaining, but the men file from the kitchen. Except for Nate. He drops back to his chair.

Micah eyes him. "You too, Nate."

"Aw, come on, Cap. I can show the ladies around." His eyebrows lift in a hopeful expression.

"Hah, no. Get up there and help your brother with the engine. If we can make good time, we should hit our first stop in about a week."

"Alright, alright," Nate grumbles as he gets up.

Once he's gone, Micah offers me a sheepish smile. "Sorry about them. I should have warned you." He rubs the back of his neck. "They don't get out much. At least that's how they act."

He rolls his eyes, and the gesture is so awkward on him I can't stop a small laugh. He rewards me with a wide grin that makes my stomach flip.

I swallow hard and stand, suddenly very uncomfortable. Jordyn hops off her chair and goes over to the dog.

"Can I touch him?" she asks, eyes wide and pleading.

If she looked at me like that, I don't think I could ever say no. And with the way Micah seems to visibly melt, I know he'll never tell her no, either.

"Of course. His name's Shep."

Jordyn pets the dog and starts talking to him. His tail flops on the floor and he licks Jordyn's face, which produces a bubbling laugh from the girl.

"Wanna see the rest of the ship?" Micah asks, drawing my attention.

What I *want* to do is figure out how to not feel like an outsider. To have a life that isn't full of evil people, who are probably now chasing me. I want to not be afraid that I'm bringing down the wrath of the Raiders on this crew who seem to be nothing but good-natured, kind men.

But I can't share any of that with Micah.

He's already shown me more kindness than he should have. I'm sure he's aware of the risks he took in helping me, at least to some extent. But I doubt he fully understands how intense the search for me is going to be. And what Carver and Grandfather will do to those who helped me.

"Uh, we don't have to," he says.

I pinch my lips together, frustration wallowing through me. Once again, I was quiet for way too long. I have to stop doing that!

"No, I'd love to see it," I say. It's not a lie. I need the diversion. And who knows? Maybe I'll find this whole sailing thing to be something I learn to enjoy.

Micah releases a whoosh of air, and his face relaxes. "Awesome."

He leads me from the room, and Jordyn and Shep trail after us. Over the next half hour, he gives us a tour of the boat, and I'm surprised at how large the vessel is. In the darkness of last night, it didn't fully register, but now as we explore the different rooms below deck, and then the main deck, I can't help but be impressed.

When we reach the deck of the ship, I'm amazed at how the crew scurries about. I don't know what any of them are doing, but they work in a seamless cadence with one another. The land passes quickly by, and the wind whips my hair.

Jordyn and Shep race past us to the railing. The little girl can barely see over the edge, but she stands on her tip-toes, pointing out different things to Shep, who seems to have made himself her companion. Micah and I move to the railing as well.

"There's something you should know," Micah says.

The seriousness in his tone makes my body tense. I shift to face him.

"We do more than just trade on the river." He pauses, eyes searching mine. "We work for Eryndale."

"Okay." I don't know what else to say. This shouldn't surprise me. After all, Micah has shared a lot about the refuge city with me. But his admission makes me uneasy. "What do you do?"

He leans his hip against the rail. "Usually we shuttle supplies and resources to new and established villages along the river." Another heavy pause.

I twist my hands together.

"But our orders changed a couple months ago to surveillance."

It takes less than a second for what he's saying to register. "That's why you were so close to our compound." The words sound normal, revealing none of the disappointment churning within me. He wasn't coming back because of me. It was just his job.

Micah nods. "There have been an increased number of attacks in the villages surrounding that area lately, so some scouts asked us to follow the river and see if we could find anything. We hadn't been able to until I went over the falls. And that just happened because I'd gone for a hike to clear my head, decided to do some fishing, slipped and got carried away."

"He's really a klutz," Davey remarks as he passes, ducking away before Micah can give him a good-natured punch.

I offer a half-smile, pushing aside my runaway emotions. "Are you a bit clumsy?" I don't try to keep the teasing tone from my voice.

Micah rubs his neck. "I have my moments."

He clears his throat, turning to ask one of the guys something, and I can't help but warm to him even more. There's an easiness to Micah, a humility with an undertone of strength, that I've never seen in a man before. His men follow his lead, respect him. And feel comfortable enough around him to tease him. No subordinate would ever consider doing such a thing to Grandfather or Carver or Briggs.

And it terrifies me, because all I want to do is trust him, let him protect me. Be free from the life I always knew.

But what if I want more than Micah does? He's a good man. Of course he would help a woman in distress. It doesn't mean he could ever care for me.

He turns back to me, and I clench my hands, willing away my warring emotions.

"As much as I'd like to sail down the river at top knot speed, it would draw too much suspicion from everyone."

I incline my head. But his words don't make sense. "Okay," I draw the word out.

"The Fearless Lady has a route down this river. We stop at different villages, deliver supplies, transport cargo and goods from one place to another, and sometimes take scouts down the river as well. If we don't do those things, I'm afraid we'll draw unnecessary attention. Only boats with something—or someone—to hide sail down the river without making a single stop."

The thought of turning into the port for one of the villages this close to the compound terrifies me, but I do my best not to show it. "Fine."

He steps closer to me. "We'll keep you safe. I promise." He gives my shoulder a quick squeeze, then steps back. "Now we just need to get you out of those clothes and into something that looks more like a sailor."

"What's wrong with my clothes?" I look down at myself.

The comfortable black leathers fit me perfectly, designed for agility and protection against the elements. I've never worn anything different than the Raider leathers, except for the gowns Grandfather makes—made—me wear for Welcoming Parties.

Micah clears his throat. "Uh, well, you pretty much scream, *Raider*. No one in any of the villages will trust you. They're all too afraid of your family. If they even *think* they saw you and are questioned, they'll likely give you up to save themselves and their families."

My stomach drops, but I nod in understanding. "Okay. What should I wear?"

Micah's face relaxes in relief, his white teeth flashing against his dark skin in a quick smile. "Great." The grin turns mischievous. "You're about the same size as Antonio," he says in a raised voice. "We'll get you some of his clothes. If we can find clean ones."

Antonio balks at the idea as laughter echoes around the ship.

I try to offer a small chuckle as my stomach drops. I understand the reasoning, but it feels like another loss.

# FOURTEEN

The next few days are filled with time aboard the boat. It'll be another three or four days until we will reach the first town on the route, according to Micah. Which is fine with me. I am tired and find the rhythm aboard a ship both soothing and frustratingly overwhelming. Everyone has a place, a job that they are doing. Except for me.

I tried to help in different ways, but I never seem to be able to do what's necessary. My hands can't perform the coordinated movements that everyone else seems able to do without any trouble. Even Jordyn's more comfortable here than me, which is frustrating.

Not to mention, Antonio's clothes are uncomfortable. The sleeves are too long, but won't stay rolled up. I'm constantly tripping over the pant legs. And if it wasn't for the rope tied around my waist, the pants would be on the ground. I asked Micah if I could wear my leathers, at least while we were on the river, but he said it was too dangerous. He promised we would find clothes that fit me at the first stop.

One sleeve rolls down, and I shove it back up. Although stopping in a strange town doesn't sound ideal, new clothes can't come soon enough.

I wash another plate, drop it into soapy water, rinse it off, and add it to the drying rack. Micah's dog sits by my side. For some reason, the animal has decided I'm its new best friend. Which has been interesting. Besides Micah and Jordyn, the only other people who appear able to control the dog and make it listen are me and Davey.

"What am I doing here, Shep?" I sigh and plunge my hand back into the tottering pile of dirty dishes.

Nate didn't want to give up his place in his kitchen, but, after a low conversation with Micah, he decided he could allow me to do dishes while he helped swab the deck. When I was in the compound, no one ever expected me to work. I helped in the Lower District, or spent time with the Inventors working on the metallic horses, but it was my choice. Here I know I need to work and make myself valuable to this crew. No one is here just for the ride. Everyone has a job. A purpose. So why do I feel like I will never belong? Maybe I shouldn't have left the compound to begin with.

As though he can read my thoughts, Shep leans closer and nuzzles his enormous head against my thigh. I drop my hand on top of it and stroke his head. I never had a pet before, but Shep's presence is soothing.

"How's it going in here?" Micah's voice behind me makes me jump and the dish in my hand clatters back into the sink.

I whirl toward him. "Fine." The word is sharp, and he lifts his eyebrow.

"You know you don't have to do this, right? Nate's pretty much beside himself up there—he hasn't swabbed the deck or worked with the radio and sonar equipment since he took over the duties in the kitchen. And no one has missed him up there either." Micah adds with raised eyebrows. "The guy can make food taste good, no matter what the rations are. But he can't clean to save his life—unless it's in his precious kitchen."

I tuck my lip between my teeth. "Oh."

As I suspected, I'm not even helping here.

Micah's brow furrows, and he strides over. "Are you okay? Being on a ship for days takes some getting used to, but you're doing great."

"Hah." I let out a mirthless laugh. "*Jordyn* is more help on this thing than I am." Tears fill my eyes, and I hate myself for them. All the emotions of the past few days weigh on me like an anchor.

I miss my home, my family, my friends. And, though I wish it wasn't true, I know I fit in better there than I do here. My sleeve rolls down again, as if to prove my point.

"You should never have helped me escape. I'm no good here and as soon as Carver and whoever else Grandfather sent with him to find me catches up to us...I'm just bringing danger to everyone." My lip trembles as the truth of the words bites at the air around us. Jordyn's probably in more danger now because I brought her with me.

Again, Shep leans against my leg, and I dig my hand into the soft fur at his neck.

Micah's face scrunches in a look that I've come to recognize as his "thinking face."

"Sorry," I blurt. "I'm fine. I'll get out of here and let Nate have his kitchen back."

"Thank you!" Nate pops through the doorway.

I blink. How much did he hear? My face warms at the thought, but I smile at him.

"If you decide you need help, let me know," I say.

But Nate doesn't answer. His eyebrows fly up on his brow.

He scurries over to the sink and immediately begins undoing everything I spent the last half-hour doing.

My shoulders droop. I'm not even sure I *want* to know what I did wrong.

"Come with me," Micah says, his large hand taking mine.

I let him lead me from the room and up to the top deck. I expect him to let go of my hand when we come into view of some of the crew, but he doesn't.

Maybe I mean more to him than just another job.

"Davey!" Micah hollers to the man who's on top of the wheelhouse and tying something off.

"What's up, Cap?"

"Your brother's doing his OCD thing in the kitchen again."

Laughter breaks out from the men nearby who hear him as Davey scrambles down the wheelhouse and drops at our feet.

"Sometimes I don't know how I'm related to the guy. Dishes can be washed a million different ways—it doesn't matter how they're stacked. As long as they're clean." Davey continues muttering to himself as he goes below deck.

Once he disappears from sight, Micah takes me to the wheelhouse. Inside, Vik is talking with Jordyn as he guides the boat down the river. Despite Vik's fear of "breaking" Jordyn our first night, the two have become fast friends. Jordyn follows him around the ship, like Shep trailing after me. At first the giant of a man didn't seem to know what to do, but now he looks for her each morning, and he often reads to her before bed at night.

"I can relieve you," Micah says.

"Aye, aye, Cap!" The massive man winks at me, then turns to Jordyn. "Shall we give the lovebirds some privacy, my young friend?"

"Uh, wait, um, we're not," I stutter over my words as

Estivik swings Jordyn up onto his shoulders and laughs as he ducks out the door.

I spin toward Micah, who just has a small smile on his face as he looks over the controls in the wheelhouse and adjusts a few things.

"Why would he call us that?" My voice is high-pitched and frantic.

Micah waves his hand through the air. "Don't worry about Vik. He's always looking for ways to poke at whoever he can." He gestures to the wheel. "Want to learn how to steer this thing?"

I blink. "What?"

Micah lifts a shoulder. "Nate doesn't know how to share his job or teach anyone to do it in his fastidious way. But I'm more than happy to share mine with you. What do you think?"

I chew on my lip, then shrug. "Okay." I join him at the wheel.

He places a hand on my shoulder, and I face him.

"I'm sorry this has been hard for you," his voice is low, warm. Soothing. "And I'm sorry I didn't stop to think that you'd need something to do to occupy yourself. You're so strong and brave and I —"

"Micah," I cut him off as my stomach flips in a way that only he's ever been able to make happen. "You've been wonderful."

The intensity in his eyes takes my breath away. He studies me as though searching the depths of my heart to see if I'm being honest with him.

I spin back toward the wheel and grab hold of it, desperate for a diversion. "So Cap, think you can teach this landlubber how to be a sailor?"

He lets out a low chuckle, and his hands come over mine.

Okay. This distraction isn't what I meant.

*What is wrong with you, Catori?*

I'm on the run, leading a crew of crazy but kind men into danger. And I'm falling for the guy who helped me escape.

---

UNDER MICAH'S SUPERVISION, I GUIDE THE BOAT INTO THE HARBOR, the same thrill tickling my spine as it does every time I can direct the vessel smoothly. Even the crew has seemed impressed at my abilities to sail the ship, some of them ribbing Micah about choosing a new captain now that they can't see his usefulness.

He laughs them off every time, and just smiles at me with pride. Like every one of my accomplishments are *his* accomplishments and he wants to see me succeed. No one has ever looked at me like that before. It's wonderful and terrifying at the same time.

We've spent a lot of time together over the past few days as he's taught me to sail and as I've worked to train Shep. The dog listens to me, and he spends most nights in the room with me and Jordyn. Which has led to the guys teasing Micah that even his *dog* thinks I should be captain. He doesn't get rattled. Just gives me that smile that flashes his brilliant white teeth against his dark skin and makes me hope he can't see how deeply he affects me.

Every Raider is fiercely proud and will do anything to maintain his position. If anyone even *hinted* that they should be the one doing something, it was considered a challenge, and there was often a duel—sometimes to the death.

But that's not how the Fearless Lady runs.

"Nice work," Micah says, at my elbow.

My cheeks warm again, and I fight the smile that wants to bloom across my face at his praise. "Thanks."

The rest of the crew moves about the deck, dropping anchors and tying us off to the dock. Shep sits at my side and I rub his head, suddenly at a loss.

My part is done, and I don't know what to do now.

"Look." Micah nudges my shoulder and points out the door.

Jordyn is scurrying behind Estivik, carrying a small part of the rope he has in his massive arms. I chuckle.

I smile at Micah. "You'd think a six-year-old would get in his way, but whenever I offer to have her sit with me or play with Shep, Vik blusters and tells me it's fine and he could use her help."

Micah lets out a full laugh. "He's all gruff, acts like a fierce warrior, but he's soft as Nate's sweet rolls."

I chuckle with him, watching as the smallest member of the crew follows the largest, her little voice echoing as she talks incessantly.

"I'm glad to see her so at ease," I admit softly. "I wasn't sure she'd ever stop jumping at every little noise, but Vik has figured out how to make her feel safe. Not sure I'll ever be able to repay him for that."

Micah doesn't say a word, but he squeezes my shoulder. He understands. I know that deep within me, and the knowledge is a greater comfort than I can put into words. I lean into his hand, allowing myself to feel his strength. What if I trusted Micah? What if he was *my* Micah?

My heart skips a beat at the thought.

Shax knocks on the door, and I jump away from Micah and busy myself with ensuring the motor is fully shut down and everything is in place.

"Courier was waiting at the dock with this," Shax says.

"Thanks, Shax." Micah takes the package, and Shax disappears to help the rest of the crew ready for port.

Micah hands the box to me. "For you."

My eyebrows scrunch together. I take the box. "What do you mean? What is it?"

Micah squirms. "I, uh, thought you might like something else to wear in port. Hope the sizes are right." He ducks his head.

I blink, then quickly open the package. Inside the box are two pairs of dark blue cotton pants, and three different loose-fitted, long-sleeved tops. "Thank you," the words are a reverent whisper.

Micah relaxes. "You like them."

I meet his gaze. "Yes."

We stare at each other for a long moment. I break eye contact first. Micah's too observant, and if he watches me long enough, he'll realize how much I'm beginning to care for him.

"I'll run below deck and change." With that, I make a quick exit from the wheelhouse and weave through the men bringing up supplies from below deck.

Once I'm in my room, I shut the door and lean against it, holding the box close to my chest. I can finally wear something other than Antonio's clothes. The thought almost brings tears to my eyes.

I change fast, throwing Antonio's clothes into the far corner of the room. I'll wash and return them later. The pants are a near perfect fit, and the top is a comfortable material. I choose one that's a rich creamy color. It feels a little strange to wear clothes that are loose and not fitted like my leathers. But as I look at myself in the mirror on the door, I find I like it. I don't look like the princess of the Raiders anymore.

Now I'm just Catori. The thought makes me feel lighter as I leave my room and head back onto the deck.

I rejoin Micah in the wheelhouse, suddenly nervous. What will he think of my new look?

He's focused on something by the radio and doesn't notice me at first. Maybe I should leave.

Then he turns. He blinks. A smile creeps over his face. "You look gorgeous."

My cheeks burn, and I smile like a fool. He's probably just being nice, but the words plant themselves in my heart.

"We're docked!" Davey announces from the doorway, rubbing his hands together. "Love the new outfit, Catori." He winks at me, then focuses on Micah. "The boys and I were thinking…" He lets the sentence hang.

Micah shakes his head, mirth bubbling in his eyes. "Fine. We can go to Finnigan's and unload later."

Davey lets out a whoop and turns back to the crew. They're all clumped together just outside the door.

"Finnigan's first!" Davey shouts.

There are cheers and hollers as the guys jostle their way to the gangplank.

"What's Finnigan's?" I ask, bewildered.

"A restaurant in town." Micah shrugs. "The guys love it there—even Nate. He always grumbles that his food is just as good, but he's also the first to head that direction whenever we're in Wisteria."

Jordyn is now atop Vik's shoulders, the smile on her face from ear to ear. Davey waves us closer.

"Let's go Cap!" Shax shouts, but his eyes are fixed on me.

"I'm coming," Micah says.

"I wasn't talking to you. You're old news! We've got ourselves a lady captain for the Fearless Lady!"

"Hoo-rah!" the other guys shout.

My eyes widen. "I'm not, I didn't—I mean." I clamp my mouth shut, unable to find words to finish any of my sentences.

Micah lets out a laugh. "Works for me."

Micah and I catch up to the men, Shep heeling at my side. Several of them grin at me, others pat me on the back. Vik and Jordyn salute simultaneously, like they've been practicing it. And, though I feel embarrassed at the attention, another part of me soaks it up.

For the first time in as long as I can remember, I feel like I actually belong.

## CHAPTER
# FIFTEEN

According to Micah, Finnigan's Restaurant is in the heart of Wisteria. As soon as we step off the pier and into the town, we're swallowed up in a bustle of people.

For a moment, I lose sight of Jordyn. I never stopped to think of the responsibility I was taking on when I left with her. The risks were obvious, but now the reality is she's *my* responsibility.

And I've lost her.

Panic surges through me, and I frantically search the crowd. I release a breath. She's in Vik's arms, rather than on his shoulders. My brow furrows. I take a step toward them, ready to carry the girl myself. She wraps her arms around Vik's neck and rests her head on his shoulder.

The tightness in my chest releases. I can trust Vik and the rest of the crew. I'm not alone in caring for Jordyn.

Many of the townspeople wave and stop to chat with the crew as we make our way down the streets and to the restaurant. I'm introduced to more people than I could ever remember as "the new lady captain of The Fearless Lady." And I try not to over-analyze how comforted I am by Micah's constant presence at my side. A few of the younger women eye me and Micah, and I can feel their jealousy. Part of me wants to tell them there's nothing going on between us, but at the same time, I find myself wishing there *was* something between us.

I shake off my uncomfortable thoughts as we draw closer to Finnigan's.

It's lunchtime, and the restaurant is crowded. Several large doors are flung wide, giving the place an open and airy feel, and the smell of meat grilling makes my mouth water.

Nate sidles up next to me. "Now, I know it smells good, but I could cook just as well as Mindy, if I had her resources of fresh supplies. Just want you to remember that."

Davey elbows his brother. "We *all* prefer Mindy's cooking over yours, you big oaf! Catori isn't gonna be any different."

Nate shoves his brother, frowning. "Whatever."

Davey doesn't seem at all bothered by his brother's irritation. "Stop swooning over the woman and marry her. Maybe she'll share a few of her recipes. That is, if she can put up with your constant griping."

Nate's face reddens, and he looks ready to clobber Davey when a short, full-figured young woman meets us at the door.

"Who's putting up with his griping now?" The woman crosses her arms, but there's a warmth in her eyes.

"Why you, Mindy-dear," Davey says with a sweeping bow. "As always, my baby brother's been pining for you since the last time we were in port, and becoming more and more woefully aware of his inability in the kitchen compared to you —oof!"

Nate jabs Davey in the stomach, cutting off his brother's speech.

"That's not true," Nate mumbles, face redder than I've ever seen it.

"Yeah it is," Davey chirps, diving out of the way before Nate can hit him again.

Mindy smiles. "I heard you were in port, so I saved you guys your normal tables." A crash comes from the back of the restaurant, and she rolls her eyes. "I'd better get back to the kitchen. Just wanted to be sure to say hi." Her gaze lingers for a moment on Nate. "If you can manage not to order me around, you're welcome to help in the kitchen with the lunch rush."

Nate tugs at his collar. "Alright then."

"Good," Mindy says. She hustles back through the restaurant.

The guys tease Nate for a moment as we make our way to a cluster of tables with a reserved sign on them.

"I think she likes you," I chime in, grinning wider as Nate's face reddens more. "And it looks like you feel the same way."

Davey lets out a yelp of laughter, tears in his eyes.

"I don't. We're professional acquaintances. Nothing more."

"Then why'd you spend an hour trying to get that ridiculous mop of hair in order?" Vik calls out. Jordyn is still in his arms.

There's more laughter as we take our seats. Nate mutters something about going where he'll be wanted. He stalks toward the kitchen, running his hands down his shirt and checking to make sure his bun is in place.

The next hour is spent laughing and enjoying Mindy's delicious cooking. Nate does a fine job on the ship, but Mindy brings food to another level. Each meal is plated in a way that's almost artful, and there isn't one bite that isn't cooked to perfection.

I enjoy my glazed pork, creamy mashed potatoes, and sautéed vegetables far more than I expected. Micah offers me a bite of his steak, and it's so tender it just about melts in my mouth.

"Good, right?" he asks.

"So good."

"Micah, dear," Davey says in a high-pitched voice. "Could you be a gem and offer me a bite, too? Don't I look beautiful today?"

Micah clears his throat and shifts awkwardly in his chair, but otherwise ignores Davey's wise-cracks.

I busy myself helping Jordyn cut a piece of her chicken. Vik is on her other side, and he leans closer.

"Ignore Davey." Vik keeps his voice low. "He's a goof, but he's got a good heart. We're all hoping you and Micah get together—we want to keep you two around." He glances down at Jordyn, his face softening, and then goes back to his own food.

But his words remain with me, both unsettling and comforting at the same time. In my wildest imaginations, I never thought I'd meet or fall for a guy like Micah. But I am. And his crew is okay with it...maybe even *wants* it to happen.

They want me around.

Does Micah feel the same way?

The rest of the food on my plate suddenly doesn't appeal. My life has already changed so dramatically, but Micah has been there through it all. A friend. An encouragement. Supportive. He's wanted the best for me more than any other person in my life up till now.

Could our friendship blossom into something even more?

---

I PASS OFF A SACK OF GRAIN TO DAVEY, WHO MAKES A WISECRACK AT his brother as he hoists the sack over his shoulder and heads down the gangplank to drop it into the waiting cart. A chuckle rumbles past my lips, and I go back into the stockroom to get another armload of supplies.

I've never worked this hard before, but I love it. This is my new life. And it's *good*.

The supply room is crowded, with Vik and Jordyn huddled right next to him. It almost looks uncomfortable for the large man, but he's all smiles as he explains to the little girl how we're divvying up the supplies and leaving certain things in Wisteria while bringing other things to the next town on our route. He barely has any elbow room, and Jordyn asks many questions, but she also helps him and does whatever he asks her to do without complaint.

I watch them for a moment, thankful Jordyn is so comfortable here.

"What next?" I ask.

Jordyn turns an adoring gaze on Vik, and he leans down to whisper something in her ear. She faces me.

"Corn seed!" she announces. She hops up and leads me to the section of the storeroom with the corn seed.

I pat her head and smile at her attempt to pick up one of the bags.

"They're heavy," Vik says.

"Here. I'll help," Micah says from the doorway. He saunters over and easily hefts the bag onto his shoulder.

Interesting version of *help*.

I raise my eyebrow at him. "What exactly am I supposed to do?"

His lips quirk. "Walk with me and keep me company." With that, he moves toward the door.

I bite my lip to keep from smiling like a fool and trail after him.

We're halfway up the stairs when a bell clangs, piercing the air. Shouts from the port rise in panicked volume.

Micah drops the bag on the stairs, corn seed spilling out. "Vik!" The urgency in his tone causes my heart to skip a beat.

The man appears in the storehouse's doorway, Jordyn in his arms.

"What's going on?" I ask as Vik charges to the stairs and passes Jordyn to me.

The child whimpers.

"Get her to safety. Lock every bolt on the door." Vik's face is a combination of fearless warrior and protector.

He moves to pass me, clearly expecting his orders to be obeyed. Micah is already almost out the door at the top of the stairs.

"What is going on?" I ask again, holding Jordyn tighter to myself—both for her comfort and my own.

Micah hesitates, lips in a thin line as he peers down at me. "The Raiders are attacking Wisteria." With those words, he disappears out the door.

Vik practically shoves me back down the stairs. "Go!" The word is a shout, and my numb limbs obey.

This can't be happening. They couldn't have found me... could they?

CHAPTER

# SIXTEEN

The shouts from the shore increase in volume and the unmistakable high-pitched whir of mechanical horses in the distance arrests my attention an instant before the door at the top of the stairs slams shut. Jordyn presses her face into my neck. I half run down the hall to our quarters.

As soon as we're inside, I shut the door and lock it with the three different bolts.

"I'm scared," Jordyn says, her voice small. All the ease she had moments before is gone.

"Shh, it's okay." I kiss the top of her head and hold her tight as I sit on the edge of the bed. The words feel meaningless.

It most certainly is *not* okay. My nerve endings are on edge. I stand again, my arms aching a little from the exertion earlier and now from holding Jordyn, but I don't put her down.

I move toward the small window on the port side of the ship and peer out, my hand on Jordyn's head both to soothe her and to keep her from watching with me.

My breath catches.

Flames leap from various buildings, and there's a cacophony as Raiders race through the streets, cutting down anyone in their way. They're not on their horses, which means they must have dismounted somewhere before entering town.

Micah is fighting with a Raider inside the port. He drives his fist into the man's face, and with a shock I realize it's Briggs.

I know these Raiders.

They're from Grandfather's compound.

Dread tightens every sinew in my body. They *are* here for me. This is my fault.

*Oh God. What do I do?*

Shax rips a young woman from the arms of one of the Raiders. The two men wrestle one another to the ground, but the girl races away. She slips into a shop and slams the door behind her.

Gunfire cracks through the air.

Jordyn whimpers and buries her face deeper into my shoulder. I lean closer to the window, heart pounding in my chest.

Then I see her.

J.

As though she can sense me staring at her, she turns and her eyes lock on mine. Her lip curls, and I'm not sure if it's a snarl or a grin. I backpedal away from the window, even as I realize it's too late. J knows where I am. If I wasn't her target already, I certainly have become it now.

My heart races, and Jordyn's arms wrap tighter around me, almost cutting off my air supply.

"It's okay," I murmur. But my voice shakes. My entire body shakes.

J's never been my friend, but before this she wouldn't have hurt me. But now, from the look on her face, that day has died and is buried in the tombs of the past. And it won't be resurrected.

"Think, Catori." My gaze whips frantically around the room, searching for a way to barricade the door. But there's nothing. Everything is bolted into place to ensure it stays secure, even on the roughest days on the river.

Each second that ticks past tightens my nerves even more until they're like an overstrung bow.

Maybe we should go into another room—

*Wham!*

Something slams into the door. I stumble backwards, falling onto the bed with Jordyn still clutched in my embrace.

"I know you're in there, Catori." Carver's voice slices through the air.

Jordyn shakes in my arms and she whimpers.

The door rattles as he slams into it again. "Open the door before more people die because of your insolence."

I pull back from Jordyn so I can look her in the eye. "Hide under the bed, okay?" I whisper.

Her lips pull down, and she shakes her head no as silent tears stream down her face.

"You have to, sweet girl." I pry her arms off of me and gently lower her to the floor.

The door shakes with the force of another blow. There's a loud *crack!*

"I'm scared." Jordyn's voice shakes.

"I know. You crawl under the bed and don't say a word until me or one of the crew comes to get you, okay?"

She nods and obeys, which brings the smallest amount of relief. I let the blankets fall back into place and step back to ensure she's totally hidden from view.

The door bursts open in a spray of wood chunks. My heart leaps into my throat.

Carver stands before me, fists bloodied, face twisted in rage. A pistol rests in his right hand. "Hello, love."

His voice grates over me like sand on sunburned skin.

"Leave me alone," I say, wishing I sounded strong and not like a simpering woman.

He stalks toward me, like he's hunting me. Feeding off my fear. I step back. The wall presses into me.

"I can't leave you alone, Catori. You're mine."

He's only a few feet from me now.

"No. Never." My hands fumble against the wall, desperately searching for something, anything, I can use as a weapon.

Why didn't I think to grab a weapon?

In a blink, he's right before me. His lips curl into a snarl. "Oh, you *are* mine, Catori."

"No." The word is strangled, but I force it out. "I'm married." The lie escapes, a desperate attempt to stop him.

Carver freezes, his eyes narrowing.

My heart pounds in my throat, ticking off interminable seconds as he processes what I just said. His face ripples in anger.

He believes me.

And we both know that, according to Raider law, if I'm married, I can no longer provide him with all he wanted. Marriage is a contract for eternity, after all. At least according to Grandfather.

His eyes narrow.

My lip trembles, fear pounding in my eardrums. What will he do with this new information? Stay and kill me anyway?

He takes a step backward. Toward the door.

My spirit lifts. It's working.

There's a roar. Micah barrels into the room, slamming into Carver.

The gun sails out of Carver's hands as the two men fight.

Carver's surprise at the attack fades almost instantly as his skills as a warrior take over. He lands an uppercut into Micah's jaw that swings his head back. Micah recovers with a right hook into Carver's face.

Micah lets out a shrill whistle. Seconds later, Shep bounds into the room.

Micah twists away from Carver.

Shep attacks him, driving him to the floor.

I scramble backwards.

Micah retrieves Carver's gun, then calls Shep off the man. The dog stands close, a deep growl emanating from him. Micah points the gun at Carver.

"This ends here," Micah says, his voice deadly calm.

"No!" The cry explodes from my lungs, and I move between the gun and Carver. "Don't. Micah. Please."

Carver lets out a laugh. I spin to see him leap to his feet.

"It's good to see you still care for your kind." Carver's eyes flick to Micah, then back to me. "Hope this doesn't make your husband too angry." Poison drips from his words.

He runs out the door.

Micah and I stare at each other for a long moment, and for the first time in the months I've known him, I see frustration in his eyes. Toward me.

"Why did you get in the way?" he asks, clearly attempting to keep his tone even.

My face burns. "I couldn't let you kill him. Then you'd be just like him."

He releases an exasperated sigh and flings his arms into the air. "I wasn't going to kill him, Catori!"

"You weren't?"

"No. I was going to bring him to those who could hold him and try him for his crimes."

"Oh." I pick at my nails, unsure of what else to say.

He tucks the gun into his pants. "I'm not like him. Don't you know that by now?"

With those words, he turns and leaves the room.

I bend down and tell Jordyn she can come out now. She flies into my arms. I rock back and forth.

"Scouts have arrived!" Davey's shout carries through the air and into the room.

Moments later, there's a yell. The Raider cry to fall back. They're leaving, and now they'll regroup.

Well, maybe Carver won't. My "marriage" has ruined his plans. He might not keep coming for me, since he can no longer get what he wants from me. At least I can hope that's the case.

But will Grandfather still want me returned to him? Will J keep hunting us?

I hold Jordyn closer.

What horror am I about to bring on this crew of good men?

---

"WHAT DO YOU MEAN, YOU KNEW THEY WERE HUNTING FOR ME?" I do my best to keep the question from coming out in a shrill tone, but barely manage it.

We remained in Wisteria for four hours after the attack, a few of the men helping to put out fires and make sure everyone was okay. The arrival of the Eryndale Scouts kept the attack from escalating and allowed us to set sail sooner than we would have otherwise.

And now I'm in a meeting with the crew while Vik steers the boat down the river and keeps Jordyn occupied.

"Come on, Catori," Micah says, still seated at the table, even though I'm standing. "You had to know they were hunting for you."

The rest of the crew stares at me with Micah. A couple of

them have cuts and bruises from the fight with the Raiders. Shax is sporting a black eye, but thankfully wasn't harmed more in his altercation. And the girl is safe.

Everyone came out of it relatively unharmed. Some of my frustration dampens.

"Yes, but I just..." I sigh. "I thought we were far enough away by now. It's been over a week since I left."

Some of the crew shift nervously, and Micah drops his gaze.

"What else aren't you telling me?"

He clears his throat. "I received word on the radio from Eryndale. They wanted us to stop in Wisteria, and they suspected there would be an attack in the hunt for you. We were supposed to draw them out, and the team of scouts would capture and stop them."

I press my hands onto the table and lean forward. Out of my peripheral vision, I notice Davey scooting away from me. "You mean to tell me you *knew* this would happen?"

Micah inclines his head, but still won't meet my eyes. "We, uh, suspected it."

I grit my teeth. "And no one thought I should be let into this bit of information?" I look around the cluster of men, but none of them look back. "I know the Raiders better than any of you! Did it ever occur to you that maybe I could have been of some help if I'd known? As far as I could tell, they all got away before the scouts could capture them." I let out a mirthless laugh. "And you know *how* they slipped out of your little trap?"

There's no answer.

"Because J is leading the hunt for me!"

At that, Micah's gaze snaps to mine. "I thought Carver was in charge."

"He probably thinks he is. But Grandfather sent J along too, and she is a master at knowing when and how to attack—and when to retreat. Every compound of Raiders knows her skills as a strategist, and it's rare to find anyone who will go against what she says. If they do, they'll regret it. Either because she makes them, or because they find she was right all along."

Davey leans forward. "Okay, so why was their attack in Wisteria a failure?"

"Carver was with her," I say. It's the logical answer. "J would have recognized the ambush much sooner—she probably would have found a way to grab me *without* attacking the village. Carver doesn't like to listen to anyone else. Plus, he loves the drama of major attacks. But I can guarantee you this: J won't be bested again." I settle back into my chair and lock eyes with Micah. "And because that's the truth of the matter, you can't leave me in the dark again. I'm our best chance at surviving this journey."

Micah tilts his head, studying me. "Fine. But, if I'm gonna bring you into all the details, you can't get in my way again. We have to trust each other."

I stare back at him. Trust. That's something I find I'm afraid to offer any man...even one as kind and caring as Micah. Especially after he kept me in the dark about this. But I give a curt nod. "Okay. What's the plan?"

Micah folds his hands together and stares down at them. "First." He clears his throat.

I blink. He's *nervous* about something.

"What?" I ask.

His dark brown eyes connect with mine, and the uncertainty in them surprises me. "Why didn't you tell me you're married?"

I stare at him with wide eyes, my mind completely blank. What?

There's shifting around the room. A nervous chuckle. But I keep my gaze focused on Micah.

"What are you talking about?"

Micah licks his lips. "Carver said something about not making your husband angry..." His words trail away, and his gaze flicks back to his hands.

Oh. That. I fall back into my chair. "I, uh. Well, I sort of told Carver I got married. But it was just because he said I was his. If he thinks I'm already married, he can't force me to marry him. According to Raider Law, Raiders can only be married once, then they're bound to their mate for eternity. They never remarry, even if their spouse dies." The over-explanation tumbles from my mouth, and I clamp my lips shut before I can say more.

Micah focuses on me again. "So it's not true?"

I shake my head no.

The relief that floods Micah's face almost makes me forget he hid this attack from me. And makes me wonder if maybe he cares for me the way I'm beginning to care for him.

"You know," Davey says, drawing both of our attention. "It's not the worst idea."

"What are you talking about?" I ask, not sure if I want to know.

"You being married."

I tense at the thought. "Carver already believes I am. Should be enough."

Davey lifts a shoulder in a half-shrug. "Seems to me like he would want to verify things. Especially if he wants to marry you as much as you say he does."

I squirm in the uncomfortable silence that follows Davey's statement. "It's unnecessary." The words fall flat. Because I know Davey's right and I'm wrong. Carver will discover I lied to him, and when he does, it will anger him all the more.

The only thing that would fully stop Carver was a true

bond between me and another man. Raider law would actually *help* me at that point. But I keep the thoughts to myself.

I'm not *ready* to get married. And who would I marry, anyway? Who would want to bind himself to the Princess of the Raiders?

Micah's hand on mine draws my attention. My heartbeat quickens.

"You're part of our crew now, Catori. We'll all protect you." He squeezes my hand and pauses for a long moment as his eyes flick back and forth between mine. "Raider law really only allows you to marry once?"

I nod since my throat is so tight I couldn't force out a word if I wanted to.

"Okay." Micah's rich voice is both soft and strong. A whisper that holds power. "I'll marry you. Tonight."

# SEVENTEEN

"What?" The word is one pathetic squeak.

"We'll give you two a little privacy to figure this out," Davey says. There are some grumbles from a couple of the guys, but I barely notice.

All I see is Micah. His handsome face is earnest. Sincere.

Does he want this? Or just think he *should* do it?

A few moments later, Micah and I are alone in the galley, and the door to the hall is shut.

I stare at him, both in shock and desperately terrified. Because a part of me *wants* to marry Micah. He's the best man I've ever known, someone I've grown to care about...even though I don't know how to trust him yet. Still, the thought of marrying him actually makes me think I could have a future I'm excited about.

But I don't want him to marry me out of pity.

Not to mention the fact that I don't really *know* him. I mean, I know his character. Know he is an outstanding leader. Compassionate, but strong. And he knows and loves God. But I don't know his past. Where he came from.

I swallow. Who is his *family*? Even if he is okay with marrying me, I doubt his mom is going to be happy to have the princess of the Raiders as her daughter-in-law.

His mouth quirks. "You're doing that thing."

I frown. "What thing?"

His smile broadens. "The thing where you go quiet and think." The grin fades, and he stands and paces the room. "But this really could work. We've known each other for a little bit now, and, although this is unconventional, I think it's the best way to keep you and Jordyn safe. Vik was a pastor before he joined my crew—he can marry us. It will just be in name only. I won't, uh—" he clears his throat—"expect anything."

I almost want to smile at his rambling and obvious embarrassment. But the reality of what he's saying stays any amusement. And dampens some of the excitement I hadn't realized was building in me. He's doing this because it's the honorable thing. Not because he wants me as his wife. "You'd be in more danger, Micah. It's not worth the risk."

He stops pacing, eyes locked on mine. "Doing what's right, honoring God by protecting those who need protecting— that's *always* worth the risk."

"What will your family think?" The question bursts from me without any preamble.

His face softens. "They'll love you."

I stand. "How can you be *sure*?"

He comes closer. "Because I know them. And I know you."

I blink at his words; the confidence woven into them. "Okay." The word falls out of my mouth. "I'll marry you." Even as I finish the statement, my pulse quickens.

Is this a good idea?

*God, am I doing the right thing?*

Micah smiles, his broad lips parting to reveal his white teeth. He actually looks...pleased.

"Good," he says.

My heart skips a beat. Could he possibly *want* this? I squash the thought before it can bloom into hope. He wants to protect me and Jordyn. That's why he's doing it.

Nothing more.

"Davey," Micah says, raising his voice, and looking toward the door. "Go tell Vik. We're having a wedding."

Excited hollers penetrate the door a moment before it bursts open. Most of the crew is right there. Grinning.

Great. They were listening the whole time. I glare at them. "Do you guys understand the word *privacy* at all?"

"We shut the door," Nate protests. "And we could barely hear the two of you because of that."

His frown is enough to bring a smile to my face. I roll my eyes.

Micah takes my hand and leads me through the crowd of guys, a smile on his lips as they pat him on the back and congratulate him.

Us.

I hold his hand tighter, not sure what else to do. This is happening. I'm about to get married.

What am I doing?

---

We drop anchor so no one has to worry about steering the ship, and within twenty minutes, everyone is gathered topside to watch the wedding take place. The sun is setting, painting the sky a riot of peaches and reds. It's beautiful, but I almost wonder if the reds are a warning. I swallow back apprehension.

This will be okay.

I stand at the front with Micah, Vik beside us, and Jordyn

next to him. There's still a haunted look in her eyes, and she crowds next to Vik like he's her personal bodyguard.

I would do anything to take the look of fear from her eyes.

Vik's Bible looks small in his hands as he explains the importance of marriage and the fact that we're making our vows as a covenant before God and these witnesses. It's different from a Raider bonding ceremony. Those almost feel ominous. Dark. Even though the man and woman are pledging to remain together for eternity, there's almost a fear that accompanies the words. At least in the ceremonies I've witnessed.

They're making a contract with one another, but both know the other will bend that contract if they want to. As long as they remain married to one person only and never marry another, they're abiding by the law. But if they break their bond by seeking to marry someone else, even years after their spouse dies, they'll be executed.

God is never mentioned, and I've never heard any marriage called a covenant.

A thousand protests crash through my mind as the weight of what I'm about to do presses on my chest. Micah deserves better than me. Doesn't matter what he said. His family will hate me because of the blood in my veins. And my family will hate him. Can I trust him? Really trust this man?

Maybe.

*God, am I doing the right thing?* Again, the prayer cries from my heart, but there's no response.

If only Miriam were here. She'd know what to do.

But she's not.

And this will protect me from Carver.

So I keep my thoughts and fears to myself. Instead, I listen as Micah vows to honor, protect, and keep me for all my days.

Until death do us part.

*What is happening?* The question chants over and over in my ears.

"Catori." Vik's deep voice arrests my attention. "Repeat after me: I, Catori, take you, Micah, to be my husband."

"I, Catori, take you, Micah, to be my husband." Miraculously, the words pass over my lips, but I keep my gaze fixed on Micah's feet.

"And I promise and covenant before God and these witnesses to be your faithful wife."

Again, I repeat the words Vik says. Words I've never heard before at any wedding I've been to. Raiders may pledge themselves to one another for eternity, but they never promise to be faithful to their spouse. It's not even expected.

"In plenty and in want, in joy and in sorrow, in sickness and in health, as long as we both shall live."

I say the final words, my voice trembling.

"With the power vested in me," Vik says, raising his voice so that it booms over us, "I pronounce you husband and wife."

The men cheer. Like this is an event they've been looking forward to for months rather than an impromptu ceremony out of desperation.

"You may kiss your bride," Vik says.

I still. I forgot about this part. My heart stutters over itself, caught between *wanting* Micah to kiss me and *not* wanting my first kiss to be an obligation.

Micah places his hand on my chin and gently lifts my head so I'm looking him in the eyes. There's a vulnerability and uncertainty reflected in the brown depths of his gaze that almost comforts me. This is scary for him too.

He leans forward, and I don't breathe. Then he kisses my cheek. A light brush, so soft I almost question if he did it or not. He steps back and smiles at me. He takes my hand and faces the guys.

They cheer again, and he squeezes my hand.

"I'm making a cake!" Nate hollers.

Micah laughs, and the guys shout their pleasure at the idea.

Some of my fear dissipates. Micah is so different from Carver. He's willingly giving up his life to marry me. And he'll never force me to do something before I'm ready.

Somehow I know that in the depths of my being. I shift so I'm standing closer to him, my shoulder brushing his. At the contact, he looks down at me and flashes a brilliant smile. I smile back.

We'll make it through this.

And maybe, one day, I'll know how to be the wife I just vowed to be.

CHAPTER

# EIGHTEEN

Two hours later, Micah and I stand in the same place where we said our vows staring out at the river. Night has fallen, and we're sailing again. Shax is in the wheelhouse steering the ship, but the rest of the guys are still below deck feasting on the cake Nate whipped up.

I think it was good, but I could barely taste it. My mind is whirling. Too much has happened today. The carnage in Wisteria, marrying Micah. How could I have faced down Carver *and* made lifelong vows with the man next to me on the same day?

I grip the railing, ready to hoist myself over the edge and into the river. My life now is so different from what it was weeks ago, yet other things haven't changed. I'm still terrified of Carver. My grandfather is using J to hunt me down. And I still abandoned the only life I really understood.

Jordyn and I escaped the compound, but how long until I'm right back there?

And now Micah is my husband. What will happen to him if we're captured?

I squeeze my eyes shut as panic bubbles through me.

"I have two brothers," Micah says.

My eyes fly open. Where is this coming from?

"Malachi is the oldest," he continues, like I asked for details. "He's twenty-five. Four years older than me. And Moses is the baby of the family. He's only twelve." There's a smile in his voice as he talks, and his words calm me down. "We all look alike, but don't worry. I'm the most handsome." He winks at me, and my cheeks warm.

"Where are they now?" I ask before I make a fool of myself by agreeing that he's the most handsome man I know.

He leans his hip against the railing. "My parents and Moses live in Eryndale. Not sure where Malachi is. He's a scout for Eryndale, so he travels a lot. My mama is the sweetest woman you'll ever meet. She'll pamper you and feed you until you can't move. But boy, if you smart talk her or do something you know isn't right,"—he shudders, but there's a soft smile on his face—"you're in trouble. My dad is a good man. Taught me and my brothers how to be men and honor God and others. Haven't seen any of them for several months now." He focuses on the river.

I lay my hand on his arm without thinking. His eyes snap back to mine, his muscles bulging beneath my fingers. I quickly drop my hand, even as my heart races.

He clears his throat and offers me a small smile. "You brought up my family earlier, and I realized I'd never told you about them." He sighs. "I just miss them more when I talk about them."

"Why don't you live near them?" I ask.

"Because I've committed my life to standing against injustice and walking humbly with God through the process. And this is the way He's given me to do that right now."

I suspect there's more to it than just that, but I can't help but admire his courage to step into difficult things. Especially since it involved leaving behind a wonderful family.

"Your family is so different from mine." I pick at the railing.

"I'm sorry for the life you had to experience growing up," Micah says.

"My grandfather isn't all evil," I protest, even as the carnage I witnessed mere hours ago threatens to overwhelm me. "And as long as I did what he wanted, he doted on me. Loved me, in his way."

Micah places his hand on mine. My breath catches as I look into his eyes that are filled with more emotions than I can understand. "Conditional love isn't love."

I swallow hard, not sure how to find a place in my heart where his words make sense or fit with *anything* I've experienced.

Miriam's face flashes in my mind. She loved me unconditionally. Even when I didn't do what she thought I should, she never once showed me anything but kindness and love. She and Micah would get along.

"But Grandfather went through a lot," I say, needing to excuse his behavior. "The Demise, everything he's experienced since...it helped shape him into who he is today. Every Raider has lost something or someone. Most of those in Grandfather's generation lost everything in the Demise. He found a few survivors in the North after the attacks. Other young men and women like himself.

"At first, the goal was just to survive. But one man, Jonas Reptation, wanted to get back the life of luxury he'd lost more than he cared about helping others survive.

"When my grandfather was out one day, Jonas murdered several people in the compound, took the little possessions they'd managed to keep, and left to find the life he'd lost. One of the people he murdered was my grandfather's sister. The two were close according to Grandfather, shared every secret." I keep my gaze on the darkness of the shoreline as I tell the story.

"When he came back, heard what Jonas had done, saw the devastation left behind...and realized he'd lost his only surviving relative, he was overcome with grief and rage. He called together the strongest men and women in their camp, and they hunted Jonas down and murdered him."

I sneak a glance at Micah, but he doesn't react. He just stands quietly beside me, watching me. Listening.

I continue, needing him to better understand who I am, where I came from. "From that day on, they decided that no one would be able to take anything from them again—that they would be the strongest, most feared, most vicious in the region to keep their families safe. The trouble is, their bitterness, anger, and hatred have poisoned them beyond what any of them ever expected.

"Families matter less now than power. Strength and fear and influence are the greatest commodities among the Raiders, and growing up in that kind of place has created men like Carver.

"Grandfather would tell me the stories of the Demise, of Jonas. Even of the things he did, always trying to impress upon me the importance of power and never forgetting the wrongs done to me. He'd say, 'You have to help yourself, Catori. No one is ever gonna help you. You do what you need to do, take what you want. It's the way things work in this blasted world.'"

Micah's brow furrows, and I release a small breath of relief. He doesn't feel the same way. I can see it etched into the lines on his face, and I suddenly feel safer with him in this moment than I ever have before.

"But as I grew older, I began to see the cruelty of what my family did. I'd go to the Lower District of the compound, talk to the captives, those Grandfather and the other Raiders had enslaved. Hear their stories. And I knew Grandfather couldn't be justified in what he was doing. No matter how much he believed it. It's in the Lower District that I met a woman named Miriam, who told me about God, the sacrifice and forgiveness of Jesus. And my life changed."

"I'm glad you had Miriam," Micah says softly.

"Me too. I wish you could meet her." The smile I want to offer fades before it can begin. I almost don't want to even think of my friend right now. Because then I'll be forced to imagine what's happened to her in the time since I've been gone.

I clear my throat. "But still, my grandfather is the only family I have left. My parents and grandmother aren't even memories in my conscience." I pause. Micah already knows what happened to them. Or what I was *told* happened to them. More and more, I don't believe it was Eryndale scouts who killed my parents and grandmother. "So, though I know he's wrong, I find I actually miss him." My words fall flat, even as a storm of emotions washes over me.

If I encounter Grandfather again, it doesn't matter that I miss him. I know I won't find any trace of tenderness in the man. Not after leaving the way I did.

Micah stands next to me, silent, as we both stare out over the water into the dark night. The engines purr gently, and the sound of the guys talking and moving about the ship is a muffled backdrop to my story. My memories. My family.

"Do you regret leaving?" Micah's voice rumbles next to me, his shoulder brushing mine as he shifts to focus on me.

I keep my gaze on the water, contemplating his question. "I dreamt of leaving as a little girl. Wanted to explore the region, go to new places. But Grandfather never allowed me to go on any missions. I was confined to the compound, and, though I was given everything I could ever want, I still felt like a prisoner." I sigh. "The more I grew to understand everything my family stands for, all they do, the more I knew I couldn't stay. Yet I remained because I didn't know how to leave." I face him now. "No. I don't regret leaving."

Even in the dark, I watch his features relax. "Good."

The one word warms me. After everything that happened earlier today, I had begun to wonder if Micah regretted helping me. If he regretted knowing me because of the trouble I've brought on them all.

Then again, he did just marry me.

Micah clears his throat. "There's something we need to discuss."

The warmth and comfort I felt seconds before melts away like snow on a summer day. "What?"

He picks at the paint chipping on the railing that I abandoned, eyes trained on the spot. "It's not safe for you and Jordyn to stay aboard The Fearless Lady."

My mouth falls open, but no words escape. I don't *have* any words.

He still doesn't look at me. "I can get you to Eryndale. You'll be well-protected there, and you can stay with my family."

"But,"—the word is a pitiful squeak, so I clear my throat. "We're married now. You saw how Carver retreated. It was because I told him I was married."

Micah finally looks at me again, his face clothed in shadows deeper than the darkness of the night. "But what if it's not enough? What if they keep coming for you?" His hand reaches out and for a moment, I think he's going to touch my cheek. But he drops it. "Don't you want to be safe?"

My automatic response to the question is *yes*. Of course I want to be safe. But another thought rises to the surface. "What about you?"

He crosses his arms over his chest. "We'll meet with a team of scouts to determine our next course of action. Most likely I'll be the one to bring you most of the way to Eryndale. I know these rivers and the passageways better than anyone. I'll get you as close as possible, then you'll be transferred to another team of scouts who will escort you the rest of the way."

A pang shoots through me. He's going to send me on my way. Without him. Our marriage really was just to protect me. And now he's taking further steps to ensure that protection.

I should feel relief, but a deep ache takes up residence in my chest.

His hand rests on my shoulder, drawing my attention. I want to lean into him, let his strength absorb into me. But I force myself to stay still.

"It's your choice, Catori." His words are soft, but rumble through me.

I look up. It's too dark for me to make out his expression.

"I won't force you to do anything." He squeezes my shoulder, then drops his hand.

I immediately miss the warmth. I don't want to leave this man I just married. A man I care about far more than I want to admit. I don't want to start a new life in Eryndale—not when I was finally getting used to being on this ship.

But he's right. Eryndale is the safest option. I stand taller. "Okay. I'll go."

# CHAPTER
# NINETEEN

I lay in the bed that has become my own, staring up at the ceiling while Jordyn's soft snores filter through the air, her little body pressed tight against mine. A few nights ago, she'd stopped waking up in the middle of the night with her nightmares. I'd thought she was healing from some of the terror she's experienced in her young life.

But hiding from Carver, being in the same room with him, it impacted her in the worst possible way.

When Vik realized Carver was one of the main ones responsible for Jordyn's night terrors, the guys had to physically restrain him from getting off the boat and hunting for the man. They'd finally convinced him that Jordyn needed him, and he'd calmed down enough to find the child and comfort her.

The wedding and the guys' impromptu celebration afterward were good temporary distractions. But the two nights since have proven to be difficult. So she's in bed with me. She moans and shifts.

"Shh, it's okay," I whisper, stroking her cheek. "You're safe. No one will hurt you."

It's the same words I've been saying to her while she's awake, and I hope her subconscious soaks it in.

Jordyn calms, and Micah's words echo through my thoughts once again. "It's your choice...I won't force you to do anything."

My choice was to run. Flee to the refuge city in the east. Leave the one place I've ever felt truly safe—the guys who have become like family. Better than my actual family.

It's what Micah thought was best. What every fear within me is screaming for me to do. But in the end, it's showing me who I really am.

A coward.

But I don't want to be. I don't want to be swayed by my fears and anxieties, or have my life blown this way and that by others and their actions toward me or opinions of me.

I want to be strong. To fight for what I know is right.

*Both our actions and our* lack *of actions determine the course of our lives.* Miriam's words from what feels like a lifetime ago wash through my mind.

Am I doing the wrong thing? Do I need to stand against my family, to fight?

The very thought sends a chill through me. I shiver. *God, what am I supposed to do?*

Silence greets my prayer.

Other crew members believe in God, but their faith seems different than mine. Deeper.

Davey and Nate have a confidence, a settledness, that seems unshakable. Vik will fight fiercely to protect those he cares about, trusting God is with him.

And Micah.

My heart flutters in my chest, and I pull Jordyn closer.

My husband. That fact is still strange and uncomfortable. But the man astounds me more every day. There's a depth of strength in him, a courage, but all clothed in a humility that takes my breath away.

Compared to them, I feel like a baby in my faith.

What if I trusted God like they do? How much would change? The thought stirs something deep within me, like I've awakened a longing I pushed aside. Like God has more for me than just trusting Him to save me.

The ship rocks gently, the creaks and sounds I've grown familiar with echoing around me like a soft cadence.

I know I need to fight, but I'm not sure *how*. How do I stand against those I've known my entire life? My friends. My family.

Not to mention, Grandfather has resources and power on his side that I'm not sure I *can* stand against.

And if I *did* fight—if I could even figure out how—who would I lose in that battle?

The family I grew up with, or this new one I'm growing to love?

A fight would come with a cost, and I'm not sure if I'm ready to pay the price.

I want to think I won't have to choose. That we'll receive word from the scouts that Grandfather is no longer hunting for me, now that he realizes I've married. But deep inside, part of me knows it's wishful thinking. Grandfather doesn't give up.

Somewhere in my struggle with my torturous thoughts, I fall into a fitful sleep.

---

"Catori," Jordyn says in a sing-song voice. "I'm hungry." The little girl shakes me, rousing me from slumber.

My eyes feel glued shut, but I pry them open. I peek out at her. "You're hungry, huh?" My voice sounds gravelly. I clear my throat and shift into a sitting position.

Jordyn's brown eyes light up. She giggles. "Your hair looks funny."

I stick my tongue out and she laughs harder.

"Your hair looks funny too," I say, smiling at her and her curls that stick out at every angle. Brushing it into some semblance of order is going to be an interesting challenge this morning.

We spend the next several minutes getting ourselves ready, and I find I have my own share of knots in my hair. When we're finally presentable, we exit our room and make our way to the galley.

We enter the kitchen, and I stop short. A woman sits at one of the tables, in deep conversation with Micah. He told me last night that a scout would board the ship before sunrise. It never occurred to me that the scout might be a woman.

Several emotions assault me, but the one that rises above all the others is one I've never experienced before. Jealousy.

They're so engrossed in conversation, they don't even seem to realize we've entered the room.

"Ah, my favorite little lady." Vik's low voice behind us makes me jump, and it draws the focus of Micah and the woman with him.

Jordyn spins around and leaps into Vik's arms. He smiles, and carries her into the room, plopping down at one of the two empty tables and settling Jordyn on his lap.

"Your finest breakfast, Natey-boy!" He calls over to Nate, who pauses what he's doing long enough to turn and scowl at Vik.

All the guys call Nate Natey-boy when they want to annoy

him. He opens his mouth—most likely to gripe about it—but before he can get the words out, Jordyn pipes up.

"Yeah! You're the best cook ever, Natey-boy!"

Nate's scowl transforms into a grin. "Anything for you, Jordyn." He glares briefly at Vik, but turns back to the stove, whistling.

Micah stands, and the woman with him does as well. She's not very tall and there isn't much about her to call her beautiful, but there's a strength and grace that emanates from her that makes her captivating. Her blond hair is woven into a thick braid, and her brown eyes are kind as she looks at me.

"I'm glad you're here." Micah waves me over.

I hesitate for a moment, before slowly making my way to their table.

"This is Zoe." Micah makes the introduction as we all settle at the table. "She's our scout contact from Eryndale, and she has news."

I clasp my hands together under the table and nod at Zoe. "Nice to meet you."

"Zoe, this is Catori. My wife."

My heart skips a beat at how easily he called me his wife, but I keep my focus on Zoe.

She gives me a wry grin. "It's good to finally meet the princess of the Raiders. And the girl who could make Micah get married."

Micah shifts uncomfortably, and gives me a shy smile that's so out of character for him I almost reach for his hand.

But I keep my fingers locked together under the table.

Zoe cocks her head. "You're not exactly what I imagined. But Micah says we can trust you and that you'll be able to provide us with some insights."

I give a half-smile but don't respond. I'm not sure I *have* a response.

"Tell her what you told me," Micah says.

Zoe sobers instantly. "The crew hunting you has increased in their violence. They know you're traveling by boat, so they've taken to ransacking towns and villages along the river."

I straighten. "But I'm married now."

Zoe gives me a sympathetic shrug. "Guess your grandfather doesn't care as much as we'd hoped he would."

I twist my fingers tighter. I expected this. At least, I thought I did. But the despair welling in me at her words reveals how much I'd hoped things would be different.

"Don't worry." She pats my shoulder. "We'll get you to Eryndale safely." She nods toward Micah. "Thankfully, you've got one of the best crews on these waters. Micah knows passageways Thaddeus is *still* trying to map out." She quirks an eyebrow at Micah. "And you know he's waiting for you to come to Eryndale to help him with that."

Micah leans back in his chair. "I'll come. Once I know Catori's safe and no longer being hunted."

I blink. That's why he's not coming with me. He wants to make sure I'm safe. Could that mean he cares about me? Hope warms my chest.

But I clear my throat, refocusing on the news Zoe just shared. "So these attacks don't change anything?"

Zoe shakes her head. "No. Like I said, we'll make sure you get to Eryndale. But we'd like to have you come ashore tonight to share whatever you can with some of our people."

I glance at Micah.

"I'll come with you," he says.

I breathe out a small breath, and turn back to Zoe. "Okay."

"Great." She stands. "Let me reach out to my team and get everything set up."

"Of course," Micah says. "Davey's in the wheelhouse. Tell

him I want to take the interior passage. That'll give us some extra cover. From there, he'll be able to help you determine a good meeting spot."

Zoe thanks him, and strides from the room.

I stand in the wheelhouse next to Micah, heart pounding in my throat. Shep leans into me. If I had realized *this* is what Micah meant by "interior passage", I would have asked if there was another option.

Here the river seems more like a stream, with the banks so close I almost feel as though I could leap from the boat to the shoreline. The crew is situated at different points on the ship, calling out any dangers they see to Micah. *The Fearless Lady* crawls through the water. We've given up speed for stealth.

And I really hope it doesn't end with us ruining the ship. Micah is confident that he can sail through the network of rivers and streams he mapped out, so that's comforting... sort of.

A low grating noise makes me jump.

"What was that?" I ask, my voice squeaking.

"Davey, report!" Micah calls out. He sounds confident and unshaken.

Despite the fact that it sounds like the ship is scraping the bottom of the river and about to break in two.

"Just a big hunk of plastic, Cap!" Davey shouts back. "All good on the starboard bow."

A small hiss of air releases from my lungs.

I'm not sure if my nerves are from the challenging boating conditions or the growing realization that I'm still being chased. Part of me wants to know more about the search for me, but I'm too afraid of what I'd learn if I asked.

Zoe enters the wheelhouse, but doesn't say anything.

After a few minutes, the river widens, and Micah's shoulders visibly lower. I guess he was more stressed about the passage than I realized. My respect for him rises. He's confident under pressure and does whatever he can to shield those under his command from becoming overwhelmed.

I chew on the inside of my lip. Every day I'm more and more impressed with the man.

Stubble clings to his jaw, giving him a rugged look, and there are shadows beneath his eyes. He bears more than anyone on this ship realizes. As though he can sense me studying him, he turns to me with a grin.

My heart flutters, and warmth spreads through me.

"Well, that was fun," he says. He focuses on Zoe. "We lost a little time back there—things are drier this year than the last time I brought her through that way. But we'll make it up on this stretch."

Zoe inclines her head. "That's fine. I've radioed out to the rest of my team. A couple of them should be ready and waiting at the rendezvous point to take us into the meeting spot, if we can get there tonight."

"We'll get there," Micah says confidently.

"Alright," Zoe says. "I'll let them know to be ready." With that, she turns on her heel and exits the wheelhouse, pressing a radio unit in her ear.

The idea of stopping and having a meeting makes me

nervous. I'd rather sail as fast as we can up the river and toward Eryndale. Find safety for myself and Jordyn.

But if I can help the scouts—and Micah—determine a way to stop these attacks in the hunt for me, then I know I need to do it. The problem is, I'm not sure what I'll be able to offer of value.

I don't know how the bands of Raiders function. I wasn't trained to become one. All I know is what I've heard, how they would brag about what they did during Welcoming Parties. Not the strategy behind it all.

Shep nudges my hand with his head, whining softly. I plunge my fingers into his coarse fur, thankful for the diversion.

"It'll be okay," Micah says without looking at me.

"What do you mean?" My voice is annoyingly higher than usual and actually cracks on the last word.

Micah looks at me and cocks an eyebrow. "We've spent the last four months together. Shep can tell when you're upset, and so can I."

That ridiculous warmth spreads over me again, and I kneel, focusing all my attention on the dog. Anything to avoid the intensity in Micah's eyes and the way his words comfort me.

Shep wags his tail, excited for me to be on the same level as him. I busy myself scratching behind his ears.

"I'm fine," I say.

"It's okay to be afraid."

Micah's words snap my head up. No one has ever said that to me before. Probably because it goes against everything the Raiders stand for. We're not afraid, because we're the ones to instill fear. Any nightmares I had as a child were dismissed, and I was told to toughen up. Being afraid meant I was weak. And that wasn't tolerated.

I stare at the back of Micah's head, unsure what to say or how to respond.

"Nervousness, fear, comes when we're about to enter something bigger than us," Micah continues. "The true test of our character, of our courage, is what we will do de*spite* our fears."

"Quoting me again, huh Micah?" Davey says, leaning on the doorframe.

Micah chuckles. "Your wisdom is always quotable, my friend."

"You know that's right." Davey's grin splits his face, but a moment later he sobers, focusing on me. "Our character and courage *are* determined in the most difficult moments. But fear can—and often does—control our lives until we surrender to the One who is greater than it."

His words remind me of Miriam, echoing the depth of her faith with his own. And leaving me wondering exactly what that surrender looks like...and if I'm brave enough to find out.

---

We make excellent time for the rest of the day as Micah sails *The Fearless Lady* down a broader and deeper portion of the river. Before I'm ready, night begins to fall and we're nearing the portion of the river where we'll be meeting with part of Zoe's crew.

My nerves hum, and the anxiety I feel over my lack of knowledge increases with every passing moment. They expect me to know what to do, know how to help them. I *should* know how to help them. But at the moment I feel worse than useless. I fear I don't actually have the information they're hoping for.

But what will that mean for me...and everyone else?

Will they still take me to Eryndale? Will Micah be at greater risk if I can't give them insight into those hunting me?

I lean against the railing, staring out into the murky water. Micah would have let me sail the boat if time wasn't of the essence. And I long for the smooth, worn wood of the wheel and the distraction that comes with navigating the waterways. I grip the railing, my knuckles whitening.

*Just breathe. Maybe you'll think of something.*

But what if my character, my courage, is as faulty as my family's?

"Hey," Zoe says, leaning against the rail next to me.

I stiffen at the intrusion, but nod. "Hi."

She's nice enough, but I haven't been able to shake my jealousy over her friendship with Micah. Which is dumb. He's allowed to have friends, to be close to others. Although he's my husband, he's not *mine*. But I can't stop the growing longing for him to *be* mine. Completely.

"This must be hard for you, sharing intel about friends and family." Zoe's words break through my chaotic thoughts.

"A little. But I know it's necessary."

"I admire you," she says. "It took guts to run from it all, and courage to recognize that all you grew up with isn't right."

I stare at Zoe, but she's focused on the river. Could she be right? Do I have some ounce of courage in me?

Before I can come up with something to say in response, Zoe lifts her hand in greeting.

"There they are," she says.

I squint at the shoreline, trying to see through the dusky shadows to whoever it is she's talking about. At first, I don't see anything. But then there's movement, and someone steps out of the shadows, a wide grin on his face.

"Thaddeus!" Nate shouts over to the shore. "Why did they send an old guy like you?"

A booming laugh echoes over the water.

"You better watch your mouth, Natey-boy," Thaddeus shouts back. "I know your mama taught you to respect your elders, and I'm sure she wouldn't want to hear a report of your sass."

"Oh, please tell her, sir," Davey jumps into the conversation. "She always thinks *I'm* the bad influence." His mischievous tone belies him, but even so, Nate shifts uncomfortably at the possibility.

A smile spreads itself over my face. I can only imagine the trouble their mother went through raising them. But the two brothers are some of the kindest men I've ever met. They might be ridiculous at times, but they have a character that's deeper than most. And their faith seems to touch every aspect of their lives.

The brothers and Thaddeus continue to shout a conversation back-and-forth to each other. Two other people crowd along the bank of the river next to Thaddeus. The rest of the crew anchors *The Fearless Lady,* a couple of the guys throwing jabs at Nate and Davey for chatting instead of working. The comments seem to have the opposite effect on the brothers as they just laugh them off and lounge at the railing.

Micah comes out of the wheelhouse and strides over to the brothers. "You two have been less help than Shep." His eyes brim with mirth. "Get the rowboat lowered and go over and bring them back."

"Aye, aye, Captain," Davey says with an exaggerated bow.

While he's bent over, Nate elbows him in the stomach, eliciting a grunt from Davey. Davey straightens, and I can tell he's about to start wrestling his brother.

"Save it," Micah says. "Go get the scouts."

The two trot over to the rowboat, but I hear Davey whisper, "You're gonna get it later, little bro."

"I thought we were going to shore?" I say to Zoe.

She nods. "We are. Thaddeus is downloading his most recent maps for Micah. Not that Micah needs them. But Thaddeus is also hoping to get some intel from your captain about the waterways he wants mapped out. The newest map download is his way of trying to bribe Micah into coming to Eryndale to help him." She leans close. "My guess is he'll be coming back sooner than later since you'll be there." She gives me a cheeky wink.

"Oh," I say, not sure what else to add to the one pathetic syllable.

The rowboat grows closer and Zoe pushes away from the rail to greet the group coming aboard.

I stay off to the side as the scouts board the ship, but one man catches my eye. He's tall and muscular, with skin as dark as Micah's and the same broad nose and full lips.

Before I hear Micah's enthusiastic greeting, I know this is his older brother, Malachi.

The two men embrace in a bear hug, and for the first time in days, I watch some of the stress ease from Micah's brow. A soft smile warms my face. He needed this—someone he trusts to be in the fight with him.

Micah steps back, his gaze skimming over those around him. He focuses on me and nods in my direction. The brothers head toward me.

I pull my lip between my teeth and my hands flutter together, then apart. My heartbeat quickens. Then they're in front of me.

"Catori, this is Malachi. My older brother." Micah slaps Malachi on the back, and Malachi grins at me with an appraising look in his eye.

Right next to each other, it's even clearer the two men are

brothers. But Micah was right. As attractive as Malachi is, Micah is more handsome.

"So, you're the girl who got my brother to marry her?" Malachi's words snap my attention and he quirks an eyebrow.

I nod, even as my face heats. "I guess. Nice to meet you." I can't believe he knows we're married.

I reach out my hand, but Malachi's grin widens. "We're huggers in this family." He steps forward and pulls me into a huge bear hug that lifts me off my feet.

"Uh, okay." I awkwardly pat his back.

"Come on, man. Put her down," Micah says.

Malachi sets me on the deck of the ship and steps back. Micah shifts so that he's closer to me, and I find myself wanting him to put his arm around me. But he doesn't. I don't think Micah and I have even *hugged*. Maybe he missed the memo that they're a family of "huggers."

"Before I forget." Malachi digs into his pocket and pulls out a simple silver band. "Here you go, bro." He tosses the ring to Micah, who easily snatches it out of the air.

"Thanks," he says. He slips the ring into his pocket. "How's everyone back home?"

Malachi leans against the rail. "Good. They miss you."

"I miss them, too."

Malachi gestures with his head to the wheelhouse. "I'd better go help Thaddeus with the download. The man is a mess around technology, and I doubt you want him bustin' up your precious boat." He claps Micah on the shoulder and strides away.

I take a step to where the others are preparing to go to shore, but Micah's hand on my arm stops me.

"I know this isn't much." He rubs the back of his neck, then pulls the ring from his pocket and looks down at it. "But I wanted you to have something. You know, uh, since we're married." He extends the ring to me, his gaze fixed on it.

My heart melts. It's strange seeing Micah nervous, but also endearing. "It's perfect." I put my left hand out, and he slides the ring onto my finger. It fits better than I expected it to, the metal cool against my skin.

"It was my grandmother's." He doesn't immediately drop my hand, and his eyes finally connect with mine. "I'm not sure what will happen next, but I want you to know I'll fight for you. Always."

My eyes burn, and I swallow hard. I nod, because it's all I can manage.

Someone calls us over, and Micah squeezes my hand, then lets go. Together, we make our way toward the group and I pull my emotions back under control.

I run my thumb along the wedding band. Who is this man I married? And why is he so wonderful?

# CHAPTER
# TWENTY-ONE

Thaddeus announces that he only needs five more minutes, then we'll head to land.

Which is what we've been planning to do. But the announcement leaves me feeling like I just ran a mile.

I go below deck to my room and close the door. Take a few deep breaths.

Jordyn is with Vik—the two of them will stay on board, and Shax and Antonio will watch things from the shore. The rest of us will head inland for the meeting. It's the safest option for Jordyn, and I know Vik will protect her, but I hate to leave her.

Still, the most important thing right now is that I actually have things ready to share with the scouts and my crew. I pause.

Since when did I start thinking of Micah's crew as *my* crew? A small smile dances at the corners of my mouth. I'd like to stick with this vessel for the long term. To sail with *The Fearless Lady,* help people, discover a new life. And I want that life to include Micah.

My face burns at the thought, but alone in my room, I have to admit it's true. I want Micah to be a part of my life, to discover if there could be *more* between us than just friends.

I wonder if he feels the same way.

We are married, after all. And somehow I know he takes those vows more seriously than any man I've known before.

The thought of leaving him and going to Eryndale sends a pang through me, but it's the safest option. Maybe once all of this ends, I can rejoin the crew and sail with them.

A knock on my door jars me from my thoughts, and I shake them off like Shep after he swims.

Right now, I need to see what intel I can provide. It will help once I know more about the attacks. At least I hope it will. I straighten my shoulders and go open the door.

Micah smiles down at me, and I can't help but smile back.

"You ready?" he asks.

I nod. "Sure."

My insides twist as I follow Micah down the hall and up the stairs. The last thing I want to do is go to a secret meeting on land. I don't want to leave the steady rocking of the boat. The familiarity of this territory.

There's a splash as the rowboat hits the river. I flinch.

It's time.

Several people clamber over the side and head to shore, but I don't register *who*. My mind is too cluttered. My heart too anxious over what's coming.

I scan the deck as Thaddeus and Micah talk. Vik is holding Jordyn as she's perched on the railing, waving at those in the rowboat. I smile. One thing's for sure: he'd die before he ever let anything happen to her.

I make my way toward them, tilting my head up to look Vik in the eye. "Will you be okay here?"

The question is silly. Of course they'll be fine. Still, I can't help but ask it.

"Yes, ma'am." Vik's muscular arms practically swallow Jordyn up as he lifts her off the rail and holds her. "We have quite a fun evening planned." He smiles at the little girl, who grins back at him with adoration in her eyes.

"Great." I try to find other words, but they fail me. I'm not sure what exactly I wanted him to say. That he *wouldn't* be okay? That he needed me to stay on board with him?

The very idea is laughable. My skills in self-defense are negligible at best, and the reality is, if they encounter trouble, I'd be more of a liability than an asset.

One of Vik's mammoth hands pats me awkwardly on the shoulder. "You'll be okay too. Our contacts along the river haven't given us any intel that would suggest the Raider crew knows where we are. This is our last stop before we make a run to Eryndale." Although he's telling me we'll all be okay, I notice an eagerness in his tone to make the journey to the refuge city. "Just tell them what you can. You'll be back here before you know it."

"Thanks." I don't know what else to say, but I give Vik a smile.

I focus on Jordyn. Her eyes are serious, and I want to berate myself for having this conversation in front of her. She's too smart. I stick my tongue out at her and cross my eyes.

She giggles, and the sound warms my heart.

"You be a good girl for Vik, okay? I'll be back soon." I cup her smooth cheek with my hand and smile.

She nods. "Okay."

"She's *always* a good girl for me." Vik tosses her in the air, and Jordyn lets out a belly laugh that spreads my grin even wider.

"Catori, you ready?" Micah calls over.

"Yeah." I wave goodbye to Jordyn and Vik. The two of them will be fine—probably have a blast.

It's time for me to go do what I need to do. Prove to all those who have helped me that I can now be useful.

I only hope it's true.

I climb over the edge of the railing, down the ladder, and into the rowboat. It rocks gently as I settle myself in one of the few remaining seats. Nate's rowing the boat, and Davey and Zoe are in this group along with me and Micah. Micah plops into the boat, and it rocks harder.

"Cap, you really need to tread lightly," Davey complains. "I almost fell in."

"Guess I didn't rock it hard enough," Micah says, giving me a wink.

He sits next to me, his broad shoulders brushing against mine. "Let's go."

At Micah's words, Nate rows us to shore. No one says anything for the few minutes we take to get to the bank of the river. The sounds of the water lapping against the shore, along with the crickets emerging for their nighttime singing, echo through the air.

It's almost peaceful.

The rowboat grates into the rocky shore, cracking through the peaceful facade. I can't let my guard down. I need to be focused, alert, ready for danger. No matter how comfortable I may feel in a moment.

Thaddeus and Malachi pull us in, and we scramble onto the riverbank.

There's low shrubbery along the river, and Shax and Antonio tie the rowboat off on it. The rest of us hike inland, toward the tree-line of a forest. A breeze blows and goose-bumps rise on my arms, despite the warmth of the evening.

The shadows of the forest swallow us up, and I step closer

to Micah, wishing I could take his hand. I clench my hands into fists until my nails bite into the skin. What is *wrong* with me? *Focus, Catori.*

We hike forward in groups of two. According to Thaddeus, we should only have to go a couple of miles before we reach the rest of the team of scouts. But in the growing darkness, that feels like further than I want to go.

Malachi and Zoe turn on low green lights that sort of illuminate the way.

I pull out my pin-light from my pocket, but Micah places a hand over mine.

"That light will be too bright and draw more attention," he says. "I know it's tough to see, but we'll be there soon enough."

"Okay." I slip the pin-light back into my pocket. I've walked through forests in the dark before, but it was a forest I knew. The path to my glen. I could have walked it blindfolded.

But this is a very different feeling.

The ground inclines, and the muscles in my calves burn. My toe catches a root. My body shifts forward and I tense, ready to make painful contact with the ground.

Then Micah's hands are on my arms, holding me up. We pause for a moment, and my heart hammers in my chest. But it's from more than just my almost fall.

Micah's hands are still on me, his rough callouses a stark contrast to the gentleness of his touch.

"You okay?" His voice is soft, close to my ear.

I nod, but he doesn't let go. And I'm glad.

"Keep moving, lovebirds." Davey prods us from behind. "We don't have all day."

I can hear the smile in his words, and I practically jump away from Micah. Heat radiates down my back. I can't be the helpless woman right now. I'm supposed to be *helping* them.

I almost jog to close the distance that's grown between us and the others, and Micah is beside me in a few quick steps.

He takes my right hand. "I'll make sure you don't fall."

My heart stops, then thunders forward. Part of me knows I should pull away, not allow myself the comfort of his touch, the security of knowing he's there, ready to help me. We'll be parting ways soon enough, after all.

But instead, I squeeze his hand, and we walk forward together.

I run my thumb over my wedding ring.

If Micah is with me, I can do this. I can share anything that might be helpful for the scouts in stopping the Raiders.

I'm not in this alone.

The rest of the hike goes quickly, and we soon come to a stop. Micah lets go of my hand, and I immediately miss his steadying touch, but I don't reach for him. I need to be a strong woman who can help these people. Prove that I'm worthy of their help in getting me safely to Eryndale.

I take a moment to look around. We've stopped in the middle of the forest, but no one else is in sight. I guess we've arrived before the rest of the team.

"In here," Thaddeus says.

He pulls aside what I *thought* were just branches from a thick grove of bushes and waves us through an opening. I blink. There's a low glow coming from inside, and it looks more spacious than I'd have ever suspected.

I'm near the back of the group with Micah and Davey. A few people exit the hideout and break off into the woods, presumably to patrol the area. Malachi, Zoe, and Thaddeus climb in, followed by Nate. I duck under the branches and enter the space.

It's cramped, but there's still some room for me, Micah, and Davey. Thaddeus, Zoe, and Malachi are settling themselves on the ground, conversing with two other scouts. I scan the group.

I stop short. Micah bumps into me. I move aside to let him in, but I don't take my eyes off two of the people inside the hidden alcove.

Two people I know. And there's no way they're scouts.

"Wasn't sure we'd be meetin' up again," Hosea says in his gruff voice.

"Is Jordyn okay?" Sienna leans forward, eyes searching the area behind me.

"How...what..." I can't find a way to finish the questions clambering in my mind.

"Find a question and spit it out," Hosea says.

"You know each other?" Micah settles himself next to me, his strength and presence instantly comforting.

I nod, but can't find my voice.

"Sure enough," Hosea says. "We had the distinct pleasure of being under her grandfather's...hospitality."

"Where's Jordyn?" Sienna asks before anyone else can say anything.

"She's on the boat," I say, finally finding my voice. "How did you...?" The question trails off as I lower myself to the floor.

"We used the tunnels and that handy exit you shared with us," Hosea says. He frowns. "But our escape wasn't without casualties. And they ain't too happy with us for it, either."

"So Jordyn's okay? She's not hurt?" Sienna's questions draw my focus, and I turn to her.

"She's safe, and the guys with her would die before she came to any harm," I assure her. I bite my lip and focus on Hosea again. "Is Miriam...okay?"

He flinches and focuses on the ground.

I hold my breath, not sure I *want* Hosea's response.

"I don't know," he finally says. "She refused to leave with us. Said she would only slow us down. Especially since...well, she needed rest."

A thousand more questions scream to be released.

"As much as I hate to break up reunions," Thaddeus says, "I think we'd better get down to business."

There's a quick round of introductions, but the names of the other scouts barely impact me. I'm still stunned to be in the same hideout with Hosea and Sienna. If Grandfather just lost a group of his captives, Hosea's right. He won't be happy. I can only imagine what horrors the remaining captives are experiencing right now.

Miriam, the closest thing to a grandmother I've ever known, is still in the compound. And based on Hosea's fractured sentence, there's even more going on. She's not safe.

Bile rises in my throat at the thought.

What if I'd tried to bring about real change sooner? What if I'd done *more* than just say things that riled people up once in a while and actually *acted*, fought for change? Would it have made a difference?

Would Miriam be safely with us right now?

I drag my focus back to the conversation at hand. Hosea's talking.

"We came upon the WUN, more by accident than anything. When me and her,"—he jabs a thumb toward Sienna—"heard that there would be a chance to stand up against the Raiders, we wanted in."

Thaddeus reaches a hand over to Hosea, and the two men grip each other's forearms. "Well, welcome. Glad to have you."

Hosea nods.

Everyone's focus shifts to Thaddeus. I tear my gaze away from Hosea and Sienna to give my attention to Thaddeus. How is it possible that they're here?

Thaddeus claps his hands together. "As you all know, the report isn't good. The Raider crew searching for you,"—his eyes lock on mine, and I fight to keep from squirming under his intensity—"is ransacking entire villages. They strike so hard and so fast that we barely have the chance to get a scouting team in there before they're gone. We've tried to determine an order and one thing has become clear." His focus shifts to Micah. "They know your shipping schedule."

I sense Micah tensing beside me and have to keep myself from reaching for his hand.

"How?" Micah asks. "That's classified. We get each schedule directly from Eryndale, and it's never the same."

Thaddeus inclines his head. "True. But you do visit certain villages more often than others. Somehow, they've determined which ones those are."

The tension in the space increases to an almost suffocating level.

Nate's face has paled as Thaddeus talked.

Davey gives his brother a concerned look. "We have friends in those villages. We need to check on them and make sure they're okay."

"There are teams in each of the villages as we speak," Thaddeus says, his tone brooking no argument. "We have other things we need to do."

"But," Nate croaks out the word, "how can we know...?" His voice trails off, not finishing the sentence.

The girl from the first village I visited with them springs to mind. I knew he cared about her, but it seems his feelings run even deeper than I realized.

"I understand your fears," Thaddeus says. "But the best way to ensure the safety of everyone moving forward is figuring out how to stop this crew."

Everyone's eyes lock on me. If I could dissolve into the floor right now, I would welcome it.

My face heats, but I clear my throat. "What do you know about them?"

"Not much," Zoe chimes in. "We believe it's the same crew that was hunting you in Wisteria. But the attacks increased in intensity a few nights ago, after one of the crew members was badly wounded."

I tense. Gabby's part of J's crew.

"The woman leading them—"

"J," I interject.

"J," Zoe repeats. She tilts her head to the side. "Well, once he was injured, she immediately called her forces back. She was crying as she took the dying man and laid him on her metal horse before riding out of the city. At first, we thought we might have done enough to stop them. But ever since that night, the attacks are swift, intense. Some survivors claim to have seen Carver still, but it's become increasingly clear that J is the one in charge."

Unease wafts over me. J is vicious, but the intensity of her attacks tells me something deeper. "Do you know who the dying man was?" I ask the question, fearing the answer I know is about to come.

"She called him Aiden moments before she rode away, but that's all we know."

"No," the word falls from my lips. A choked whisper.

I can feel the eyes of everyone boring into me, but no one says anything.

"Aiden was her brother." My throat thickens, a lump lodging there.

Memories of my last moments with Aiden, his jokes and laughter, cloud my thoughts.

He could make anyone laugh, and he was always getting into trouble by playing a prank on someone he shouldn't. J got him out of any real issues every time. I clear my throat and press my eyes closed for a moment. I need to keep it together— at least for long enough to help Micah and Zoe with the next part in our plan.

I'll never hear his laugh again or try to keep my laughter in as Gabby yells at him for doing something annoying.

A friend. Gone.

I want to hope that maybe he survived, but with the way J's acting—

"Catori." Thaddeus's voice breaks into my pain. "You seem to know this crew well. Is there anything you can tell us that will help us stop them?"

I swallow the lump in my throat, and scan the cramped space. They're all here hoping I can help them, share something that might save more innocent lives from being taken in the hunt for me. They're willing to risk their lives while helping me get to Eryndale so that I'll be safe.

The least I can do is share what little I know.

I straighten. "J is poised, brilliant, and she's able to out-think anyone. At least that I've seen. She plays the long-game, and she's willing to wait until the optimal moment to attack, ensuring that her attack is executed with as much precision as possible. Grandfather always knew that any time J was out on a mission he could expect her to return with whatever it was he'd sent her out for—supplies, slaves, intel."

I lift a shoulder, let it drop. "She's the best. Not everyone loved working with her because she won't tolerate actions that go against her commands. But over the years, she formed a crew that would follow her to the end of time. At least that's how it seemed to me. They obey her every command, act only when she gives the order. Most of the other Raider groups vie for position, want to take over leadership, but not J's crew."

I squeeze my hands together, and press forward, even though by doing so I'm betraying not just J, but Gabby. "They function like a machine. Trust each other. Her brother and sister joined her crew when they were old enough—Aiden and Gabby. They were the only real soft spot anyone ever saw with J. Aiden is...was,"—I swallow again—"a goofball. Gabby is different from J, but brilliant in her own ways." The memory of her with Carver pushes aside any warm thoughts of our friendship. She's better at deceiving people than I ever realized.

I focus on Thaddeus. "If Aiden is dead, I can guarantee this: J will stop at nothing to complete her mission and avenge her brother's death. She just became more fierce and deadly than you can imagine."

The words settle over the group with a choking intensity.

After a moment, Thaddeus nods. "We've gathered that they function differently than other crews. And they seem to be everywhere. Her crew will hit a village further south on the river, and then a few days later, hit the lake region. It's so sporadic, we can't figure out how to stop them. Hopefully, since we know the target,"—he gives me an apologetic look—"we'll finally be able to stop her."

I bite my lip.

"What is it?" Micah asks.

"It's, well." I clear my throat. "J and her crew are the best

I've heard of. But I've never known them to travel in the lake region." I shrug. "I mean, Grandfather didn't tell me everything, but most of the raids he ordered, as far as I knew, were to the south. He left the lake region be. I'm not sure why J would have gone up there."

"Huh." Thaddeus rubs his beard. "Well, that's an issue for another day. For now, what do we do to stop her?"

I rub my palms against my legs. "The weak point is Carver. He never rides with them. That and the fact that Aiden..." I swallow. "If he's gone, she might be a little more reckless."

"How many members of her crew are there?" Thaddeus asks.

"Um, she has a smaller crew than some—she's picky about who she lets join her. There's probably about seven of them."

Malachi leans back and links his hands behind his head. "We'll be able to take them."

"There's a factor you need to add in now," Hosea interjects. "The Raiders ain't gonna take anything lying down. They've lost over a dozen captives—nine of us escaped. The others..." his voice trials off.

I want to ask who didn't make it, but keep my mouth shut. Now's not the time. But my heart aches to know more about Miriam, to be assured she's alive and okay.

"Anyway, it's always a pride thing with them." Hosea juts his chin at me. "They want Catori in a bad way, and I doubt stopping one crew will be enough. They'll send others."

Chills prickle my arms. His words so closely echo my own fears. I'm half-tempted to jump up, end the meeting, and start running to Eryndale immediately.

"Which is why we're going to ensure she is safe in Eryndale as soon as possible." Thaddeus says in a voice that brooks no argument.

Hosea grunts and focuses on me. "Not sure runnin' is gonna solve all your problems."

I shift.

"We're removing her from the equation," Micah interjects, his tone fierce. "Which will allow us to focus on stopping them, knowing we don't have to worry about her safety."

Thaddeus raises his arms in the air. "Easy, everyone. We're a team. Catori, thank you for sharing what you know."

"It seems like we need more current intel, though," Malachi says.

My stomach dips. He's right.

Zoe sighs. "True. What if we bring in Broche? He's always got more intel than he should. That might help give us an edge."

"No." Micah frowns. "I don't trust that guy. He works for whoever will pay him the most."

Some others nod, and there's silence for a few moments. I'm not sure who Broche is, but something about the name is familiar. Like I've heard him mentioned before.

"What if we bring the WUN in?" Thaddeus suggests. "Some of our best assets are close to the compound."

"It could blow their covers," Zoe says. "Are you willing to risk that?"

Thaddeus rubs his beard, eyes distant. Everyone watches him, waiting for his determination. Thaddeus is an interesting man, and it's clear everyone around me respects him. I'm inclined to do the same, just because Micah and his crew do.

"Let's at least meet with them," Thaddeus finally says. "They've got some of the best intel, and hearing it from them firsthand will keep us from any miscommunication." He pauses. "If they decide they want in on this fight, then we'll let them."

There are nods and murmurs of agreement.

"Who is the WUN?" I ask, even as warmth spreads up my neck. I'm embarrassed that I don't know, especially since Hosea already mentioned them.

"I'm not sure she's cleared for that intel," one of the female scouts says.

My face flushes even hotter.

"Catori is trustworthy," Micah says. "I'd stake my life on it. And we need her help."

"For sure!" Davey chimes in, and Nate nods emphatically at his side.

"I gotta trust my sister-in-law," Malachi says, tossing me a grin.

Now my embarrassment is from their accolades more than not being trusted. Even Zoe agrees.

Thaddeus puts up his hands, and the conversation dies down. "Okay, okay. We're all here because we trust each other." He looks at the woman who spoke. "No matter where we've come from, right now we all have the same purpose." He doesn't look away until the woman inclines her head in agreement.

Although she agrees, I'm uncomfortable as I realize a few of the scouts are eyeing me as though I'm more trouble than I'm worth.

"The WUN is the Western Underground Network," Thaddeus says. "They help get people safely to Eryndale—especially those who are at high risk of being sought by the Raiders."

I nod, my brain hardly able to keep up. There's so much more in this world outside of the compound than I ever realized.

Thaddeus turns to Zoe. "I'll contact the WUN tonight. We'll meet with them tomorrow to get an idea of what type of chatter they're hearing and what they've seen of recent Raider movements." His intense gaze collides with mine, and I shift but don't look away. "Once we have a clearer idea of what we're up against, we'll mount an attack. Take out the key players. It won't be worth it to them to keep coming after you at that point, but we'll have you remain in Eryndale until we're confident they'll leave you alone."

I swallow hard but nod. It makes sense. If the attack goes the way Thaddeus thinks it will, Grandfather will lose many of his top men and women.

Will it be enough to stop him? Or just make him angrier?

I stand with everyone else as Thaddeus ends the meeting. I walk out of the hideout and into the warmth of the night.

Micah emerges, touches my elbow, and nods for me to follow him. I do, even though my swirling thoughts need some time to slow down. He leads me several feet away from the entrance of the hideout and the others who are still exiting.

He stops and faces me. Shadows obscure my view of him, but his solid presence makes me feel like maybe things will be okay.

"I know this is a lot," he says. "But we'll take it one day at a time, alright? I'll be with you every step of the way, all the way to Eryndale. And I'll keep you safe, whatever it takes."

A lump lodges in my throat, and I can't find a response. Without giving myself time to weigh out the consequences or overthink things, I step forward and hug Micah. He stiffens in surprise. I almost pull back, but before I can, his strong arms wrap around me, his heart beating steadily in my ear.

Even with all the uncertainty of what's to come, for the first time in my life, I actually feel *safe*.

# TWENTY-THREE

Unease tightens my stomach as we come closer to the river. Something doesn't feel right. But I can't say what it is, so I keep my mouth shut. There's no need to worry Micah, or anyone else for that matter.

It's probably just my apprehension and overwhelm after everything I learned tonight.

Something rustles to my right. I spin toward it, staring into the darkness. But there's nothing there.

"You okay?" Micah asks.

"Yeah?" The word sounds like a question more than anything. *Pull it together, Catori.* "I thought I heard something."

Micah stands next to me a for another moment, staring with me into the darkness of the forest. "I don't see anything. Probably just an animal. All our senses are on high alert after that conversation." He squeezes my shoulder. "But we should keep moving. We're close to the river now. The sooner we can get you and Jordyn to Eryndale, the better."

I nod and continue hiking forward. There's only four of us now: Micah, me, Nate, and Davey. Thaddeus and his team remained with the rest of their team and Hosea and Sienna to finalize their parts in the plan and work out how to bring in members of the WUN. Part of me assumed I'd be happy once it was back to just me and the crew of *The Fearless Lady,* but now I miss the added layer of protection Thaddeus and his scouts brought.

My shoulders tense as we break out of the tree line and onto the bank of the river. We're exposed now. Which should be fine. But something still feels...off. Like the sounds I should be hearing aren't there. Like someone is watching us.

But that's ridiculous.

Antonio and Shax wave as we head toward the rowboat, each approaching from different sides of the riverbank. They've been patrolling the area the whole time we were in the meeting, and they're far more alert and attuned to dangers than I am.

So why am I so on edge?

Part of me wants to stop Micah from heading toward the rowboat, but I'm not sure why. It's time to board the ship again. I'll be able to see Jordyn, confirm she and Vik are as safe as when we left them. There's no reason to be freaked out right now.

But I can't shake the sensation.

My boots crunch over the rocky shoreline as I make my way toward the rowboat Nate and Davey are situating in the water. It'll be crammed with all six of us in it for the short ride back to the ship, but the guys are clearly preparing for just that.

My stomach tightens and an ugly memory surfaces, like debris on the river. A dark night in the forest. A lonely walk back from my glen. The unwanted advance of Carver as he materialized out of nowhere. His men surrounding me. Their laughter.

Chills wash over me like someone doused me with water.

That night was horrifying. They didn't do anything to me, but they laughed at my fear. Taunted me. When I'd finally gotten away from them and raced back to my grandfather to tell him, he'd laughed. Thought the whole thing was hysterical.

Then he'd berated me for my fears.

That was two years ago now, but this feeling...this moment. It's just like how I felt before they surrounded me.

I cross my arms over my chest and rub my hands up and down my biceps. I turn in a slow circle, inspecting the area.

"Catori."

I jump, heart racing. Micah is a few feet away, eyes wide.

"You okay?" Concern mingles with the shadows of the night on his face.

I swallow. "I just felt..." I shake the thought away. There's no way to explain this feeling without sounding silly or paranoid. "You just startled me."

"I'm so sorry. The boat's ready." He gestures to it. "Should we go?"

"Sure. Of course."

He waits for me to go ahead of him, and his solid presence at my back eases some of my anxiety. Unlike that night, tonight I'm not alone.

The other guys are chatting as we approach. Antonio and Shax are in the boat and Davey and Nate are still waiting on shore, probably preparing to push us further into the water.

Micah offers me a hand to help me aboard, and I accept it. I half-crawl my way past Shax and Antonio, who are on the middle seat and to the back seat. I'm not sure *why* they decided to get in before Micah and I did.

"Why'd you get on here already?" Micah asks as he squeezes past them. "You could've at least taken the back seat."

"Didn't want you to have to row, Cap," Antonio says, laughter in his voice.

Micah thuds into the seat next to me, the boat rocking far more than I'm comfortable with. I grip his arm without thinking. His muscles tense beneath my fingers.

"Plus, we've been standing all night," Shax adds. "We earned our seats."

Micah sighs dramatically, but I can tell he's not upset. This man cares deeply for those under him, and I know he'd gladly take any inconvenience if it meant it would help his crew.

It's one of the things I'm beginning to love about him.

My heart lurches as Davey and Nate push the boat into the river, then scramble aboard. I release Micah's arm.

With everything going on right now, I can't *possibly* be falling for Micah. It's impractical, distracting. Dangerous even.

But as he laughs at something Davey said, his shoulder pressed against mine, I can't deny the feelings growing inside me like a weed.

Plus, he *is* my husband now. Maybe it's not the worst thing...unless he doesn't feel anything for me.

In a few brief moments, we're back at the ship. Micah grabs hold of the rope hanging off the side and anchors the rowboat in place. I climb aboard.

Low lights illuminate the deck, but Vik and Jordyn aren't topside, which was to be expected. It's long past Jordyn's bedtime and Vik would have brought her below deck and settled her. He's probably camping right outside the door to our room at this moment. The tension in my chest eases a notch.

I run my hand along the rail as the men board the boat behind me. The night sky is clear and covered with stars, and there's a light breeze that perfumes the air with the lilac bushes from shore.

Everything is quiet and in order. Peaceful.

Safe.

Why was I worried? I must need rest or something.

Micah approaches, and I shift to look at him.

The low lights of the deck illuminate his face, and he smiles. My stomach flips, and I bite my lip. I really need to get this under control.

"You ready to get to Eryndale?" Micah asks, leaning his hip against the rail.

I shrug. "Yeah, sure." In reality, I'm worried about what they'll think of me there. But there's not much of a choice. I can't stay around here. Not with J and Grandfather hunting for me.

He stares at me for a long moment, but I don't look away.

"Catori." His voice cracks, and he clears it. "I, uh, I know we've only known each other for a few months..." He pauses and squirms.

I almost smile. I've never seen Micah so uncomfortable and unsure of himself, and the sight is endearing. He reminds me of Jordyn when she's acting shy. I stay quiet and wait for him to continue, curious.

He blows out a slow breath. "I'm not very good at this. Anyway, I uh, just, well, I care about you. A lot. And after everything's done...I...well...would it be okay..."

My cheeks warm as what he's saying registers. I offer him a small smile, hoping it's enough encouragement for him to continue. I think I know what he wants, and it's what I want, but I need him to continue. To make sure I'm not just imagining this moment.

He stays quiet.

"Just ask, Micah," I say softly, my words barely above a whisper.

He rubs the back of his neck. "What I want to know is, would you —"

"Captain! Get down here now!" Davey's frantic voice shatters the peaceful and hope-filled moment, dragging me back to the reality of *now*.

I whirl toward Davey and find him at the door to the stairs below deck. His face is ashen, but that's not what freezes my breath in my lungs and makes every inhale painful.

His shirt is covered in blood.

# TWENTY-FOUR

Micah reacts before I can make my legs obey the frantic screams of my brain. Then I'm racing after him. Davey has already disappeared below deck. Nausea rolls over me like rapids.

Jordyn.

Vik.

Whose blood is Davey wearing?

What happened?

The questions pound through my mind. I shove them back and scramble down the stairs after Micah.

Something sticky on the railing causes me to pause.

More blood.

I yank my hand from the rail and almost leap the rest of the way down to the lower deck.

Davey, Antonio, and Shax crowd the hallway, obstructing my view.

I want to scream, force my way through. But I'm frozen. I need to know what happened, yet a part of me is terrified of seeing whatever I'm about to see.

We pass the galley, and my gaze catches on Shep laying just inside. His belly moves up and down as he breathes, but he doesn't move his head. Is he drugged? Dying?

My stomach clenches, but I move on. I have to check on Jordyn before I can care for the dog.

The men part for Micah, and I stay close behind him. His broad shoulders continue to block my view, but I'm almost glad.

He stops. Shifts.

And what I see sends me to my knees.

Vik is laying on the ground, blood pooling around him, and he's unconscious. At least I hope he's unconscious.

Nate kneels next to him, his shirt stripped off and pressed against Vik's abdomen.

"Is he...?" Micah doesn't finish the question.

Nate remains focused on Vik. "He's still alive, but I'm not sure he would have been if we'd arrived any later."

Micah whirls so fast he almost collides with me. "Davey, radio Thaddeus. We need more medical supplies than what we have in stock."

Davey clambers up the steps.

Micah turns to Antonio and Shax. "Did either of you see *anything* tonight while you were patrolling?"

"No, Captain," Shax says. "It was quiet. Nothing out of the ordinary." He looks with wide eyes at Antonio, who nods his agreement.

Micah's lips compress. "Well, something happened."

Adrenaline shoots through me. "Jordyn!"

I scramble to my feet, leap over Vik, and burst through the door to the room I share with the little girl.

It's empty.

"Micah." My voice is choked. Air rushes out of my lungs and I can't bring any back in.

She's gone.

Micah is at my side. His eyes rove the room. He drops to the floor and looks under the beds. I follow suit, unsure why I didn't think to do so earlier.

Something shifts.

"Jordyn, sweetie. It's me." I crawl closer and reach my hand under the bed.

The little girl crawls out, face blotchy with tears. She flies into my arms and sobs.

I cling to her, tears pressing against my own eyes.

She's here. In my arms.

Micah kneels next to me. "What happened, little one?" His voice is tender as he rubs her back.

But she doesn't stop crying or respond to the question.

"Ah, there's the little brat." J's voice steals the breath from my lungs.

I whirl to face her, clutching Jordyn tighter. Micah leaps to his feet, stepping between us, and pulling a gun.

There's scurrying in the hall. Over Micah's shoulder, I see Antonio and Shax pull weapons and train them at J.

Jordyn's sobs become whimpers as she quiets, her little arms clinging to me. Tremors run from my head to my toes.

J is surrounded. Nate's working on Vik. Jordyn is in my arms.

Even though she's aboard the ship, it doesn't mean she's won. But all the logic in the world doesn't stop the shaking in my body.

"Put your hands up." Micah gestures with his gun. "You're surrounded."

J crosses her arms over her chest and cocks an eyebrow. "I'm not foolish enough to be here without a plan." Her eyes find mine, and I involuntarily shift further behind Micah. "Haven't you told them *anything* about me, dear Princess?" The words drip with sarcasm. Her gaze dips to my ring, then back to my eyes. "Huh. So you *did* get married. Guess I should say congratulations."

The hair on the back of my neck stands up, and I hold Jordyn tighter.

"What do you want?" Micah asks. His gun remains steady, but I know he won't shoot her. Not unless she provokes him.

He and his men arrest those who commit crimes. They don't kill them. Which is far less of a comfort to me now than it was before.

J sighs. "I would have thought that was fairly obvious. I want Catori. Her grandfather wants her back, and I get paid a lot more if I deliver her alive." She shrugs. "But really, I'll take her however I can get her." There's a hard, bitter edge to her words.

She sounds nothing like the woman I knew. How is it possible that I counted her as a friend?

"No." Micah steps toward her.

J pulls her own gun. "You're close enough, honey. I can guarantee you, I'm an excellent shot. And I'm not aiming at you. So unless you want your lover here to die, I suggest you listen to what I have to say." She flicks a hand behind her. "And tell your goons not to do anything stupid."

Micah raises his free hand toward Antonio and Shax, and the two men stay where they are.

"Good boys." J smirks. "Now, I know you're not likely to give Catori to me right now. But feel free to shock me by proving me wrong." She pauses, then shrugs at Micah's glare. "Fine. So here's the deal. We know your plans to bring Catori and the kid to Eryndale, and it won't work. We have ambushes set for every possible route you could take from here to the east." She tilts her head. "And your friends' plan to draw us into a fight won't work either. You have no options."

Chills inch up my spine. How could she know? She's good... but even J couldn't have imagined what we're planning. There must be a leak.

J shrugs. "We just want Catori. You can even keep the kid if you want her." She gestures to Jordyn, and I squeeze her tighter. "I never understood why Carver took her, anyway. And, because I'm enormously generous, you have forty-eight hours to deliver her as close to the compound as you want to take her. If you don't deliver her within that time, I can personally guarantee that you'll have more than one injured man to deal with." Her perfectly formed eyebrows lift. "Not to mention the countless people we'll kill or capture in every village you've stopped in. The choice is yours."

"Your options are unacceptable," Micah says through clenched teeth. "Besides. There's no way we're letting you off this ship alive. Your threats are empty promises."

J shakes her head, her many braids moving in rhythm. "Oh dear captain, I do not make empty promises. Do I, Catori?"

Her eyes find mine again, and I shiver. "Just leave us alone," I beg. "I won't go back."

"Then people will die. All because of you." She smirks. "Guess you really are a Raider after all—letting innocent lives get taken just so you can get what you want."

Air whooshes from my lungs. No. She can't be right.

"And to address your...concerns for me," J continues, her focus back on Micah. "Which I do appreciate. Living is my pref-erence, after all." She flashes a grin, then grows serious. "If I don't leave this ship within the next thirty minutes, unscathed, you'll be overrun by Raiders. And trust me, you'll lose."

For the first time, Micah's gun seems to waver. The thought of Raiders, of Carver, boarding *The Fearless Lady* and harming this crew is more than I can bear. But I don't know what to do. I can't go with her. I can't go back.

J seems to sense that we believe her. She tucks her weapon into the holster in her leather pants. "Catori, I've left a little note for you on your bed. Enjoy." She wipes her gloved hands together. "Well, I've delivered my message. So it'll be time for me to go."

Micah lowers his gun fully now, his shoulders rigid. "We won't give her over to you."

J sighs. "Then prepare to see a lot of death."

She moves toward the exit, then stops, eyes locked on mine. "I could take you now if I wanted. Kill all of your friends. But you get this one favor because of what you did for Gabby. Don't waste it. Because now we're even."

She leaves the room, and Micah and I follow her.

She pauses, focusing on Vik and Nate working on a large gash in the man's abdomen.

J leans down. "Don't miss the cuts on his back. They might not be as deep as that one there, but we wouldn't want to see them infected, would we?"

She pats Nate's shoulder, and the man's entire body tenses, but he doesn't stop working on Vik.

Blood pounds in my ears. I want to attack the woman. Silence her forever. But I know that in a fight with J, I would never win.

"Well, gentlemen, goodbye for now." J smirks, strides past Antonio and Shax and up the stairs, her braids swinging in rhythm behind her.

Micah follows her, and Antonio and Shax go with him.

"Hey!" Davey's voice filters below deck.

"Let her go," Micah responds.

There's a splash.

J's gone.

But her threats linger in the air, promising to stain everything as permanently as Vik's blood is staining the wood of the hallway.

"Where's my Vik?" Jordyn's small, shaky voice draws my attention.

I back further into the room, not wanting her to see Vik this way. Unconscious.

Dying.

*Oh God, please don't let him die.*

"He's hurt, baby," I say, doing my best to remain calm.

Davey clambers down the stairs. "What was she doing here? And why in blue blaze did we just let her *off the ship*?"

"We didn't have a choice," Micah states in a tone that brooks no arguments. "Did you reach Thaddeus?"

Davey presses his lips together. He nods. "Yes. He's sending Raul and Zoe. They're using Skinter Suits, so they should arrive within the hour."

I have no clue what Skinter Suits are, but at least they'll allow the scouts to get here soon.

Micah runs a hand over his short hair. "Good. Radio him again and tell him to hold off on preparing the ambush. We have a major problem."

Davey's eyebrows draw down, but he turns and jogs back up the stairs.

"Antonio and Shax, get the ship ready to move. I want to get out of here as soon as Raul and Zoe arrive. No sense in sticking around when Raiders are so close."

Shax turns to go, but Antonio hesitates.

"Why wouldn't they just attack now if they're so confident their forces could overwhelm us?" Antonio asks.

Shax stops, waiting for an answer.

"I don't know." Micah looks back at me.

Jordyn's sobs have finally slowed, and I rock her gently in

my arms. "Because of something I did for her sister, Gabby." The memory of sticking up for my friend and taking the demerit feels like a lifetime ago. But it was only several months.

An ache builds in my chest at the thought of my best friend. No. Not my best friend. Not even my friend. And this is the only kindness J will give me for years of friendship with her sister and keeping her from exile.

There's no doubt in my mind that the next time I see J, she'll destroy everyone in her way in order to get to me. Including my husband.

"Come on, Vik," Nate mumbles. "Stay with me, brother."

I sink onto the nearest bed, staring out at the men in the hall that I can see...and envisioning the two men I can't see. The weight of everything drags me down like an anchor.

"How did this happen?" The words squeeze themselves past my numb lips. "How did she know so much?"

Shax crosses his arms over his chest and stares at me in a way that's almost scary. Like he doesn't trust me. "That's a good question. And I suspect I'm looking at the answer to it."

My stomach drops.

Micah steps toward him. "Don't talk like that. Catori is *not* the reason this happened."

Shax's mouth bunches. "There's clearly a leak. And all I'm saying is she's the most likely one for it to come from."

I inhale sharply. I would have been less shocked if he'd slapped me across the face. He can't believe that.

Micah's hands clench into fists. "She's running from them, man. Why would she leak sensitive intel?" He's trying to keep his voice calm, but I hear the anger boiling beneath the surface.

Antonio puts a hand on Shax's arm. "Let's not assume the worst of anyone. We'll go get the ship ready, Captain."

He steps on the first stair, almost dragging Shax with him.

But Shax doesn't move right away. He stares at me for a

long moment. I drop my gaze. A second later, the sound of the two men climbing the stairs fills the room. I bury my head in Jordyn's curls. How could Shax think I'd do this?

It doesn't matter.

J knows our plans. She's taunting us, waiting to see what we'll do. Probably hoping to uncover more intel about the scouts as a result of whatever move we make.

And is she right? Am I willing to sacrifice innocent lives in order to save myself? Am I really just like my grandfather, Carver, Briggs—all the Raiders I grew up with?

There's a low moan.

"Uh, Micah!" Nate's voice is panicked. "I need help!"

# TWENTY-FIVE

Micah shuts the door to my room, muffling the sounds from the hallway. Protecting Jordyn from hearing or seeing whatever's happening. Her chest rises and falls evenly, and I realize she's fallen asleep. I gently turn and settle her on the bed, pulling the covers up to her chin.

As much as I want to go see what's happening with Vik, reassure myself that he's still alive, I remain in the room. If and when Jordyn wakes up, I need to be here.

And I can't run from whatever message J left behind for me. I need to find it. Read it. See if there's some way I can outwit her, get to safety, even though I know there's little hope of that.

I scan the room for a moment and catch sight of an envelope on my bed. My breath snags in my lungs. There it is. With shaking hands, I pick it up.

My name is on the front, written in Grandfather's handwriting.

I squeeze my eyes shut. J and Carver are threatening. Terrifying even. But Grandfather, as much as we didn't always see eye-to-eye, he loved me. It was a conditional love, one I constantly had to earn. But still love...right?

Maybe he just wants me back. Misses me. A pang ricochets through my chest. Part of me misses him. I open my eyes and unfold the letter.

Catori,

After all I have given you, all I have done for you, I am disgusted by your behavior. You are a spoiled, ungrateful wretch, and no grand-daughter of mine.

Carver couldn't bring you back, so he's dead.

I have no doubt I will fulfill my orders. But until you return, I'll kill a captive every day. Starting with the ones you visited most.

You wanted to befriend those so beneath your station? Fine. They'll pay the price.

And I want you to know that this is all because of you and your act of rebellion.

Jehoram, Chief of the Raiders

THE NOTE FALLS FROM MY NUMB FINGERS. HE'S COMPLETELY disowned me, and yet he'll stop at nothing to get me back, restore whatever he sees as his *honor*. Even if it means killing Carver. And murdering innocent captives.

Miriam's face comes to mind. Will he kill her? Has he already killed her?

But what can I do? If I go back, he'll execute me or make me a slave. Just like he does with every other person who defies him. I sink to the floor, hands pressed against my face. Even if I return and do exactly what he wants, there's no saying he won't still murder everyone just to prove his point and show his power.

I've always wanted to see the best in him, justify the man who raised me. Believe he was more than the evil of the compound. Different from the other Raiders. How could I be so foolish?

He's their leader.

Who they are, how they act, it all stems from him.

He wants me back. And he'll stop at nothing to bring me back, even if it means destroying everyone and everything in his path.

Since I escaped the compound, I've wanted my fight to be with Carver, or even J. Any of the Raiders hunting for me. But the reality is, my fight has always been against my grandfather and his forces.

My body trembles, and I rock back and forth.

I can't go back. I can't return to that life. This time with Micah, the crew, even the scouts, has all shown me that a different type of existence is possible. One that's not built around bitterness and hurting others. Some part of me always knew there was more, knew the life of a Raider was wrong. And there's no way I can put myself back into that life.

J's words from earlier echo in my mind again: *Guess you really are a Raider after all—letting innocent lives get taken just so you can get what you want.*

I rock back and forth faster. No. She can't be right.

But the truth is, I won't go back.

Again I see Miriam's beautiful, wrinkled face. Her smile. Grandfather knew I cared for the elderly woman. I fought for her hours to change, for her to be given some preferential treatment in order to keep her from getting hurt in one of the factories. He'll kill her. All because of me.

Maybe he already has.

The door to my room opens, but I don't look up. I can't look up. I'm shaking too hard.

"Catori?" Micah's steps echo softly in the room. Hands grasp mine and pull them away from my face. "It's okay. You're safe." He pulls me into his arms and I let him.

For now.

He rubs my back, murmuring comforting words in my hair, but I'm numb. I'm not safe. And he's not safe because he's with me.

No one is safe who's associated with me.

After a while, Micah stands, and helps me to my feet. My shaking has stopped, but my mind still wrestles with everything, unsure of what to do.

Micah tilts my head to look up at him. "Raul and Zoe arrived. They've stabilized Vik."

I release a gasp as some of the weight on my chest lifts. "He's okay?"

Micah hesitates, and the weight returns instantly. "They're optimistic. But he's in critical condition. How he responds to the treatment in the next couple hours will tell us a lot."

I swallow hard. "Oh."

"Why don't you get some rest?" He nods to my bed.

I shake my head no. "What happens now?"

He glances at Jordyn, who's still sleeping, then gestures to the door. I follow him.

"We're not sure. There's a leak in our intel. The Raiders

know far more than they should. The problem is we don't know where the leak came from."

Shax's untrusting gaze creeps into my mind. "And everyone thinks it's me." I don't mean for the words to sound as bitter as they do.

"No," Micah says quickly. Too quickly. He rubs a hand over his jaw. "But we have to recalculate things. Figure out what to do. For now, I have Davey setting our course back through waterways that are less traveled. We'll find a place to rendezvous with Thaddeus and his team, and figure out a new plan."

For the first time, I realize the boat is moving. But it feels pointless. "Even if we get to some meeting place with Thaddeus and his team of scouts, what happens then? My grandfather..." I struggle to say the word, "won't stop at anything until he gets me back."

I pass him the note with a shaking hand. He skims the words and his jaw bunches.

"I won't let him have you." Micah folds the note and focuses on me. "We'll find a way through this. Get you to Eryndale, where you'll be safe."

He puts his hands on my shoulders, but I shrug them off. The look of hurt in his eyes sends a pang through my chest, but I harden myself against it. I can't let myself get close to Micah or anyone else. It will only bring pain and death.

And I can't handle that.

"Eryndale's out of the question now," I say. "We both know that."

"Catori," Jordyn whimpers from the room before Micah can argue with me.

Not that there's anything to argue about. He knows I'm right.

I turn away from Micah and go to Jordyn. "It's okay, Jor. I'm right here."

I sink onto the bed next to her and pull her into my arms. Her small hands grasp the loose fabric of my shirt.

"Where's my Vik? I want him."

Her words shred me. My eyes burn, but I blink back the tears. "He can't come right now, honey. He's busy."

She pulls back to look me in the eye. Her eyebrows scrunch together, lips in a frown. "I want to go to him."

"We can't."

"Why? My Vik always lets me come to him, even when he's busy."

"Because he's hurt. And he needs to feel better before we can see him."

Jordyn scrambles into a sitting position. "The mean lady hurt him?" She sounds close to panic.

I stare at her for a moment, unsure what to say. What to do. How am I supposed to explain what's going on to a child when I can't grasp it myself?

"Yes she did," Micah says.

I give him a quick look. I'd thought he left, but apparently he didn't.

"Should I pray for him?" Jordyn asks.

*It won't work*, the thought whispers through my mind, and I instantly feel guilty. Miriam would gently rebuke me if I *ever* said something like that. Yet I can't deny that it's exactly how I feel right now.

"That's a great idea," Micah says.

Jordyn nods, a small line between her brows. "Dear Jesus, help my Vik to feel better and to not be hurt anymore. And help the mean lady to not come again and scare us. Amen."

She looks up at us with eyes that seem brighter and more at peace. There's still some twinge of uncertainty, but it's not the same. How does that work? I want to ask her why she believes Jesus can make it all better—because she clearly believes that—but I can't find the words.

She's a child, but her faith seems so much stronger than mine. My chest aches. I would give anything to have Miriam here right now.

"How about you get some sleep, little one?" Micah says. There's a gravelly sound to his voice, like he's suppressing emotions.

"Okay." Jordyn looks at me. "Will you stay with me?"

"Of course," I say. "I just need to talk to Micah for one second, okay?"

She hesitates, then gives me a small nod. I tuck her under the covers, smooth her hair back, and then walk to the hall. Micah follows me.

I pull the door, but leave it open a crack. Vik's blood on the floor makes my stomach turn. I drag my gaze away. He's still alive, and he's being taken care of. There's hope. He'll make it... he has to make it.

"She can't be put through more trauma." I stare at Micah. Whatever else we're about to walk into, whatever else I have to do, there's no way I want Jordyn to be a part of it.

She's already gone through more than she ever should have at such a young age.

Micah nods. "I agree. What do you want to do?"

I bite my lip. "I don't know." The phrase ripples over my lips, an echo of my heart.

I don't know what to do about anything right now.

"Well, I could see if Thaddeus can get her to someone in the WUN."

The fact that he doesn't so much as mention Eryndale twists my stomach. I knew he wouldn't, knew it wasn't an option anymore since the Raiders will have multiple ambushes in place. But some part of me still hoped.

"She wouldn't know anyone."

A low moan comes from a nearby room, and I stare at the closed door.

"Vik," Micah explains. "The moans are good. It means he's alive."

My pulse thrums in my throat. How is this all happening right now? I pull my mind back to Micah's suggestion. "I don't know." Again, I say the loathsome words. "She'll be dragged away from everything and everyone she knows. Again." I look toward the room I share with her. "What will that do to her?"

"She could stay with us, with people she knows. But whatever decision we make in the next several hours is going to bring her into danger."

I squeeze my hands into fists. "What are we going to do, Micah? What *can* we do? My grandfather is leaving us with no options. I'll have to go back, or people will die." Tears clog my throat. "But I can't go back."

My jaw trembles and I press my eyes together. The tears leak out.

Micah's strong hands clasp my shoulders. He pulls me to himself. This time, I let him.

"Everything is falling apart." I clutch his shirt, wanting him to deny the words.

He doesn't say anything. He just holds me. I want to be comforted in his embrace, to feel better because I'm in his arms. But I don't. The ache inside me expands, filling my chest. I inhale, trying to pull myself back under control.

I can't lose it. There's more to figure out. I step away from Micah.

"I should get back to Jordyn. Goodnight." I move to enter the room, but he grabs my hand.

"We'll figure this out. I promise."

I attempt to smile at him, but the effort is too much. I enter the room and close the door.

J's words.

My grandfather's note.

Vik dying just down the hall.

I want to believe what Micah said, that we'll figure this out. But I don't think I can.

CHAPTER

# TWENTY-SIX

I stare out the small porthole, watching the landscape pass by. The sky has brightened, and it looks like it will be a beautiful day. But inside, I feel like I've fallen into a pit of darkness. One I'll never escape from.

My night consisted of little sleep, comforting Jordyn when she'd wake from a nightmare, and thinking. The conclusion I've come to is as murky as the parts of the river most cluttered with debris from the Demise.

Somewhere in the middle of the night, I realized I'm *happy* Carver is dead. Glad I'll never have to see his face again, no matter what happens next. When that realization hit, another wasn't far behind.

I'm just like my grandfather.

I'll do whatever it takes to get what I want.

How many people have been hurt, homes destroyed, lives lost, all because I wanted a life different from the one I was born into? Running away seemed better than fighting. So I ran. It seemed like the right decision. The *only* option. But was it?

Was there a point, somewhere along the way, where I

should have stood up and done something different? Not been the *princess* everyone in the compound considered me? What if, instead of just occasionally saying something and visiting the captives, I'd actually used the position I had to try to make a difference?

It may not have worked. But what if it had?

Maybe Miriam wouldn't be in danger.

Now it's too late.

Soft whimpers draw my attention, and I go to Jordyn.

"Good morning, Jor Jor." I settle on the bed next to her, attempting to push away my dark thoughts.

"Where's my Vik?" The words come out with a tremor. "Is he better?"

I close my eyes. I'm so self-consumed that I haven't even gone to check on Vik to find out if anything has changed. What is wrong with me?

"Catori?"

I open my eyes. "Let me go find out, okay?"

She shakes her head. "No. Don't leave me alone. I want to come too." She scurries out of the covers and jumps to the floor before I can respond.

"I don't know." I stand. "How about I get you breakfast first? Then we'll check on Vik."

Jordyn's brow lowers. "No. I want my Vik."

She marches to the door, and I trail after her, trying to find a way to redirect her attention. I don't even know if Vik made it through the night. I can't let Jordyn just walk into his room.

She steps into the hallway and stops. Nate is on his hands and knees, scrubbing the floor. His hair has fallen out of his normally tidy bun, dark circles rim his eyes, and every motion is slower than it should be.

He pauses his scrubbing. "Morning, ladies."

"Where's Vik?" Jordyn asks.

Nate blinks. "He's resting."

I let myself breathe. If he's resting, that means he's alive.

"Is he all better?" Jordyn asks, kneeling on the floor next to Nate.

"Not all better, but he's getting better," Nate says. "Did you pray for him?"

Jordyn nods so emphatically it looks painful. "Yes! I prayed and asked Jesus to make him better."

Nate smiles, and it transforms his exhausted features for a moment. "Good girl. And Jesus heard your prayers. Vik wasn't doing so good, but he's starting to feel better now."

Jordyn sighs, her little shoulders bouncing up, then down. "Good. I'm glad I have Jesus in my heart like you, Natey-boy."

"Me too." Nate pulls Jordyn into his arms.

Bitterness coats my tongue, and I walk away. I should stay with Jordyn, but I can't keep listening to them. To their talk about God, Jesus.

Miriam taught me about Jesus. I accepted Him as my Savior, just like Jordyn and Nate. But I don't understand how my faith fits in with life right now.

All I can see is the dark evil of my family, of my own actions, tainting my blood.

I go topside. Nate will be fine with Jordyn. He'll probably feed her, give her some distraction.

And I need space.

The deck is relatively quiet, and I wander around to the back, almost hiding myself behind the rowboat.

I stare out at the water, unsure of where we are. Or what the plan is.

Does it even matter?

I drop my head to my hands as I lean against the rail.

Voices drift toward me.

"...and it wasn't until she knew." Shax. "I'm telling you,

she's not safe. And we need to give up whatever foolish plans we come up with and just turn her in."

I freeze. Is he talking about me?

"I don't know," a voice I don't recognize says. "The Raiders have always been a threat in this area. I don't think it's her."

"I agree with Shax," Antonio says. "Plus, she's their family. And they know exactly what our plans are. You think that's just coincidence?"

I shift, so I'm more in the shadows. They're definitely talking about me, and I don't want to try to explain myself.

"All I'm saying is that she seemed ready to help us at the meeting, and give up any intel she could," the man I don't know says.

"If she's willing to give up her family to get what she wants, what makes you think she won't give us up when it suits her?" Shax asks.

The men continue to talk, but the rushing in my ears keeps me from hearing them.

His words feel like a knife in my stomach. How could he think that about me?

But even worse, I can't help but wonder if he's *right*. I don't know that I'm any different from my family who will sell out anyone to gain power, position, comfort. And J knows far more than she should.

There's a leak, and, according to Shax, I'm the most likely culprit. What if others think so, too? What happens then?

I drop silently onto the deck and bury my head in my arms.

Everything is falling apart, and I'm inclined to agree with Shax.

It's all my fault.

"Have you guys seen Catori?" Micah's voice cuts through the air.

My head snaps up.

What if Micah has begun to think like Shax and Antonio? What if this crew that's become more of a family to me than my own family ever was now wants nothing to do with me?

It would be what I deserve.

I should have never believed I could have more than the life of a Raider. Never hoped for the love of a man like Micah.

I ease to my feet and climb over some equipment, and move away from the back of the ship.

"There you are." Micah's voice behind me causes me to jump.

I whirl toward him. "Oh."

He steps closer, and I take a step back. "What's wrong?"

"What's *wrong?*" I throw my hands in the air. "Everything, Micah. Everything is wrong." I snap my mouth shut. Take a breath. "What do you need?"

"I just wanted to check on you." His dark eyes search my face. "Jordyn was with Nate, and I couldn't find you. I was just worried."

His rambling disarms me. I know Micah is a good man, that he cares about me. But I'm too dangerous, and the best thing I can do for him is push him away. As painful as the thought is.

"I'm fine. No need to worry about me. Before long, you'll be rid of me for good."

"What? Catori, what are you talking about? We're married." He reaches for me, but I pull away.

The hurt in his eyes almost undoes me, but the reality of what my grandfather will do if I stay with Micah...I let the thought build within me. Desperate for it to give me the strength to do what I need to do.

He steps toward me. "There are some enemies you can't outwit or outrun. You just have to be prepared to fight."

I flinch. Could I fight? Could that be the answer?

No.

Because I could never win. I push aside his words. He doesn't understand.

I pull the ring from my finger, instantly missing its familiarity, and thrust it toward Micah.

His eyes widen.

"Just leave me alone."

His forehead wrinkles. "But..." The word is choked.

I drop the ring, and it clinks against the wood of the deck.

I walk away before he can see the tears ready to burst from me.

Once I reach the stairs that lead below deck, I swipe an arm over my wet face. I need to keep it together. And figure out how to not be the woman I am.

The woman I hate.

Pots clang, and the scent of bacon comes from the galley. Nate's cooking. But the idea of food turns my stomach.

I stride down the hall, keeping my head low.

The door to Vik's room is open, and I stop. Jordyn is inside with him and Davey. She's perched on the edge of his bed and talking to the massive man, who's awake.

A small weight lifts from my shoulders. At least I won't have Vik's death on my hands.

I continue on before any of them notice me. Although part of me wants to ask Vik what happened last night, how J managed to get on the boat and do the damage she did. But does any of it matter?

I enter my room, close the door behind me, and lean against it. The tears I'd forgotten threaten again. My chest tightens. This is too much. There's no way forward without loss, pain, and death. And the more I recognize the depths of my own darkness, the more painful it all becomes.

The letter from my grandfather lies on my bed, mocking

me. I suck in a shuddering breath, grit my teeth, and march over to it. I swipe it off the bed and rip it to shreds. The words are already implanted in my soul, scarring me. I don't need the note to remember them.

Bits of pieces of paper cascade to the ground. Sobs crack through my chest.

What am I going to do?

Once the letter is so shredded I can't find a piece big enough to tear in half, I collapse to the floor. My tears dry up. I stare unseeing at the wall. Everything feels numb. Like when the pain from an injury becomes so excruciating, you just pass out.

I'll have to act. Do something. But at the moment, I let the numbness cocoon me.

# CHAPTER
# TWENTY-SEVEN

A soft knock on my door draws my attention, but I don't get up to answer it. It's most likely Micah, and I can't let him close or I'll hurt him.

The knock comes again. Then the door opens, and Davey pokes his head in.

"Found you." His voice is light, but his eyes are serious.

He pushes the door the rest of the way open and steps into the room.

I stand. "Do you need something?"

"This isn't your fault, Catori," he says. "You *needed* to get away from the compound. And none of us would ever deny you our help."

A mirthless laugh scrapes out of me. "I'm not so sure about that." Antonio and Shax's accusations are still too close to the surface for me to allow Davey's words to be at all comforting.

His eyes search mine. "What happened?"

The question is so soft, it's almost a breath. And it breaks me.

I tell him what I heard Shax and Antonio say. His face hardens, but he doesn't interrupt.

"I'm not the leak," I say. "But the truth is, every difficult thing all of you have gone through these past months is because of me. It would have been better for everyone if I'd just married Carver, lived the life my grandfather demanded I live."

The bitterness from my soul seeps itself into the words, coating my mouth.

Davey shakes his head. "Don't talk like that. All of us live the lives we live, *knowing* the risks we're taking. Every time we help someone enter the WUN, or work with a village to rebuild after a Raider attack, or choose to stand up for what's right, we take a risk that the dark and evil things of this world will rise in an attempt to silence us and stop us forever. But we do it anyway."

I swallow hard, avoiding Davey's gaze. "I'm just as much responsible for being a dark and evil person." I lift one shoulder, and it drops like a weight. "As much as I want to blame my grandfather or Carver or J, the reality is that I've added my evil to this world. My complacency has brought destruction, and my need to protect myself,"—my voice wavers, and a tear slips down my cheek—"it's come at a cost. I've chosen to look out for myself above every other person." I spread my arms. "And people have died."

With a painful effort, I look Davey in the eye. The compassion in his gaze takes my breath away.

"You're right. Your own darkness, complacency, and evil have added their marks to the brokenness of this world."

The words pierce me, ripping me into finer pieces than the remnants of Grandfather's letter.

"But, Catori, that's true for every single one of us. No one is good on their own. No one can stand against evil, because the truth is we *all* have evil within us."

"Then what's the point of any of this?" My words echo the hopelessness deep within me. "If we're all evil, why not just live like my grandfather and every other Raider?"

It's the logic I'm sure my grandfather would give, but it feels flimsy. A deep part of my soul *knows* I'm wrong.

Davey approaches, his face earnest. "Because it's not what we were created for. God made us to know Him, love Him, and find in Him a life that has hope and meaning and purpose. The problem is, we could never have that life on our own, because we're too evil. Too broken. No matter what we do, we can never earn God's love or live in the way He wants us to. And because of our rebellion against God and His ways, our evil needs to be punished. It's why we need Jesus."

I fall to the bed. I know what he's saying is true. They echo words Miriam spoke to me over and over again. The hope of salvation that I accepted a few years ago in her tiny home. "I trusted in Jesus. Asked Him to save me. But I am still so broken, Davey."

He sits on the bed near me and stays quiet for a long moment. "I'm thankful you know God," he finally says. "But our faith isn't a stagnant faith. God doesn't just save us and then give up on us and leave us to figure out the rest."

"Maybe I'm worth giving up on." I stand before he can respond. "All I want is to keep myself safe, and try not to see anyone else hurt in the process." I glance out the door toward where Vik is.

Thankfully, the man is still alive, but what will happen next time? Who will die because of me?

"Catori, you can't always try to save yourself," Davey says. There's an earnestness in his gaze that contradicts the somewhat ridiculous man he normally is.

I'm not sure what to do with it.

I pace toward the small window, and stare unseeing at the

passing landscape. "It's what I've done my whole life." As the words leave my mouth, I realize how true they are. "It's who my family is—always look out for yourself. And it's who I am."

"You don't have to be defined by your family or your own struggles anymore," Davey says. "Jesus saved you. He has a different life for you."

A bitter laugh escapes. "Right."

He gets to his feet. "He proved it was true for me."

I spin toward him, fists clenched, ready to chuck something across the room. "Oh really? What have you done, Davey? You and your brother come from a good family. You help people all the time. You have no *idea* what my life has been like or what I've done."

Davey's lips compress for a moment. "You don't know what I've done. Or where I've been." He hesitates, as though weighing whether or not to continue. He inclines his head. "I did grow up in a great family. Both of my parents taught me and my brother and sister about God, loved us unconditionally."

The thought of unconditional love is one I can barely grasp, but I remain quiet.

"I loved my life. But one day, everything changed. Raiders invaded our town, murdered my dad and my sister." His voice is thick with emotion, and something in me cracks.

Davey knows pain. A depth of which I never expected, and it came at the hand of Raiders. Probably my family. Yet he still trusts me and wants to help me. My hands unclench.

"I was fifteen, and I never knew how deep and controlling hatred could be until that happened. My whole life became about revenge. I pulled away from my mother, from my brother, and plotted how I would find the Raiders who killed my father and sister. Make them pay. I changed so much, but didn't even see it. I was angry all the time, cruel even. Before I knew it, I was becoming the very type of man I hated."

I stare at him, but remain silent, unsure how to process what I'm hearing. Davey is nothing like the man he's describing now.

"God had always been my parents' God, a normal part of my life. I even asked Him to save me as a kid. But in the depths of my hatred, the last thing I wanted was God or anyone talking about Him." His jaw clenches. "One day I cursed out my mom for bringing Him up, shoved her so hard she fell, and stormed out of the house." He hangs his head. "Nate found me later, ready to beat me up. He told me our mom was in the infirmary because of a head injury. It looked like she would be fine, but..." His voice trails off.

He clears his throat. "It was in that moment that I realized who I'd become, the path I was on. I could have killed my mother, destroyed the part of my family I had left. I was headed for destruction. It was in that lowest and darkest moment that I knew I needed the God my parents had always taught me about to not just save me, but to take my whole life. So I turned to Him."

Silence stretches between us, but I can't find words to fill it. Davey isn't the man he was before, and part of me can't believe what he's talking about is true. That it actually happened.

"A man can't change that much," I blurt, then clap a hand over my mouth.

Davey's lips quirk. "On our own, no one has the power to change themselves completely. To change from the very depths of who they are and become who they were destined to be. But with God, change isn't only possible. It's part of the process." He shrugs. "And you can go talk to Nate. He loves sharing what a jerk I was. Claims that's why he'll always be our mom's favorite."

I smile a bit at that. But it fades. "But your family...it was different than mine. I'm stained by the countless lives my grandfather and his people have murdered. I grew up learning how to only care about myself, my wants, and to take what I needed, no matter who got hurt. I knew it wasn't the best way, but at the end of the day, it's what I *always* resort to."

"It doesn't matter who our families are. We're all capable of the darkest of evil, and even if we don't give into it, just those tendencies will keep us from God. Every one of us needs a Savior *and* a Shepherd who will lead us day by day."

"My Vik is sleeping," Jordyn says from the doorway.

Davey and I turn to her.

I'm not sure if I'm relieved or upset at the interruption. Davey's words, his story, call to something within me, beckoning it out. But I'm terrified of what it would look like to surrender to God in the way he talks about.

Miriam would love Davey.

The thought sends a pang through me.

Will she ever be able to meet these incredible men?

"That's good," Davey says to Jordyn. He strides to the little girl and scoops her into his arms. "It means he's healing and getting better."

I shake myself out of my fog. Time to focus on Jordyn. Anything to distract myself from all the things I don't know how to deal with at the moment.

"Are you hungry?" I ask.

Jordyn nods. "Maybe Natey-boy has something yummy cooking."

I force a smile. "Let's go see."

Davey spins Jordyn around, and she giggles. He sets her back on the floor. "You two go get yourselves some food. I've got to see the captain and find out what the plan is." He walks out the door.

I take Jordyn's hand, and we head to the galley. Nate serves up scrambled eggs, bacon, and fried potatoes for us, and I'm thankful that he seems able to chat with Jordyn since I'm not sure how to at the moment.

One thing has become increasingly clear. I have to stop doing everything I can to distract myself. It's time to fight, really fight, and try to be different from my family. Maybe I'll always be stained in my soul by who they are, but if there's a chance I can at least *act* differently…

*God, can You do anything with my life?*

I sigh, and both Nate and Jordyn look at me with concern.

"You okay?" Nate asks, with a pointed look at my full plate of food.

"Sure, yeah. I'm fine."

He quirks an eyebrow, but doesn't say a word.

"Catori, can I talk to you?" Micah says from the entrance to the galley.

I look at Nate, and he nods. "I've got Jordie-girl."

"That's not my name!" Jordyn protests with a giggle.

"Oh, it's not?" Nate gives her a look of mock horror, and Jordyn laughs harder.

I stand and leave my untouched breakfast to follow Micah from the room. He leads me topside, and to the wheelhouse.

The rest of the crew is working, and the look Shax gives me when our eyes connect makes me shiver.

I shake it off and enter the wheelhouse behind Micah. Davey's steering the boat, but he leaves when we enter and closes the door behind him.

Shep is inside and he trots over to me, nuzzling my hand with his head. The dog's presence is almost stabilizing.

"I've connected with Thaddeus," Micah says as he takes over steering the boat. "He's agreed to meet us fifteen miles down the river. You and Jordyn can enter the underground."

My head springs up. "What?"

"He'll get you to Eryndale. And you'll be safe there. My mama knows you're coming, and she'll take good care of you." Micah gives me a look so filled with longing it takes my breath away. Then he turns to the wheel, focusing on the river in front of us.

I shake my head. "It won't work. J knew I was planning to go to Eryndale. Anything we try to do to get me there is sure to have too high of a risk of failure."

"The WUN should be able—"

"It's too much of a risk," I repeat, more firmly this time. "You know that." I hesitate, then press forward. "And what about you?" I ask. As much as I know I need to push Micah away, the idea of leaving him, not having him as a part of my daily life, is more painful than anything I've ever considered.

He doesn't respond for a long moment. "I'll fight for you. Until you can know you're safe for good."

The reality of what Micah is willing to face for me is difficult to bear. His words from a few hours earlier come back to me.

"I can't let you take all the risk for me." I take a slow, deliberate breath and say the words that have been churning within me since J left. "I need to fight. Otherwise, I'll be running for the rest of my life."

Micah looks over his shoulder at me. His dark eyes gaze into mine, his focus intense. I don't drop my eyes. "Are you sure you're ready for that?"

I stand taller. "I'm done running and always looking out for myself above everyone else. This is my battle, and I need to fight it."

As I say the words, a sense of certainty fills me, along with fear.

He turns back to the river. "You don't have to, Catori."

"Yes. I do. I've lived my whole life looking out for myself, no matter what it cost others. As much as I hate it, I'm more like my family than I've ever wanted to admit. Now it's time for me to be different. To do what I have to do."

Micah nods once. "Okay. The plan right now is to meet with Thaddeus and a select group of others tonight. If you want to join us, we'll take any insight you may have to offer."

I clench a handful of Shep's coarse fur. What possible plan could we concoct that would be successful against *J?*

Micah navigates around a piece of metal sticking out of the river and then continues. "Tomorrow, we'll share some of our plan widely. We're assuming J will find out." His shoulders are tense, but his words are firm. "We know there's a leak somewhere. I hate to believe it could be anyone that's been planning this with us, but..." he clears his throat. "We're keeping a tight lid on who knows the real details. Only me, Davey, Thaddeus, Zoe, and some high-level leaders in the WUN will be in on the plans. And now you. It'll work. I've seen God bring us through crazy things before. He'll do it again."

It feels like he's trying to convince himself more than anything. But the fact that he trusts me enough to include me in the plans, that he doesn't believe I'm the leak, warms me. Maybe we can do this.

A dark thought occurs to me.

"Even if we defeat J, my grandfather won't stop coming after me. I've wounded his pride. You saw the letter."

He stays silent for a long moment. "We'll discuss it more tonight. But our priority will be stopping the force he has coming at us now. If we can defeat J and those working with her, we'll handicap him."

"Which will make him dangerous," I say.

If Grandfather feels cornered, like he's going to lose, I can only imagine how reckless...and savage...he'll become.

# CHAPTER
# TWENTY-EIGHT

Micah brings the boat to a stop, and the crew sets about anchoring the vessel and preparing to bring the small group on shore aboard. We've crisscrossed through a series of streams and waterways—some far more narrow than I ever want to experience again—to get to this portion of the river. Trees line the land on either side of us in thick groves, and it's difficult to make out much of anything in the gathering dusk. We're far enough from land that the rowboat will have to be sent to bring in Thaddeus and the others, but the river is calm here.

I peer out across the dark water, searching the tree line for a sign of the men and women waiting within. But all I see are the thick branches of the trees, some birds flitting about, preparing to settle in for the night. A bat flying in its irregular pattern. Hunks of debris clinging to roots of trees in the shallow water by the shore.

No people.

A breeze blows and the tree branches bend and twist, leaves rustling. The reality of what I'm about to do hits me. I clench my hand until my nails bite into my palms. The icy fingers of anxiety clamp themselves on my neck. They're all trained for a battle like this, but I'm not.

What happens if I fail them? If I can't do what's necessary?

"Hey."

I flinch at the sudden sound as Zoe plops herself next to me. She acts as though she doesn't notice, which I'm grateful for.

"Micah said you're gonna fight with us." She looks at me out of the side of her eye. "I'm glad."

I spin to face her fully. "Really?"

Her face softens. "Course. I'm always happy to have a friend I can trust. We need people who've go our backs, right?"

I gape at her, unable to form a response. So I nod, even as her words careen through my brain.

Friends. Trust. Have each other's backs. How does this woman—who I barely know—feel this way about me? All I've felt toward her is jealousy of her ease and friendship with Micah.

Which is unfair. She's only ever been kind to me.

There's a splash as the guys lower the rowboat into the river, saving me from trying to figure out how to respond to Zoe.

"I should gather my notes," I mumble.

Zoe smiles, and I push away from the rail and head below deck.

I pause and peer in the room that's now being used as an infirmary. Jordyn is curled up next to Vik, chatting away. The giant of a man is healing well, and it's been nearly impossible to tear Jordyn from his side since she joined him early this morning. I've asked him several times if he wants me to occupy the little girl so he can rest, but his answer is always an emphatic no.

Vik catches me watching them and lifts his fingers in a wave. I wave back, then go to my room to retrieve my notebook.

Since making the determination to fight, I've worked on putting together as much information as possible to share in tonight's meeting. Micah and Zoe might be ready to trust me, but I fear others will be inclined to feel the same way as Shax and Antonio. The more I prove my loyalty to those fighting the Raiders, the better.

I grab my notebook from the desk and flip through it quickly.

Detailed profiles on each of the Raiders I know to be in J's crew and profiles on different Raiders my grandfather trusts. Those I suspect are hunting for me as well. Information on most commonly used weaponry. Approximations on the size of various crews.

I even have a rough drawing of Grandfather's compound, with notes on cameras, sensors, weaponry—the stuff I know about at least—and the access points into the compound. My shoulders tense just thinking about the place I called home for my entire life. I'll give them the intel in case they need it, but I never want to set foot in there again.

---

THE GALLEY IS FULL OF PEOPLE. THADDEUS, MALACHI, ZOE, RAUL, and other WUN members, along with Micah, me, and Davey, have been discussing our next moves for twenty minutes. No one else was permitted to be a part of this meeting, which was met with some frustration by the members of the crew.

Shax's words before the door closed still ring in my ear: "You let someone like *her* be a part of the planning, but leave out the rest of us?"

I've never seen Micah so angry, but Davey restrained him before he did anything, and Nate led Shax away. Micah gave orders to each member of the crew to keep them occupied during the meeting, and Nate's job was to remain on guard outside of the room.

It feels strange to not have all the guys in here, but this core group is for everyone's safety. Which Thaddeus keeps reminding us.

Another argument breaks out between the three groups as they try to determine where the leak could have come from.

Thaddeus stands and motions for everyone to quiet down. It takes a moment, but soon everyone's silent.

"I know none of us want to believe the leak could come from someone within our command." He turns slowly, taking time to make eye contact with everyone. "But the leak came from somewhere. We won't be able to move forward if we can't all at least *try* to come to an understanding."

It feels like getting reprimanded by a father. Not that I've ever really experienced that. Maybe it's Thaddeus's age, or the obvious respect every person in the room has for him, but before long, he's elicited nods of agreement from Micah and the leaders of the WUN.

"Now. At this point, we won't be able to fully identify the leak unless we catch him or her in action. Continuing to argue about the possibilities is pointless."

"But don't we need to know?" A woman from the WUN—Felicia, I think—asks. "How can we move forward with a plan if someone is just going to share it with our enemies?"

There are a couple grunts of agreement.

Thaddeus settles back into his seat, then leans forward, arms resting on his legs. "We'll come up with four plans."

My lips part slightly. He can't be serious.

"We're not sure we can figure out *one* solid plan," Zoe says. "Now you want us to create four? Why?"

"We'll give a fake plan to each of the groups: my scouts, the WUN, and Micah's crew. And then we'll have a real plan that we'll actually use. We'll know which group the Raiders have received their intel from based on what they do next."

Silence descends on the group, and there are nervous glances around the room. Part of me can understand why. It's one thing to *say* everyone is innocent. Another thing entirely to put every person you trust to the test.

"The problem is, we need to coordinate everyone's efforts if we're going to have any chance of defeating the Raiders," Micah says. His face is expressionless, and I wish I could tell what he's thinking.

The two of us have been on rocky ground ever since we returned to the ship, and I miss the ease of our relationship. Maybe I shouldn't have given him back his ring.

Thaddeus inclines his head. "True. So the question becomes, can we all work together on a single plan, knowing there's a spy in our midst? Is it worth the risk?"

"Of course it's worth the risk," Davey says. "We can't let Catori be left to the mercy of the Raiders. And it's time we took a stand. Wisteria and all the villages close to the Raiders compound have experienced more terror than they ever should have. We need to take a risk and stop playing it safe."

A small smile dances on Thaddeus's lips, like that's the exact reaction he was looking for.

"But how many lives will be lost if we're reckless?" Felicia asks. "This is already far more dangerous than anything else we've encountered. The Raiders have a vendetta against you," she says to me. "I'm sorry you have to live with that." Her expression softens ever so slightly, showing her sorrow is real. But she continues, focusing on the others. "But is one life worth risking so many others and our entire operation in the area?"

Heat floods my body. Her words should feel abrasive, cruel. But all I can think is *she's right.*

"It's not." The words fall from my lips with both certainty and fear. I keep my focus on my hands clenched in my lap, but I can feel the eyes of the room boring into me.

"You're wrong," Davey says. "One life is always worth the risk. Because it's one life at a time, one *choice* at a time that determines who we will be. As soon as we start to disregard human life, start to defend our decisions to *not* help others, no matter what the risk, we'll find ourselves becoming so similar to the Raiders we won't recognize ourselves." He sounds so resolute, so passionate, that I can't help but look up.

In the past twenty-four hours, Davey has surprised me. I've known since I met him that there was a depth to him, but I didn't realize *how* strong his convictions are. Or how deep his faith runs.

"But this is dangerous," Davey continues. "And I don't want to march into the battle with anyone but those who are ready to die for what is right. If you're not, I don't judge you. This mission will be dangerous, one of the most dangerous any of us have ever encountered."

Now that I know the depths of what Davey has experienced in his life, the weight of his words is even heavier.

"Some will be hurt, some may die. If this isn't the battle you want to lay your life down for, I think we should let you leave." Davey looks at Thaddeus as though waiting to see if he'll agree with him.

Thaddeus nods. "Well stated, Davey." He casts a somber look around the room. "None of you or your people are obligated to continue forward. If this mission is too much for you,

you can retract your team now before we move into further planning."

Felicia stands and gives me an apologetic look. "I'm withdrawing my resources. If you fail, there still needs to be those in the region who can help people escape to safety. The Templeton branch of the WUN won't be available."

Thaddeus inclines his head. "Understood. Thank you for what you've done so far."

Felicia exits the room.

My heart drops. What now? We need all the resources we can get, all the teams who were strong enough to lend men and women for this fight. What if more of those in this room decide to leave?

"Anyone else?" Thaddeus asks. "There will be no judgment. You have all proven you care for those who are oppressed. This is a different type of battle."

There are a few exchanged looks. Some nod. But no one else stands.

"We're in," Zoe says. "Let's get this plan going."

"Yeah," Malachi agrees. "Catori is family now." He winks at me. "Can't get rid of us, no matter how hard you try."

My throat thickens. They're willing to do this for *me*. To risk their lives to stop my grandfather and his forces from terrorizing villages in his hunt for me. I know he's been ruthless before now, taken many captives, and left even more to die. This is bigger than me. But it's also coming to a head now because of me.

And the men and women in this room are willing to fight for what's right. No matter what the cost.

I straighten my shoulders. If they're willing to, so will I.

Thaddeus stands. "Our plan will unfold in two stages. First, we'll make it well-known that The Fearless Lady is heading back to Wisteria and we'll prepare an ambush there for J and her crew. And any other crews in the area."

My body tenses at the thought of traveling closer to the place I most fear. I stay silent. But as Thaddeus details plans to attack the compound and bring an end to Grandfather's reign of terror in this region, my shoulders scrunch together so tight it's painful.

The plan makes sense. Attacking the compound is the way to stop my grandfather. And that's the only way to truly bring this hunt for me to an end.

Thaddeus removes a map of Wisteria and the surrounding area from his bag, and for the next hour we work through a plan. I share what I know about the compound, the Raiders, weaponry in the compound. My notebook with all the details I could think of gets passed around, and everyone seems to appreciate the work I put in. None of them look at me like I'm a traitor, and that fact alone helps me breathe a little easier.

Even with Felicia removing her branch of the WUN, there're more of us than I expected. And others who might be willing to join the fight once asked. A seed of hope that maybe this will work grows.

"There's one thing we don't have a plan for," Malachi says, effectively squashing the hope desperate to bloom inside me. "The metallic horses they ride are always our biggest issue. If they can access those metal monstrosities, they get away. Even our Skinter Suits don't seem to be able to keep up."

I sit straighter. Why didn't I think about the metallic horses sooner? "I can help with that." My voice practically squeaks, and everyone's focus swivels to me. But I find I don't mind. Confidence swells in me for the first time since this whole planning session started.

"How?" Micah asks, eyebrows scrunched together.

I stand. "Because I know how they work. I used to train

with the Inventors occasionally since I loved riding." I turn to Malachi. "Do they ride the horses into town?"

"Not usually," Malachi says, and the other scouts nod their agreement. "They'll leave them outside of the town, powered down and with a guard or two, and enter on foot. We think it's because they don't want us getting hold of one. We've *tried* to get one, but even our best tech guys can't turn the things on— at least not in the time we have."

"I can teach you what to do." I grin at my brother-in-law, and he smiles back. But his grin doesn't make my knees weak the way Micah's does. I force the thought away and focus on the task at hand. "I know how they work. How to turn them on, and how to completely disable them."

At that, Thaddeus chuckles. "I believe, ladies and gentle-man, that we have ourselves a plan."

# TWENTY-NINE

Over the next two hours, we discuss a plan that involves drawing the forces of the Raiders deeper into Wisteria than we'd originally planned and having most of the team fighting from within the town. I'll stay back with a much smaller group of those who are best at handling technical and mechanical elements. Together, we'll work at disabling the metallic horses.

If we're able to gather as many forces as Thaddeus hopes to, they'll be able to overpower the Raiders, and they won't have a means to escape, since their horses will be disabled.

The goal is to arrest and stop as many of Grandfather's Raiders as possible. Once they've been immobilized, an elite team will be sent to hit the compound directly. Grandfather's forces will be weakened from the attack in Wisteria, and this blow should mean the end of the compound for good.

It's a few days' journey from Wisteria to the compound. But with the metallic horses and the scouts Skinter Suits—which are some kind of personal transportation devices with wheeled feet and an ability to fly over short distances—Thaddeus and Malachi believe they could have an attack set within two days of the battle in Wisteria.

Then it will all be over.

"It's risky," Micah says without looking in my direction. "What if they can't disable all the horses? They'd be able to get away and the enemy forces in the compound would be stronger than we'd like to imagine."

"We'll be able to disable the metallic horses," I say with more confidence than I feel. The truth is, it will be a lot of work, and I don't know how many horses we'll have to deal with. But this is something I can do.

I can't let Micah convince everyone to let me stay on the sidelines. For once in my life, it's time I stopped running and started acting.

"It's the best plan we've got," Thaddeus says.

Micah opens his mouth to protest, but Thaddeus continues.

"Every plan we come up with will have its risks. If Catori is as good with the metallic horses as she claims, she'll be fine."

Micah presses his lips together, looking none too happy, but he doesn't argue.

"How can we be sure they'll hit Wisteria?" Davey asks.

It's a good point.

"We'll make it clear that we're making it our base," Thaddeus says. "Hopefully that will be enough to surprise them into attacking before they're ready."

Unease spreads over me.

It would have been enough to surprise Carver into an attack...but will J go for it?

WE'RE ABOUT AN HOUR OUTSIDE OF WISTERIA BY BOAT, AND A THREE-hour hike with the route we plan to take. *The Fearless Lady* is anchored. It was a late night of meetings, and I was shocked to realize that we've been heading back toward the compound ever since J's attack.

As much as it makes me uneasy, I'm glad we were. It meant less ground to cover through the night and early this morning.

Members of the WUN began secretly evacuating villagers from Wisteria after Thaddeus decided to use the town as our base. At least innocent lives won't be in the crossfires of this battle.

Vik and Jordyn will stay on board again, along with Shax, as the rest of us leave and head toward Wisteria, meeting up with others along the way. Vik has an arsenal of weapons at his side, and the guys added two additional deadbolts to his door. Shep is in the room with Vik and Jordyn as well, which brings an added comfort. J may have been able to drug him last time, but he appeared more alert than I've ever seen him when we locked him in the room with Vik and Jordyn.

Shax will guard the boat and radio Vik at the first sign of trouble.

They're as safe as they could be. I hope.

Shax is still not happy with me. I tried to talk to him, convince him I wasn't the leak, that I want to keep everyone I care about safe. But he didn't want to hear it.

For some reason, his anger is almost more than I can take. Maybe it's because I understand it. I wouldn't trust me either if I were him.

My nerves are a tangled mess, but I swallow them back as I hike behind Micah.

Our plan is to connect with a few of the branches of the WUN on our way to Wisteria, share parts of our plan—though not all of it—and then continue forward to Wisteria.

We've already contacted two groups, and they're making a direct line to the town as we head further inland to connect with three other branches. So far, the reactions to me have been...varied.

I suppose that's to be expected.

"How you holding up?" Davey asks.

I jump. I've been so lost in thought, I didn't even hear him approach.

"Fine."

He lifts a branch out of the way and motions for me to go ahead of him, so I do.

"You sure?"

I sigh. "I'm ready to stand up to my grandfather. But what if I can't do what I need to with the horses?" The words gush out of my mouth faster than the river.

I've learned to trust Davey and respect his advice. Part of me would rather be talking this over with Micah, but I've pushed him away, and he's considerate enough to give me space.

Which is good. I guess.

"It's as solid of a plan as we're gonna get at this point," Davey says.

Micah glances back, and our eyes connect. My heart leaps, but I look away.

"But I can see the plan isn't the only thing bothering you," Davey says with a smile in his voice.

My face warms. "I don't know what you mean."

There's a snort of laughter from behind. Zoe is much closer than I realized. I really need to pull myself together.

"My friend, the two of you look like lovesick puppies." Zoe chuckles. "If this lug can see it, it's obvious."

Davey gives her a look of mock horror, but doesn't seem offended.

"Just let the man back in." Zoe sighs. "We don't know what we're heading into and you don't want to live with regrets. Trust me."

The way she says the words hints at a deeper story, but she gives no indication of wanting to share what that story may be.

"It's dangerous," I say. There's more I should say, greater clarification I should give.

But Zoe just nods, like she completely understands. Davey opens his mouth, but she silences him with a look. Which I appreciate.

After our strange conversation on the boat, I decided to count Zoe as a friend.

It's comforting to have another woman around. A woman who understands how dangerous and terrifying it is to let a man in. Somehow, I know she gets that that's just as scary to me as the battle we're about to face in Wisteria.

I shake away the thoughts. "Maybe after Wisteria." I say the words more to myself than anyone else, but Zoe puts a hand on my arm and pulls me to a stop.

Davey stops too, but she shoos him away. He pouts, but it swiftly moves into a grin and he hikes away.

"We are never guaranteed another breath," Zoe says. "If there's something you feel for Micah, some sort of reconciliation you two need, don't waste time. Talk to him, work it out. And know that, whatever happens in Wisteria, you have nothing to regret with him."

Her gaze is intense, passionate.

And I find myself nodding. "Okay."

She's right. If the worst happens...if Micah doesn't make it out of Wisteria...I wouldn't want my last moments with him to be like this.

The group stops several yards ahead of us.

"Guess we're at the next contact point," Zoe says.

The two of us half-jog to catch up with the rest of the group.

As we approach, I hesitate for a moment, staring at Micah. Zoe shoves me in that direction. I move toward him and stop when I'm right next to him. Micah glances down at me, and his eyes widen. When I smile up at him, relief floods his face and he smiles back.

Thaddeus steps forward and raps on the door of a small hut, using the knocking pattern I've heard him use at the last two contacts.

The door opens, and a short man with glasses and a beard that looks too big for him scowls out at us. "Whatcha want?"

Thaddeus's eyebrows rise. "Well, Heraldo, that's not the typical password."

Heraldo rolls his eyes and crosses his arms over his chest. "I know you. You know me. Why go through the ceremony?"

Thaddeus chuckles, but the look Heraldo gives him has him changing the chuckle to a cough.

"You know I hate asking questions twice, Thaddeus." Heraldo's foot taps out his impatience.

"Right. It's been a long time, my friend."

Another harrumph from Heraldo.

Thaddeus clears his throat and grows serious. "We have a situation brewing. And we could use your help."

Heraldo casts a condescending glance over the rest of us. "I'm listening."

"The Raiders are on the move. And we're taking a stand against them in Wisteria. Will you join us with your people?"

Heraldo again looks over at us, and his eyes land on me. It takes everything in me not to shift behind Micah and use him as a human shield.

So much for bravery. But the little man is...a little terrifying.

"She's one of 'em, ain't she?" He juts his bearded chin at me.

"Not anymore," Thaddeus says with a finality.

Something washes over me. He's right. I'm not a Raider anymore. Another emotion quickly replaces the relief. Uncertainty.

If I'm not a Raider, who am I?

Heraldo's scowl remains in place for so long, I'm not sure if he'll help us, or run me through with the knife he's caressing at his hip.

He gives a curt nod and turns inside.

Thaddeus stares after him, then shrugs at us.

"Well, what're y'all waiting for? Get in here before ya let in critters."

Something about the man inspires action, and we all scurry after him. A smile plays at my lips. He's grouchy and rude, but I like him.

And we'll need all his cantankerousness if we have any hope of standing against J and whatever we're about to face.

My smile fades at the thought.

The six of us cram into the small hut. Heraldo is sitting on an oversized chair that's so high his feet don't touch the ground. But he appears completely in control, despite the ridiculous image.

We spend the next fifteen minutes sharing what we need him to do. Before we're out the door, he's radioing his contacts, telling them to converge at a specified location immediately.

I inhale the fresh scent of pine as we exit, my spirits buoyed.

Help is coming.

We can do this.

## CHAPTER
# THIRTY

The next two contacts we make don't go quite as well as our contact with Heraldo. It seems Felicia communicated with more than one of them and shared her concerns about this endeavor and what it could do to the WUN.

My confidence in our abilities has wilted.

Maybe this *won't* go well.

We're a few miles from Wisteria now, and everyone is on high alert. J and her crew could be here already, for all we know.

I've stayed close to Micah, and we're near the back of the group. Soon we'll split off with Zoe and meet up with the crew we'll be working with to disable the mechanical horses.

If I'm going to talk to him, now's the time. "Micah." My throat thickens with emotion as I say his name.

He looks over at me.

"I'm sorry for everything I've brought into your life. All the pain." I can't look him in the eye. "And I'm sorry for how I've treated you."

He's silent as we continue following the others through the forest and to our destination. Something inside me wilts.

I waited too long.

"When I was twelve, a band of Raiders murdered my best friend." Micah's voice is low, but his words pierce my eardrums. "She was full of life, so much fun." He nods toward Davey. "A lot like her brothers."

My heart aches, and I don't know what to say.

"I heard her scream, and I ran to get to her. But by the time I arrived, she was dead." His words are a whisper. "Davey told me he shared a little of his story with you."

I nod.

"When Laney died, our worlds were shattered." He pauses, and I can feel his gaze on me. "Davey went into a spiral, and we all feared he'd never recover. But it was that same event that God used to propel me into this life. One where I fight for justice and mercy and stand for those who can't stand up for themselves." He puts his hand on my arm and we both stop.

But I can't look at him. How could he ever care for me after what my family did to him, to those he cared about? And after all he's gone through since I came into his life.

"I never thought the Raiders could bring anything but pain and death."

I squeeze my eyes shut at his words.

"But God has used you to show me He can bring beauty even from the darkest of places."

A breath hitches in my throat, and I dare a glance up at him.

Micah exhales, his eyes tender but serious. "I don't like fighting with you."

"I'm sorry, Micah. For everything you've been through, everything my family did to cause you so much pain." I press my lips together for a moment. "And I'm really am sorry for how I've treated you. You've been nothing but amazing to me since I first met you. You haven't deserved my frustration or anger. I just thought…"

I swallow hard, unsure how to voice the thoughts without exposing too much of my heart. Zoe's words spring to mind.

No regrets.

I press on. "Pushing you away seemed like the only way I could keep you safe." I hesitate for an instant, then take his hand in mine.

His eyes widen, but he tightens his grip and stays quiet.

"But all I wanted was to hide in your arms. You're different from every man I've ever known, and I don't want to go into this fight at odds with you."

A smile warms his face, stealing my breath. He cups my cheek with his free hand, and I lean into it. "I will *always* be there to hold you and protect you. If you'll let me."

Tears flood my eyes, and I squeeze them shut. One leaks out.

Micah brushes it away with his finger. He kisses my forehead. "You are nothing like your family, Catori. And as for the pain you've brought into my life."

My eyes fly open, breath catching in my throat. But the tender smile in his eyes stops me from completely panicking at his words.

"The only pain I've experienced at your hand is from the fear of losing you." He leans forward until our foreheads are pressed together. "Because you have captured my heart."

My jaw trembles, but words escape me. We stand there for a long moment, and I forget everything else.

I love this man. My husband.

The realization sweeps over me with a force so breathtaking, I don't know what to do with it. I squeeze his hand tighter.

"Ehh hemm." Davey clears his throat so loudly a bird squawks out of a nearby tree.

Micah and I straighten, but I don't let go of his hand.

"Thrilled to see you two together, but we have some work to do." He points with his thumb over his shoulder.

I smile, and Micah and I follow him.

Micah pauses and pulls something from his pocket. My ring.

"May I?"

I can only manage a nod, but that's enough. A moment later, he slides the wedding band onto my finger. We continue after Davey.

I feel lighter than I have in my whole life. Whatever may come, I have Micah's heart. And he has mine.

***

We arrive at the staging point and find five others waiting for us, making nine total in our group. I only hope that we're a small enough group to stay hidden and a large enough group to do the work necessary to disable the metallic horses.

There's a quick round of introductions, and then we hide ourselves in a site the others have prepared. I've already shared the plans on how to disable the metallic horses with Micah, Zoe, and Davey, so the four of us quietly explain what to do to the others. The five Thaddeus sent to work with us don't seem at all intimidated by what we share, and I breathe a little easier.

"Makes sense," a guy who goes by Wolf says. "What do you plan to do about the recalibration effect?"

"If we short circuit it the way I've outlined, that shouldn't be an issue," I say. "We'll essentially be resetting it to manufacturer settings. The Inventors in the compound create the horses to be disabled if they're taken out of the compound. The only way they can leave is when they're upgraded for Raiders who go on missions. If it's reset, the Raiders won't be able to move the steeds at all." I speak with confidence, but hope I'm getting everything right.

Wolf opens his mouth, but a shrill whistle pierces the air.

The signal.

The Raiders have arrived.

Everything seems to still. Even the forest sounds go quiet. Then the piercing whir of the engines filling the air. The ground beneath us rumbles. It's a feeling I've known countless times, the thunder of dozens of mechanical horses racing together. A thrill zips through me at the thought. I miss racing, miss the feel of going faster than I ever could on my own.

There's a cry. The thundering grows to an almost deafening roar. Like we expected, they're approaching Wisteria from the north. They'll ride right past us.

My heart skips a beat. Hopefully, they ride past us. The hideout looks like a crop of bushes. Nothing more.

Still, my pulse throbs in my throat.

The sound fades, and there are distant shouts and gunfire cracks through the air. We wait, each second interminable. But this is the plan. Wait until we're sure all the riders have passed, then sneak to their horses.

A new thought collides in my mind.

We've been assuming they'd dismount and leave the metallic horses outside of the town like they always do. But what if some ride in? Then there will be horses unaccounted for.

My hands are slick with sweat. There are too many unknowns.

Wolf pokes his head out of the hideout and scans the area. "Let's go."

No one argues, and we file out into the open.

The hair on the back of my neck rises and my heart races. We're exposed. If anyone's watching, they'll see us.

The distant sounds of the fight zap at my nerves. I want to go join in, help there. Do whatever I can. Prove to everyone—to myself—that I am not a Raider.

But I have a job to do, one that will prove my allegiance.

We split into three groups of three and spread out. Based on my understanding of the area, I made an educated guess on where the horses would be, but there's no assurance that will be the case. So each group is checking a likely area, and the first group to find the horses will radio the others.

I hike with Davey and Micah, all of us crouched low as we move over the terrain as quietly and quickly as possible.

"Okay, God, help this to work," Davey whispers under his breath.

I bite my lip. *Yes, God. Please help this to work.* My faith isn't as strong as Davey's. I feel like a baby compared to him. But I want my faith to grow like his and be intrinsically tied to my life.

We climb a crest. Wisteria is in view. Smoke rises from buildings, and the shouts of the battle are overwhelming, even from here. My limbs shake, but I press forward with Micah and Davey, half-running down the incline.

There's an old farm a quarter mile or so from the town, and we come closer to it. If I'm correct, the horses should be right on the other side.

My heart pounds in my ears, drowning out every other sound. *Please be there, please be there.*

Davey and I pause at the barn, and Micah jogs ahead to peek around the corner. If the horses are there, they'd have left at least one guard. Maybe two.

Before Micah can come back to report to Davey and me, the radio lets out a low buzz.

"We've got horses," Zoe says, the words barely audible.

My shoulders sag. I was wrong. They didn't leave them here.

Micah runs back. "The horses are here." His eyes are bright. "Only one guard."

Davey and I look at each other.

"Zoe said they have the horses," Davey says.

Micah blinks, then gestures for the radio. Davey hands it to him.

"We've got a group of horses here, too," Micah says. "Wolf, your team have a report?"

"Horses here too, man," Wolf says.

"They spread them out." Micah's lips compress for a moment. "Alright. We all know what to do."

"Right-o," Wolf says. "We've got one guard and about a dozen of the metal guys."

"Same," Zoe says.

"Looked like closer to two dozen here," Micah says.

I clench my hands into fists. That doesn't add up.

"I doubt they'd only send four dozen Raiders in," Zoe says, echoing my thoughts.

"Which means we've got to work fast and find where they've left the rest of their horses," Wolf says.

"Let's do it," Micah says.

"Godspeed, my friends," Wolf says. The radio clicks off.

Micah looks at me and Davey. "Ready?"

I nod. There's nothing else I can do. We were supposed to have the entire team in one place, but the Raiders have spread us out. As though J expected something like this.

What else has she prepared for?

As I race with Micah and Davey to the corner of the barn, I

can't help but be thankful they're the two I'm with. Because I don't think anyone else would believe I didn't leak intel.

We come to the corner, and Micah gestures for me to wait.

He signals Davey to go to the left, while he goes to the right.

The two drop to the ground and crawl away.

Every part of me screams to follow them, but I stay where I am.

There's a muffled cry. It cuts off. I risk looking around the corner, and Micah waves me closer.

I jog to the men, and find Davey tying up an unconscious Raider. Again, I'm reminded of the difference between these men and those I grew up with. If they don't have to take a life, they let the person live so they can be tried for their crimes. Something no Raider would dare do.

"Let's get to work," Micah says.

The three of us separate, and I go to the closest horse. I swing myself into the saddle, relishing the feel of the cool metal beneath me. It feels wrong to miss anything from my old life, but I miss this.

I pop open the panel on the neck of the horse, push a sequence of buttons, then pull out one of the wires. The horse shudders underneath me, then its head bows.

Done.

I spring off and go to the next one. Each second feels too long, especially knowing there are more groupings of horses. Micah and Davey ask a few questions on their first horses, which slows me down. But once they each get to their third horse, they appear more confident. Part of me wants to check their work, make sure the horses weren't just put in sleep mode to preserve power. I shake off the idea.

There isn't time. I have to trust my partners.

Zoe's voice comes over the radio a few minutes later to say

they've finished and are moving to check for other horses. Wolf says the same thing moments later. I panic, then remember that they had fewer horses to disable than we do.

There are only four left here.

Micah, Davey, and I each mount another horse, and before long, I've disabled mine. The two men aren't far behind me.

I mount the last horse and hesitate. Part of me doesn't want to disable it. It might be helpful to have one still able to ride. And we don't know if we'll find any other groupings.

"Everything okay?" Micah asks.

"Yes, I just—"

"They're coming!" Davey says.

My heart lurches. No. It's too soon. But as I stare off in the direction Davey's looking, there they are. Raiders leaving Wisteria and coming this way.

## CHAPTER
# THIRTY-ONE

I power on the horse. I won't be caught. Can't be. Not after all we've been through.

"Catori?" Micah gives me a quizzical look. He holds his gun, but the sound of the horse draws his attention to me.

"There she is!" Someone shouts.

And the voice sends chills down my spine. Carver.

Grandfather lied.

Carver isn't dead.

A Raider launches an arrow at us. I kick the horse into gear and race away.

"Cator—" Micah's voice cuts off.

I risk looking back and see the arrow has hit its mark.

Micah collapses to the ground.

"No!" I cry in a choked voice as tears rush down my cheeks.

But I don't turn back. I can't. If I do, they'll get me, too.

Instead, I shift the horse into high gear and race through the trees.

Away from the Raiders hunting me.

Away from Carver.

Away from capture.

And away from Micah.

A mix of pain and fear makes me nauseous, but I don't stop.

I crest a hill, weaving in and out of trees as I lean low over the horse's neck. I push as fast as I can, ignoring the branches whipping my arms and face.

*Get away. Just get away.*

But where am I going?

Tears blur my vision. I swipe at them. My past and what I wanted for my future are colliding in a battle behind me.

And my past is going to win.

I cut around the ruins of an old neighborhood. This isn't right.

I should go back.

I round a crumbling building, then pull the horse up so hard it shuts off.

Standing before me is a line of a dozen Raiders, weapons drawn. Like they were just waiting for me.

J leaps off her horse, pulls a gun from one of her holsters, and strides toward me.

"Great to see you again, Princess."

I try to turn the horse back on, but it's still rebooting after my hard stop. The Raiders surround me.

My panic ebbs away as realization dawns. In my attempt to save my life, protect myself, I've left behind the man I love, my friends, and walked right into a trap. I was going to turn around. Go back. But now it's too late.

If I had stayed. If I had *fought*, I might have died. But it would have been worth it.

*God, what have I done?*

"Get down." J gestures with her gun.

I dismount, almost falling to my knees as I land on the ground.

J crowds close to me, eyes narrow as she stares me down. "Time to go home."

Before I can respond, she brings her pistol up and whips me across the face.

My head snaps to the side, pain ripping through me. I crumble to the ground as everything goes black.

---

Cold water rushes over me, and I sit up, gasping for breath. My head pounds, the ache intensifying as I realize where I am.

Water drips from my lashes, but not enough to obscure my vision.

I'm in the Upper District.

Cheers erupt from the crowd, and I dig my fingers into the dirt under me. This can't be happening. But it is.

I'm surrounded by Raiders. Everyone is dressed like they're here for a Welcoming Party.

My gaze collides with J's. She's staring at me, still in her Raider leathers, arms crossed. Frowning. Her crew stands behind her, and after a quick assessment, I realize it's smaller than it was before. And not only is Aiden unaccounted for. Gabby is nowhere to be seen.

Did she die too?

A pang ricochets through me. She betrayed me, but I don't want her dead.

"Silence!" Grandfather's voice booms over the crowd, and an instant later everyone goes quiet. He stands on the platform I once joined him on, and his commanding presence is like a shadow over the entire clearing.

The familiarity of this moment strikes me a second before

Grandfather's heavy gaze lands on me. My jaw quivers. Gone is any hint of care in his eyes or the smile he would give me that let me know he was pleased. I'm not staring at Grandfather.

This is Jehoram, Chief of the Raiders.

And he's going to make an example out of me.

The silence in the clearing throbs in my ears, but I just continue to stare at my grandfather.

Finally, he speaks. "Bring her up here."

J grabs my arm and hauls me to my feet, propelling me toward the platform. Her grip pinches my skin, but I don't flinch. I stand as straight as possible and walk toward the one man in the world who's my family.

My heart skips a beat.

No. That's not true. He's not my only family. Not anymore. Now I have the crew of *The Fearless Lady*. Jordyn and Vik, Davey and Nate.

Micah.

I stumble, and my mind viciously replays the moment the arrow struck him.

Is he dead?

*God, please. Don't let him be gone.*

I stagger up the stairs, and J shoves me forward. I stumble. Fall. And don't get up as a sickening realization dawns.

We lost.

*I* lost.

We walked right into a trap. J knew our plan and was prepared for everything. I raced into her arms and left behind my husband. My friends.

"Bring in the informant." Grandfather's words crack through my pain, and my head snaps up.

I get to my feet, searching the crowd.

Who did this? Who betrayed us?

Grandfather steps into my line of sight. "I didn't think I

could be *more* ashamed of you than I was." He releases a bitter laugh. "But you proved me wrong." He backhands me across the face, and my head jerks to the side.

Pain crashes over me. I stagger, but manage to stay standing.

"Not only did you defy your people. You walked right into a trap." He leans into my face. "How does my blood run in your unworthy veins?"

I force myself to look him in the eye, desperate to see a glimpse of the man I grew up with. But he's gone.

"Please. Just let me leave." The words are desperate and barely over a whisper.

Grandfather's lip curls. He turns and faces the crowd. "Do we offer mercy?"

"No!" the crowd shouts.

"Right. We are Raiders, and no one escapes our rule." Grandfather faces me. "You thought you could run, escape your destiny, defy me. But you. Were. Wrong."

There's a stir in the crowd, pulling Grandfather's—Jehoram's—focus from me. I turn to see what's happening, my nails digging into my palms.

Three men clamber onto the platform, and I gasp.

Shax is standing alongside Carver. Unbound. Unharmed.

He's the leak.

Jehoram approaches him and reaches out his hand. Shax grasps his forearm. Like they're old friends.

Jehoram whirls and faces the crowd. "We don't offer mercy. But we do give...opportunities."

There are some murmurs through the crowd, and my eyes narrow. Where's he going with this?

"This man," he gestures back to Shax, "was faced with an opportunity several nights ago: let J board the riverboat safely, or die." Jehoram smirks. "We can all see what choice he made."

Laughter ripples over the crowd.

"But he didn't stop there," Jehoram continues. "He continued to supply us with vital intel, which aided in our resounding triumph!"

He goes on, detailing their victory and belittling all who dared stand against the might of the Raiders.

But I barely hear a word. Anger pulses through me.

Vik almost died, all because Shax didn't step up and fight when he should have.

I almost choke.

How can I judge Shax for doing the very thing I always do?

*Oh God. Forgive me. I hate who I am on my own. I'm a coward and care more about protecting myself than courageously standing for what's right. But I can't stand on my own. Change me. Make me who You want me to be, like You did with Davey. And please give me courage to do whatever I need to do, even if this is the last day of my life.*

A weight lifts off me. I release a slow breath, and look at Shax. He's watching me, his eyes haunted. Maybe he felt like I did: trapped and forced to make choices he hates himself for.

Although I can't grasp why he would continue to leak intel to the Raiders.

My forehead scrunches, and I hope he can read the question in my eyes. His jaw tenses, and he looks away.

"Where's the old lady?" Jehoram's question freezes my blood.

"Here," a Roamer in the crowd responds. He drags a staggering Miriam closer to the platform. She cradles her right arm close to her body and walks with a heavy limp.

"No!" I shout. I rush toward them.

J intercepts me. I struggle against her grasp, but she's stronger than me.

Tears blur my vision. I swipe them away.

"She's an old woman. Don't hurt her," I plead, even as I realize they've already harmed her.

Jehoram grins, but it doesn't reach his calculating eyes. "You've always had a soft spot for the crone."

I flinch at the disrespect in his words. "Just let her go. Please."

Miriam catches my frantic gaze. Her one eye is blackened and scrapes mar her left cheek. But she smiles at me. Her soft, gracious smile and eyes alight with years of wisdom and clarity.

My Miriam.

The woman who taught me, helped me. Showed me God.

"You are not unlike us, Catori," Jehoram says. "So, in my benevolence, I will offer you one opportunity."

My heart hammers in my chest, but I don't take my eyes off Miriam.

"Kill the informant, marry Carver, and take your place as the princess of the Raiders, and save this slave. Or become a slave and watch her die."

"Wait, what?" Shax says.

The raider nearest him punches him in the stomach, and Shax doubles over with a gasp.

*What do I do? What do I do?*

"I'm already married," I blurt out. "By Raider law, I cannot marry another."

Jehoram's nostrils flare. He strides closer, and I cower. But he doesn't strike. "You dare quote Raider law to me?" His voice is fierce. "Your marriage is void here. My proposition stands as stated."

He glares at me until I bow my head.

"You have until tomorrow at dawn to make your choice." Jehoram claps his hands. "Lock them up."

J drags me from the stage, and I strain to look past her and continue to watch Miriam. The Roamer with her is hauling her in the same direction as me.

Shax struggles behind us. "I did what you wanted! You said I could have a new life!"

"Shut up." Briggs punches him in the face. Then he's shoving him in our direction.

Toward the dungeons.

I stumble as J pulls me along. I pick up my pace. Miriam is coming too. I'll see her soon. Which means Jehoram hopes that by being with her, he'll be able to encourage me to make the choice he wants. To become more like him by killing someone to save myself.

The dungeon is between the Upper and Lower Districts, and we arrive moments later. I know this compound better than most. But I've never been in the dungeons. It's rare for *anyone* to be kept in the cells below the compound. Raiders don't take prisoners. They take slaves.

But Jehoram wants to show his power and make a point with me.

*God, what do I do?*

J leads me to a crumbling staircase that goes underground. Halfway down, the air grows thick and damp, and the scent of mold is suffocating. I blink, trying to get my eyes to adjust to the low lighting after being in the sun.

We pass a few empty cells. J stops and shoves me into one. The space is cramped, and an instant later there's a clang as she shuts and locks the door.

"J. Wait." I grip the bars.

She pauses. "What could you possibly want with me?" Her words hold a bite that causes me to step back.

"Is Gabby—"

"Don't you *dare* say her name." She spins to face me. "Gabby's gone. And Aiden may never recover."

My breath hitches. Aiden isn't dead.

J stalks to the barred door. "I can't believe you have the option to live." She looks me up and down. "If somehow you survive, I promise, one day, I will kill you."

With that, she turns and marches from the dungeon.

My body shakes, damp clothes clinging to me, and I collapse to the dirty concrete floor. A tear leaks out, and I squeeze my eyes shut even as emotions burn in my lungs. Gabby's gone.

She's probably not the only friend I lost today. Micah… Jordyn. The rest of the crew, the scouts. Are they alive?

A few moments pass, and then Shax is brought in, breaking me from my thoughts. He's locked in a cell across from me.

Miriam stumbles down the last stair.

Even as she's dragged forward, she appears dignified. My cell is opened, and the Roamer shoves her inside.

I clamber to my feet and steady her before she falls.

When the Roamer shuts the door, I recognize him as Parreu. The Roamer who made me join my grandfather on the stage at the Welcoming Party months ago.

He glares at me. The same disdain I remember coating his face then is even more apparent now. He turns on his heel and leaves.

Miriam leans back, her worn hands on my cheeks. "Oh, my daughter. I longed to see you again, but not like this."

Tears fall from my eyes, and I step into her embrace.

Even though I'm now in prison with no hope of escape, as I cling to this woman who has loved me so well, I feel at home.

How could I ever make a decision that would lead to her death? But how can I do what Jehoram demands?

# THIRTY-TWO

"Let me look at you," Miriam says. She steps back, taking both my hands.

I study her as she studies me, and my stomach twists. She's thinner than when I left, and more than one bruise marks her exposed skin.

"I'm sorry for whatever they did to you." I press my lips together. "It's my fault."

"Shh," Miriam says. She tugs me over to a rickety bench in the back of the cell. Once we're settled, she takes my left hand in hers. She pats it, then looks down. "You're married. To Micah?"

My face heats, and I nod. "Yes. He did it to protect me. But now..." My voice breaks as I fight to find words to express how much he means to me.

A deep ache builds until I feel as though I'll shatter into a million pieces. Even if he miraculously survived, I'll probably never see him again. The ache moves to my throat, intense as I try to hold back tears. Sobs. My eyes burn. *Oh, Micah.*

"Tell me," Miriam murmurs. "I want to hear how my girl has been all these months."

So I do.

I share with her about my time aboard The Fearless Lady, the close encounters we faced. Marrying Micah. How he has helped me understand what love—true unconditional love—looks like. My longing for her to meet him.

I keep my voice low, not wanting to expose the depths of my heart to Shax, who's watching us from his cell.

Especially as I tell Miriam about the final stand in Wisteria...and how utterly I failed. "I should have stayed. Fought. Died even. But I ran."

I can't look at her as I say the words. Tears aren't flowing freely from me, but I almost wish they were. Instead, I feel hollow. Like a dried and shriveled husk after the grain has been beaten from it.

She squeezes my hand, her weathered fingers gentle and familiar.

"Fear gets the best of all of us at times. But what will you choose to do *now*? For it is how we stand after failure that determines our character."

I lean back against the concrete wall. "I want to be courageous. I even asked God to help me. I'm tired of letting my fears rule me." My eyes slide shut. "But how am I supposed to make a decision after the ultimatum Jehoram gave?"

"Please don't let me die." Shax's plea echoes through the cavernous space.

I open my eyes and stare through the low-lit space toward the man who betrayed me. Betrayed Micah and every person he called his friend. He's standing at the door to his cell, clinging to the bars.

"Why did you do it?" I ask.

Shax drops his gaze. "After I let J onboard, and she hurt Vik,

I knew I needed to find a way to another life. Once you all learned what I had done, that I was responsible...” His words trail off, and he rests his forehead on the bars. “I didn't have a choice.”

“There's always a choice,” I say. I blink. Those were the words Miriam said to me months ago. Words I was sure couldn't possibly be true.

But now I see how right she is.

“I won't obey Jehoram,” I say. “Never again.”

Shax's head snaps up. “Really?”

I nod, even as uncertainty threatens to smother me. I turn toward Miriam. “But I can't let you die.”

“I've lived many years, dear girl.” She tucks a strand of hair behind my ear. “And God has been with me through every moment. In the best of times, and in the most painful.” She pauses, eyes searching mine. “Take your stand, and trust me into God's hands. Whether I live or die, He is still in control. You need to do what is *right*.”

A lump chokes me, cutting off any response.

“Seeing you live courageously is what I have prayed for.” She smiles. “If I die tomorrow, I will be with the One whom my soul loves. But who knows what God will do?”

I lean into her, and she wraps her arms around me. My tears are hot as they track their way unchecked down my cheeks. I cling to Miriam.

Can I do it? Can I make the choice to save the man who betrayed me and the people I care about and lose this woman who I love so dearly? And then become a *slave*?

I press my eyes shut and breathe in. Out.

Yes. I can.

Because I no longer want to live attempting to keep myself safe, when all I've really done is become more bound by my fears and harm the people I love.

*God, help me.*

"I'm scared," I whisper.

Miriam leans back. A loud scraping noise cuts through the air before she can respond.

The wall behind me shifts, and I jump up, pulling Miriam with me.

My heart pounds against my ribs, and I position myself in front of Miriam.

Hosea pokes his head through the opening. "Guess this tunnel wasn't a waste after all."

"What..." my voice trails off.

Hosea pulls himself out of the opening and brushes debris off his clothes. "Ya gonna finish the question?"

I blink. "Why are you here?"

He crosses his arms over his chest. "I'd think there's a pretty obvious answer to that question. Did you *want* to stick around here?"

I shake my head no.

He grunts. "Then let's get out of here. I ain't loving being back."

"Still brimming with charm, aren't you, Hosea?" Miriam chuckles.

"What about me?" Shax asks.

I glance toward him. If we leave, Shax will die. And they'll hunt us down.

I take a step back. "I can't go."

Hosea rolls his eyes. "You being in here is gonna make the next part of the plan harder than necessary."

"What do you mean?"

"Wisteria was never the only operation in play. You knew that." Hosea shakes his head.

"But attacking the compound was supposed to come *after* we weakened their forces." I say.

Hosea grunts. "We had a contingency in place, and when it was clear we'd been played, that plan was activated."

My head is spinning. And aching. "Okay. So what does that mean?"

Hosea looks past me toward the exit of the dungeon. "I really ain't comfortable chatting about this out in the open." He gives a sweeping gesture toward the hole he climbed out of. "Can we get below ground?"

"Whatever your plan is, they'll be tipped off if we're gone." I wish it wasn't true, but as I say the words, I know that's exactly what will happen.

Hosea makes a noise that sounds far more like a growl.

"She's right," Miriam says. "We should stay where we are. Whatever plan you have in place needs the element of surprise."

Hosea runs a hand over his hair. "Perfect. Just what I needed today," he grouches. But I think he's pleased with our response.

He sighs. "Fine. I'll leave you be. But just know I'm not looking forward to letting Micah know you're still in this place."

"Micah's alive?" The words are a breath. I hadn't even wanted to consider asking the question sooner for fear of what Hosea's answer would be.

"Banged up a bit, but yeah."

My knees weaken as hope billows through me. Maybe I'll see him again. Maybe whatever plan Hosea and the others have will work.

"What about Jordyn?" I ask, holding my breath as I wait for him to respond.

"She's okay too. Still on The Fearless Lady, far as I know."

"And the rest of the crew and the scouts? Those from the WUN who helped us?"

Hosea holds his hands up, as though to staunch my flow of questions. "Alive. Some have sustained serious injuries, but they're breathin'. Seems the Raiders wanted you most of all. Once they had you, they retreated." He snorts. "With a couple dozen less mechanical horses than they came with."

Relief courses through me.

"If I'm gonna leave you, there're a few things you need to know," Hosea says. He turns and focuses on Shax. "And if you so much as hint at what you see, I can guarantee the first bullet I fire will find its mark in you."

"I just want to get out of here," Shax says, desperation lacing his words.

Hosea stares at him for a long moment, then nods. "Fine."

He leans back into the opening. "Tell Leroy I need five minutes. If anyone's approaching, git word to me right away."

"Yes sir," a woman says. But I can't see her through the murky darkness of the tunnel.

There's some shuffling for a moment, then the distinct click of a radio. The woman relays Hosea's message to Leroy.

All I want to do is ask him more about Micah, but I focus on what Hosea is saying.

"We've brought in trained men and women through the passageway you discovered. Dozens of them are waiting in the tunnels below the Lower District, and we're preparing to attack." He details plans for the attack, and Miriam and I just listen.

Hosea's keeping his voice low, so I doubt Shax can hear anything. I look over at him. He's slumped on the floor, head in his hands. Pity rises in me, but I tamp it down. Shax made the choices that led him to where he is right now. Same as me.

I turn back to Hosea. "When will you attack?"

"There're a dozen or so scouts coming in within the next couple hours. Right now, the plan is midnight tonight."

"That's dangerous," I say. "There are Roamers who patrol throughout the evening and they monitor the security cameras more closely at night. You won't know where everyone is, but they'll spot you right away. Can you hold off the attack until dawn?"

"Maybe. Why?"

"Because that's when Jehoram,"—the name feels strange on my tongue, but I can't say Grandfather—"will have everyone gathered in the center of the Upper District. All the Raiders in the compound will be there, as well as the slaves from the Lower District. Which means far less Roamers patrolling. He wants everyone to witness his cunning and ruthlessness."

Hosea nods. "Alright." He looks between me and Miriam. "You sure you both want to stay in this place? I can't guarantee someone will be able to keep you safe once the attack starts."

I turn to Miriam, her weathered face shining in support even before she tilts her head.

"We'll stay," I say for both of us. "Your plan will only work if you have an element of surprise. If we're gone, they'll know something is happening."

"Fine." He steps toward the opening, then pauses and focuses on me. "You've changed."

I want to squirm under his gaze, but stay still.

"Never woulda thought you'd give up a chance at safety. Goes to show people can surprise ya." With that, he crawls through the opening.

A moment later, the slab of concrete shifts back into place, sealing us into our cell.

But not for long.

There's a plan.

Micah, Jordyn, and the others are all alive.

And Hosea's right. I have changed, and, by God's grace, I'm

going to stay on this path. Because I would rather coura-geously do what's right, no matter what the cost, than face the shame I've felt time and time again after doing what was easy.

---

MIRIAM AND I SPEND THE NEXT COUPLE OF HOURS QUIETLY DISCUSSING what Hosea shared, and sorting through our own plan. This attack comes with a lot of risk. No matter what, there's a high likelihood that I'll lose people I care about within the next twelve hours.

My body aches, and the moldy scent of the dungeon only intensifies the pounding in my head.

I twist my ring around my finger.

"Tell me about Micah," Miriam says.

"What? Shouldn't we discuss what we're going to do?"

She pats my leg. "We have a plan—as much of one as we can, anyway. We *should* get some rest. But I sense you're not quite ready for that."

I focus on my ring. Our plan seems feeble, which I guess makes sense. We don't know how the Raiders are going to handle things in the morning—if they'll keep us together or separate us. Or how much pomp and ceremony Jehoram plans to bring to the event.

We don't even know exactly how Hosea and the others will attack. There wasn't time for him to give us that information. Plus, some details are still getting figured out since I suggested a change in the attack location.

So many unknowns.

Not to mention, we're going against J. The hatred in her eyes...her promise...how will I face her and live to tell about it?

"Tell me about Micah," Miriam says again.

"He's handsome and brave and courageous. He loves God

and cares for others." My throat thickens. "I want you to meet him."

The possibility that the two most important people in my life may never meet each other feels like more than I can bear, but I press my eyes together. I will not dissolve into tears right now.

"I hope I get to meet him, too." Miriam takes my hand in hers. "The man who won the heart of my girl must be a special one indeed."

I shift so I can lay my head on her shoulder, and we sit quietly for several moments.

"You should have left when you had the chance," Shax says.

I sit up.

"Should have saved yourselves. There's no way we're getting out of this alive." The bitter hopelessness in his words makes me cringe.

I open my mouth, but Miriam places a hand on my arm, and I stop.

Shax continues. "I'm sorry. I shouldn't have done what I did. Or blamed you for betraying us." His voice is raw. "I'd rather be dead now than face Micah and the guys like this. Like the traitor I am."

Miriam stands and goes toward the bars of our cell. "From what Catori has told me of Micah and his crew, they will forgive you."

Shax hangs his head. "I deserve to rot forever for what I've done."

Miriam settles herself on the floor next to the bars, and I can tell from the look in her eyes that Shax is about to be the recipient of her insights. Whether or not he wants to be.

A small smile tilts the corners of my mouth, even as

exhaustion sweeps through me. I yawn and drop to one of the dirty mats on the floor.

I close my eyes and drift to sleep, listening to Miriam share about Jesus and forgiveness with Shax.

*God, please don't take her. Not yet.* The prayer whispers from my heart a moment before sleep takes me completely.

# THIRTY-THREE

I wake a few hours later to find Miriam and Shax sleeping. The lights in the dungeon have been dimmed even more, and the murky darkness combined with the musky scent is consuming. It can't be long until someone comes and gets us.

And we're brought before the crowd of Raiders.

At this moment, I wish I'd spent more time learning how to use weapons.

We're about to enter a fight. A battle. I'll probably be more of a liability than a help.

I roll onto my side and stare at the concrete wall, barely making out the cracks that would indicate the opening Hosea came through.

The scouts are well trained, I think. But I *know* every Raider and Roamer knows how to wield their weapon of choice. Not to mention, the scouts look to capture and preserve life. The Raiders always seek to kill.

My heartbeat picks up, and I breathe in and out slowly.

The one thing we have going for us is the element of surprise. It will make a difference. It has to.

If I ever get out of this mess, I'm going to ask Micah to teach me how to defend myself. I sit up, my body too energized to stay still.

Will Micah be in this battle? Will he even want anything to do with me after I ran?

I chew on the inside of my cheek.

I don't deserve a man like him, but today I will show him I've changed. And maybe, maybe he'll forgive me.

Boots clomping down the stairs brings me to my feet. I knew it was soon, but I don't feel ready.

Parreu and J round the corner, along with a handful of Raiders and Roamers. Someone turns up the lights and I squint against the increased brightness and bursts of pain it causes. I bend down and gently shake Miriam's shoulder.

"It's time," I whisper. My voice quivers.

Miriam sits up, and I help her to her feet.

J unlocks our cell and thrusts the door open so hard it crashes against the wall and shudders.

"Let's get this over with." Her chilling gaze lands on me and it takes more willpower than I wish it did to hold her stare.

J always intimidated me, but I never thought she could hate me this much.

My chest tightens. Gabby is gone. And I'm not sure how bad Aiden's injuries are, or even where he is. They were her world...and two of my closest friends in this prison.

"I said, let's go." J reaches out and grabs Miriam, yanking her forward.

Miriam gasps, and I rush to her side. "You're hurting her."

J backhands me across the face, hitting the same spot she struck before. Pain explodes through me, dancing spots before my eyes.

I manage to stay standing and hold back tears. I take Miriam's hand, and we leave the cell.

Shax is already out of his cell and being led by two Roamers toward the exit. For an instant, I wonder how his conversation with Miriam ended.

Can we trust him, or will he betray us again?

J pushes me from behind, and I take a stuttering step forward, then pick up my pace.

She's waiting for an excuse to hit me again. Or worse, hurt Miriam to get to me. And I refuse to do anything to give her that excuse.

We climb the stairs out of the dungeon and enter the crisp air of early morning. A breeze lifts my hair off my neck and sends goosebumps rippling over my skin. The street lamps are still on, and the sky is barely softening with the hints of dawn.

It's earlier than I thought.

Will Hosea and the others be ready?

Miriam squeezes my hand, like she can sense my growing anxiety, and it calms me. What will I do if she dies?

"Be courageous, my girl," Miriam says, so soft I barely make out the words as they're carried away on the breeze.

"Shut up," Parreu says, his voice loud in the early morning.

Another squeeze of my hand from Miriam.

The only sound for several minutes is our feet crunching against the gravel as we make our way past houses and shops and into the Upper District. But Miriam's words pulse through me, and I want to rise to them more now than I ever have before in my life.

I want courage to *define* my life.

The sky has lightened more as we pass palatial houses and near the center of the Upper District. Miriam leans more heavily on me as the walk wears on her weakened body, but I don't mind the pressure. It means she's here. Alive.

I hear the crowd gathered long before I see them.

It sounds like a Welcoming Party that went through the night. Which means many of them are drunk.

If the scouts time this right, maybe we'll be able to stop them.

The roar of the crowd is deafening as we step into the center square. Raucous laughter. Shouting. A gun goes off.

I freeze.

Then realize it's a drunk Briggs firing his weapon into the air. Cackling as those nearby jump.

J shoves people out of the way so we can make our way to the platform. The hair on the back of my neck rises. I glance up to find Jehoram's gaze on me as he sits like a king on his throne.

I meet his gaze. My jaw quivers, but I clench it. Even if I'm terrified, I will do the right thing today.

Jehoram continues to stare at me as we draw closer to the platform, and I can't read anything in his expression. I drop my eyes, afraid of the treason he might read in their depths.

Another squeeze of my hand from Miriam.

Then we're climbing the stairs onto the platform.

Shax is bound and standing between two Roamers, their weapons drawn.

Our eyes connect. There's a stalwart resolution in his face that reminds me of the man I watched fight off a Raider to save a woman from slavery during the first fight in Wisteria.

I give a small nod.

"Do what you need to do," Shax says. "Miriam deserves to live."

Parreu drives the butt of his gun into Shax's stomach, and the man doubles over.

Jehoram rises from his seat and the noise in the square dampens, then dies as Raiders quiet their drunken friends.

Even in their inebriated state, they seem to understand they can't cross their chief.

"There is no place we aren't feared!" Jehoram shouts, arms raised into the air.

The crowd cheers.

He gestures for them to be quiet, and it takes a moment longer than usual. He continues. "Wisteria is burning. The traitor has been apprehended." He points to me. "And now we will allow her to make her choice. Live and embrace the blood in her veins. Or become a slave and watch the old woman she claims to care about die." Venom drips from his words.

My palms are slick with sweat, but I don't release Miriam's hand.

Jehoram faces me. "What is your decision?"

The square that was once throbbing with noise is now deathly silent. All I hear is the thundering in my ears. My vision blurs. I blink to clear it.

Where are they?

It wasn't supposed to get to this moment. The scouts should be here now. But it's earlier than I expected.

So they're not.

Miriam squeezes my hand. I take a shuddering breath. This is the moment I need to stand. *God, help me.*

"I refuse your offer." I sound stronger than I feel.

"What? No," Shax says.

Parreu strikes him again.

Jehoram's face twists, turning a mix of purple and red. He draws his pistol.

Shouts rise from the crowd, but I don't understand any of them.

The seconds tick by, interminable.

He loads a bullet.

Gunfire explodes through the air.

I dive at Miriam, taking us both down to the ground.

Screams erupt through the square.

"Are you okay?" I shout the words.

"Yes. He didn't shoot me," Miriam says.

She sounds winded, but relief courses through me.

He missed.

But he'll try again. I spin to face him, but Jehoram is distracted.

My heart skips a beat.

Scouts are entering the square from every angle, and the Raiders are fighting with one another in their drunken confusion.

I get to my feet and help Miriam up. "Get out of the square and go to the tunnels. I'll find you once this is done."

A Raider rushes toward us, then drops mere feet away.

Miriam bends down and pulls his gun from his hand. "Just because I'm old doesn't mean I can't fight."

I hesitate. I want her to be safe, but how could I ever expect the woman who taught me about courage to be anything but courageous?

I retrieve a short sword from the fallen Raider's belt.

Miriam and I put our backs to each other and face the battle. I swallow my fear, eyes careening around the place. Where do I go? How do I fight?

Then I see Micah.

My heart skips a beat.

He's wrestling Parreu fifty feet from the platform. They're battling for a gun a few feet away on the ground. I race toward the edge of the platform, ready to spring on them.

Someone grabs my arm a moment before I leap, yanking me backward. I almost drop the knife, but manage to keep hold.

I spin, waving my weapon toward my attacker.

Jehoram grabs my hand and squeezes until I cry out and drop the knife. His lips turn up in a smile, but his eyes seem dead.

"You've never known your place," he says through gritted teeth.

The battle rages all around us. Someone calls my name, but I don't take my gaze from the man I called grandfather.

"Your way isn't right," I say.

His lip twitches, and his grip on my arms tightens. I gasp.

"My way makes sense." He shakes me. "You know what it means to look out for yourself above everyone else."

I'm trembling, but I shake my head no. "Not anymore. I won't be like you."

He spits in my face. Then he throws me to the ground, pinning me in place with his boot on the center of my chest. He points his gun at me.

All I can see is its muzzle.

"You will watch everything and everyone you love die." He leans down. I squirm, but can't free myself. "I promise you."

"Not today," Micah says. He tackles Jehoram, knocking him off me and off the platform.

I scramble to my feet.

Micah throws a punch. Deflects one. Jehoram lands a blow to Micah's open side.

Micah grunts, but doesn't stop.

I scan the area for a weapon. Something I can use. Jehoram's gun lays discarded near the edge of the platform. I leap toward it.

"Catori!" Shax shouts from behind me.

I hesitate for a fraction of a second, then whirl toward him. Blood oozes down his vest as Carver pulls out the knife he thrust in. Shax is on his knees, struggling to get up. Carver cuts him again, and Shax cries out.

Carver turns and stalks toward me.

I aim the gun at Carver.

He smiles the ugliest smile I've ever seen, but doesn't stop his advance.

"I will always find you, Catori. And you will be mine." He nods behind him at Shax, who's attempting to follow Carver, even as blood flows from open wounds. "All that one's attempt to keep me from you did was make me want you more."

Shax was fighting for me.

The gun shakes in my hand. "Stop."

"You won't shoot me." Carver takes another step toward me.

I pull the trigger.

The bullet catches him in the arm. His eyes widen, then narrow.

He pulls his own gun.

Shax is on his feet now, stumbling toward me.

I pull the trigger again, but the chamber clicks. Empty.

My heart pulses in my throat.

Carver aims at me. "You're dead."

"No!" Shax shouts as Carver pulls the trigger.

Shax dives in front of me. His body quakes as Carver's bullet hits him in the chest. He crumbles to the ground.

Before Carver can aim again, an arrow strikes him in the neck. Wolf stands on the roof of a nearby building, crossbow in hand. He reloads and fires at another Raider an instant later.

Carver drops, the gun clattering on the platform.

"Shax." I drop to the man laying at my feet.

The man who took a bullet for me.

Gently, I roll him over. He's barely breathing.

"Don't die. Come on, Shax," I say.

His eyes flutter, then open. He swallows. "At least...I can end...a better man than I was."

Tears stream down my cheeks. "No. Stay with me."

He releases a rattling breath. Then nothing.

I swipe my hand over my face and stand.

I swirl to find the battle behind me has ebbed. Smoke rises from fires throughout the compound, and Raiders lie scattered on the ground, some wounded, some dead. Scouts are restraining those who still live.

And Micah has a gun trained on Jehoram—who is also surrounded by Hosea, Wolf, and Zoe.

Hosea is the closest to him.

Jehoram spins in a circle, chest heaving. Blood trickles from a cut above his eye. "Just kill me! If you don't, I promise you, you will regret it." He focuses on Hosea. "Once a slave, always a slave."

I know what's going to happen an instant before it does.

Jehoram pulls a knife from his waistband.

I leap from the platform as Jehoram rushes Hosea.

I land between the two men. Jehoram thrusts his knife out.

Hot pain rips through my side.

A gun is fired.

My knees buckle.

Everything fades.

CHAPTER

# THIRTY-FOUR

I sit up straight and gasp, clutching my side. I squeeze my eyes shut and breathe until the pain subsides.

Memories march through my mind. My grandfather stabbed me.

Shax is dead.

Carver is dead.

The battle for the compound was victorious.

I open my eyes. Blink.

Why am I in my old room?

I scan the familiar and yet strange surroundings. The windows are open, letting in a cool breeze, and everything is the same as it was when I left. Undisturbed. My closet door is ajar, providing a view of hangers holding various pieces of Raider leathers. A desk with bookshelves rests in the other corner of the room. The book on the desk is one of J's. I shudder.

What happened to her? And why is one of her books in my room?

I swallow back the apprehension and push the uncomfortable questions aside. I grasp the thick comforter over my legs. I feel like an intruder here. This isn't my home. Not anymore.

A longing for my cabin on *The Fearless Lady* steals my breath. A thousand more questions erupt in my brain. But two rise above the others: what is going on?

And, more importantly, who survived...and who didn't?

We won.

I think.

So why am I still within the walls of the compound?

Easing the blankets off my body, I get out of bed, careful to not put any pressure or bend over the cut on my side. I hesitate once I'm standing next to the bed. I'm in soft pants and a flowing shirt. It would make sense to look at the wound. Yet I'm not ready to view it.

There are too many questions I need answered. Now.

I take an aggressive step forward and wince. Slow and steady, it is.

The hallway outside of my room is empty, but voices coming from Grandfather—Jehoram's—study catch my attention. I make my way down the hall and push open the slightly ajar door.

The group of men and women inside stop talking, and all eyes focus on me. But the only one I care to see is Micah.

His face seems to melt in relief. He strides toward me, squirming around those in his path. "You're awake," he says as he comes to a stop in front of me.

I nod. Which seems as silly as his obvious observation that I'm awake. "And you're okay?"

He takes my hand in his. "Yes." He flashes his brilliant smile, and all I want to do is fall into his embrace.

We stare at each other. I can't believe he's here. And happy to see me.

"Eh hem," Davey clears his throat. And my face heats.

Micah drapes an arm over my shoulders and tucks me against his side. I wrap my arm around his waist as he turns us to face the others in the room.

Jehoram's office is enormous, but it suddenly feels cramped when I see how many men and women are in the room.

"Glad to see you're okay," Davey says with a wink.

My face burns hotter, but I smile at him. Then search the other faces. Tension I didn't realize I was holding releases and tears well behind my eyelids.

My friends, my *family,* are here. Next to Davey is Nate. Thaddeus and Malachi and Zoe are here. So is Vik.

I focus on him. "Jordyn?"

"Can't wait to see you," he says.

My throat thickens, and I continue looking around the room. Wolf is here, and so is Antonio. And Hosea.

When I look at him, he steps forward and extends his hand. I step away from Micah to grasp his forearm, his work-roughened fingers curling around my arm.

"Can't say as I always thought much of you. Or that I wanted to help ya." He cocks his head and gives me the first smile I've ever seen from him. It transforms his features. "But you risked your life for me. Anytime you have a need, know I can be one you call on to help."

"Um, thanks?"

He gives a short laugh, then releases my arm.

I go back to Micah, and his arm is around me again an instant later.

"What happened?" I freeze. "Miriam. Is she...?" I can't bring myself to finish the question.

"She was wounded," Micah says, his voice rumbling through his strong body.

I shift away to look at him, ignoring the pain in my side. "Will she be okay?"

He nods, and I can breathe again. "The doctors expect her to make a full recovery."

"If she rests," a woman I don't know says, with a frown on her face.

"It takes more than a couple of bruises to keep me down." Miriam's voice behind us brings a smile to my face.

I turn as she hobbles into the room, moving slower than I've ever seen her. But she's alive.

Nate brings a chair over and settles Miriam.

"We've lost some good people," Thaddeus says. "But our victory here is better than anyone in Eryndale ever could have hoped for."

Then, for what I'm assuming is for Miriam's and my benefit, he goes onto explain the details of the attack and how they were able to overcome the Raiders with inferior forces. They staged the attack in such a way that it appeared there were far more of them than there were, causing great confusion among the ranks of Raiders and Roamers at the Welcoming Party. Because many of the Raiders fought each other, the battle ended faster than Thaddeus had dreamed possible.

Nate grins. "I told you, man. It worked here like it did with Gideon. God was with us."

Thaddeus shifts in his seat. "Uh, okay." He clears his throat. "Anyway, now that we've taken the compound, the next few weeks will be spent getting the captives back to their homes and families or to Eryndale if they so choose, and helping the wounded recover."

"If they'll rest," the woman who spoke earlier—who I now assume is one of the physicians—says.

Thaddeus shares how Jehoram was fatally shot when he

attacked me, which brings so much relief I almost feel ashamed. He won't be able to hurt anyone else ever again. Several Raiders who were captured, including Briggs, are to be brought to Eryndale to be tried for their crimes. J isn't among the list of casualties or prisoners. I try not to squirm too much at that information.

He focuses on Micah. "You and your crew have done more than we ever could have asked for." He pauses. "I'm sorry for what happened with Shax. No one expected him to be the leak."

Micah and every man from his crew hangs their heads. Ashamed the leak could have been from our crew.

"Shax blew it," I say. "But he regretted his choice. And he saved my life."

That brings each of the men's heads up.

"What do you mean?" Micah asks. His deep brown eyes search my face, as though desperate for a reason to remember Shax as more than a traitor.

I quickly describe how Shax tried to keep Carver away from me and then dove in front of me, taking the bullet that should have ended my life.

Micah's jaw bunches, and he cups my cheek with his hand. "I'm glad he won't be able to hunt you ever again."

There are grunts of agreement, and then Thaddeus goes back into the next steps.

"Micah, I'm sure you and your guys could use some rest…" Thaddeus hesitates.

"Just spit it out," Davey says, wiggling his eyebrows.

Thaddeus tries to scowl at him, but his lips twitch. "We could use *The Fearless Lady* to get some supplies to Wisteria to help them rebuild, and then continue onto Eryndale to bring some captives to the refuge city. You can all have a few minutes to discuss it if you want."

Micah nods. "We'll let you know. But if my guys are tired..." He shrugs. "I'd say they've earned their rest."

"Tired?" Nate scoffs. "Speak for yourself, old man."

"I'm only a year older than you," Micah argues.

Davey looks at each of the men in the crew, then focuses on Micah. "We're good to go if you are, Cap."

I grasp Micah's hand. "Yeah, Cap. Let's do it."

I hold my breath for an instant after I say the words, desperately hoping I can still be part of this crew. This family.

The grin Micah gives me explodes every fear. "Okay." With his focus still on me, he says to Thaddeus. "You've got your crew."

Thaddeus says something, but I'm too lost in Micah's gaze. Suddenly, all I want is to be alone with this man. Apologize for leaving him. And beg him to give me another chance.

Because as much as I want to be part of his crew, I want even more to be in his heart.

# THIRTY-FIVE

Before long, Thaddeus dismisses everyone. Micah takes my hand and leads me out of the office, through the halls, and the out of Jehoram's mansion.

"How are you feeling?" he asks.

"Okay, I guess. But I think I should be asking *you* that question. You were shot." I can still envision the moment with sickening clarity.

He takes my other hand in his. "And you were stabbed. If I'd lost you..." his voice cuts off and he clears his throat.

"Catori!" Jordyn's little voice breaks into the moment, and we turn to find her racing through the doorway.

I release Micah's hand an instant before she crashes into me. A breath hitches as she hits my side, but I ignore the pain and pull her toward me.

"Hi Jor Jor." I stroke her hair, thankful to have her in my arms. I pull back slightly to look at her. "How are you?"

She offers me a brave smile. "I'm okay. My Vik and I prayed for you."

My heart melts and I kiss her forehead. "God heard your prayers, baby girl."

She wraps her arms around my neck and squeezes. "I love you."

Her words bring tears to my eyes. "I love you too."

I glance up to find Micah watching us. His lips quirk in a half-smile, but he almost seems...disappointed.

Before I can ask him if he's okay, Davey calls for him.

"Be right there," Micah yells back. He focuses on me. "I'll find you later." The words are a promise.

"Okay," I say as warmth spreads through my chest. He's alive. And he doesn't hate me.

I stare after him as he walks away, wishing I could follow him. He brought me out of the meeting with such purpose, but I don't know *why*.

Jordyn starts jabbering, and I force my attention back to her.

Later. Micah and I will find time together later.

---

THIS IS MY LAST DAY IN THIS ROOM.

Under the care of Dr. Rosa, I've been healing well, so in a few hours, I'll be joining the other members of the crew of *The Fearless Lady* for our journey to Eryndale. And I'm ready to leave this place and never come back.

Jordyn waltzes into the room. "I'm hungry." She flops onto the bed.

I smile at her. "I just have to finish packing. Then we'll see if Nate has anything yummy for you."

"Okay." She hops off the bed and heads over to the book-shelves.

Ever since she and I were reunited a few days ago, the little girl has barely left my side, other than a few outings with Vik. She sleeps curled up next to me and still has nightmares, but she's not as scared as she once was.

Because of my adorable shadow, Micah and I haven't been able to find anytime alone. Which is something I didn't anticipate. Based on the longing in his eyes whenever he looks at me, I don't think he was expecting it either.

My face warms at the thought, and I go into the closet to see if there's anything I need to bring.

I miss him. Which is another reason I'm looking forward to being on *The Fearless Lady*. At least there we won't be busy with meetings and gathering supplies. We can steer the ship together. And finally have a conversation.

I turn in a circle in my closet, surveying the rows of Raider leathers. Other than a pair of gloves and warm boots, which will be beneficial now that the weather's cooling, there's nothing in here I want. I'm done being a Raider and have no desire to look like one.

"What's this?" Jordyn asks, stepping into the cramped closet.

"What, sweetie?"

She hands me an envelope with my name on it. In J's handwriting. I freeze. "Where did you find this?"

I sound choked, and Jordyn's face crumples. "I'm sorry."

"It's okay, Jor." I pull her into my arms, the envelope shaking in my hand. "Can you just tell me where you found this?"

"In the book on your desk," she mumbles into my stomach.

"Right, okay." I clear my throat. With everything else going on, I'd completely forgotten about J's book on my desk. "Let's go find you a snack." I sound overly cheery, but Jordyn pulls back slightly with a small smile.

She nods.

I take her hand in mine and lead her out of the room. I tuck the envelope into my pocket. I'll look at it later, when I'm not around a little girl who has already known far more trauma than she ever should have.

Once again, I'm thankful Micah's mom and dad are willing to take her in. He spoke with them via radio two days ago, and they both insisted Jordyn make her new home with them. I'll miss having her around, but she needs stability and safety. Two things Micah's parents can provide.

And we'll visit her regularly.

Vik plans to stay in Eryndale for a stretch as well. He says he wants to train with the scouts, but all of us know he's just looking for an excuse to be close to Jordyn and make sure she gets settled.

Nate is in the kitchen, packing food for our journey. He smiles as soon as he sees us, and I leave Jordyn in his care. I just need a moment to read whatever is in this envelope.

I slip outside and find a bench in Jehoram's garden. It's secluded for the moment, so I pull the envelope from my pocket and stare at it. No one knows what happened to J. Her crew was either captured or killed, and her house burned down. Aiden is apparently in a different Raider compound recovering from his injuries.

But J disappeared.

With shaking fingers, I open the envelope.

*I'll never forget.*

I turn the paper over, but those are the only words. My hands fall into my lap. That's all. She went out of her way to leave a note in the book for me, and this is all she wrote.

It seems like too much of a risk.

But I am confident that I never want to see J again.

<hr>

"Where are we going?" I ask Micah as he weaves us through the streets of the Upper District like he knows them as well as I do.

He looks down at me with a shy smile. "You'll see."

He practically stole me from eating lunch, but I was happy to let him. Vik had Jordyn so preoccupied that she barely noticed me leaving. Now my hand is securely in his as he leads me to some unknown destination.

We pause a couple of times to answer questions from former captives preparing to leave later today. A few of them smile at me. Others still seem wary.

But, over time, I will prove to them I am not the girl I once was.

When we get to the edge of the Upper District and no one is around, Micah stops.

"Are you packed?" he asks.

I blink. He wanted to walk me all the way out here to ask me that? "Um, yeah. Ready to get out of here."

"Good."

We set off again, and then we are entering the forest. I tuck my lip between my teeth to keep from grinning like a fool. I know where he's taking us now. And, although my side is aching more than it has been with the additional movement, I can think of no place I'd rather be.

In silence, we walk hand in hand through the forest, down a path I could walk with my eyes closed. The scent of pine wafts through the air, and the crunch of leaves underneath our boots becomes the percussion to the melody of the birds singing.

I never thought I'd get to enjoy this walk with Micah, but here we are. And although there are things we need to discuss, the last thing I want to do is break the perfection of this moment.

When we arrive at the edge of the cliff and the rope ladder that leads down into my glen, Micah stops.

He rubs the back of his neck. "I forgot about the ladder." He peers down the drop to the glen and river below and sighs. "We can talk here."

I shake my head. "No. Let's go down. I'll be okay." Hopefully. I think I've healed enough for the climb down.

"You sure?"

I nod.

He gives me another of his dazzling grins, and my stomach flips. Then he eases himself over the ladder and we begin a painfully slow climb down.

By the time we've reached the bottom, we're both breathing harder than we should be and a thin sheen of sweat coats my face. Micah winces, and I realize he still isn't in prime shape either.

He leads me to the fallen log I used as my bench for more visits than I could ever remember.

Once we're settled, he shifts to face me, and I follow suit. I want to see him. Prove to myself that he's okay. He's alive. Here with me, even if we're both a little banged up.

"The day I found you changed my life," I say.

His face softens into a smile. I let my eyes wander over his features. The strong jaw, broad nose, full lips, gorgeous dark skin. The cuts on his face are almost all healed. A bruise mingling with the stubble on his jaw is fading.

He's here. Alive.

"It changed my life too." He traces his finger along my jaw and sends shivers down my spine.

"I'm sorry." I press my lips together for a moment. "Running and leaving you was a huge mistake." A tear escapes, and he catches it with his thumb. "I've regretted it every moment since."

He doesn't say anything for several long moments, and I can't read his thoughts in his eyes. Which scares me more than I want to admit. The river gurgles nearby, filling the silence.

"It was hard to see you run away," he finally says, and my heart breaks at his admission. "But somehow I know that the woman I fought with a week ago, the woman I watched leap from the platform to save Hosea—she's not going to run again."

All I can manage is a nod.

He shifts, so he's closer to me, and takes my left hand. The side of his mouth tilts up when he sees the ring, and he twists it around my finger. "I wanted to get you something nicer than this. Fancier."

I shake my head. "No. It's perfect. How can the wife of a riverboat captain wear something fancy? There's too much work to do." The words feel bold as they parade themselves out of my mouth.

Micah looks up at that, his eyes serious. "Catori, I love you. I will fail you and make mistakes. But before God, I will love you the best I can and be faithful to you all my days." He interlaces his fingers through mine and stares down at them. "When I thought I'd lost you, I begged God for an opportunity to tell you that." The words are a whisper. Raw and vulnerable.

I place my free hand against his cheek. "I love you too."

His eyes meet mine, and my chest feels like it's going to explode as I see the love I have for him mirrored back to me. He releases my hand, then captures my face in his strong and gentle grasp.

My heart beat quickens as he leans toward me, and my eyes slide shut. He presses a kiss against against my cheek.

Disappointment swirls through me, a longing for more than a peck on the cheek.

Then his lips capture mine in a kiss so sweet, tender and full of love that my heart feels ready to burst. I lean into the kiss, my arms reaching up to circle his neck. He pulls me closer, his arms strong and solid as he holds me.

The kiss deepens and the thrill of realization sweeps through me.

He's *my* Micah.

He ends the kiss before I'm ready, but he doesn't release his hold on me. Instead he shifts, hugging me to himself. I rest my head on his chest, his steady heartbeat in my ear.

Whatever may come, he's mine, and I'm his.

I tilt my head to look up at him, and he drops a kiss on the tip of my nose. He gives me a dazzling smile, and everything around us fades as he leans down and kisses me again.

# WHAT'S NEXT?

READY TO DIVE DEEPER INTO THE POST-DEMISE WORLD? CHECK OUT THE TALIONIS SERIES!

**When the world falls apart, one girl must find hope in the darkness.**

# About the Author

Award-winning author CJ Milacci writes stories for teens and young adults with heart-pounding action and hope. As the podcast host for Read Clean YA with CJ, she loves talking about books and the deeper themes woven into the pages of each novel. She's passionate about crafting stories of good overcoming evil, finding hope in the midst of seemingly hopeless circumstances, and true acceptance.

Always willing to get real about hard issues, C.J. also enjoys the cheesiest of puns. She chats about writing, her faith, bubble tea, and other fun adventures online (@cjmilacci) and at cjmilacci.com.

*Subscribe to C.J.'s newsletter to receive a free short story and get the latest updates and exclusive freebies!*

# SPREAD THE WORD

Can you think of two people who could use this book in their lives? Maybe they are your friends, teens in your church, someone you know who loves young adult fiction. Maybe they are avid readers and always looking for a new book. Or maybe it's someone you know who needs an escape from the crazy life she is immersed in, someone desperate for hope.

If so, I would love it if you could connect them to this book so they can experience the hope found in this book.

Thanks again for reading!

# ACKNOWLEDGMENTS

This book began as a short story. Then it became a novella. Then it was a full blown novel. And what an adventure it's been! I've loved diving deeper into Catori's history, discovering more of the world of the Raiders, and watching Catori and Micah's love grow. And my favorite part is that I get to take you on this adventure with me!

But a book like this can't be written alone! And there are so many amazing people who I have to thank for believing in this story and helping it become all it is today.

First and always foremost, thank you to my Savior and King, Jesus Christ. You breathed a life and depth into this story that I could have never achieved on my own, and I praise You!

Mom, thank you for reading this book so. Many. Times. And loving it every step of the way. I can't imagine writing a story without you being there to listen and encourage me throughout the process!

Dad, thank you for loving my stories, encouraging me, and always being more excited than I am whenever I hear a good review from someone.

Ani, my little sister, this book (and its marriage of convenience!) is one I knew you would love. Thanks for cheering me on each step of the way! Even when you're annoyed because a character died.

To Erica, the one who dreamed up Catori with me. From plays at Mommom's house, to writing a book based on a character we created together, I'm thankful we've been able to dream up adventures for all these years.

To my editor, Becca Weirwille, and my amazing beta readers: Mom, Katie Robles, Ani, Katie Briggs, Karah Little, and Uncle Paul. Your feedback, encouragement, and insights helped make this book so much better.

Jewell, I loved creating J with you and it's been so fun watching her character develop!

And to my incredible family. Rarely is someone as richly blessed as I am with aunts and uncles and cousins who love and support the way you guys do. Thanks for being in this with me. I love you!

# ALSO BY CJ MILACCI

**Talionis Series**

Recruit of Talionis

Fugitive of Talionis

**Talionis Series Short Stories**

Dying Embers

Shattered Ashes

Differing Paths

Rise from the Ashes

**Talionis Series Companion Novel**

Abandoned Shores